=o=o=o=o=
=o=o=o=o
=o=o=o=
=o=o=
=o=o=

COME BACK MY LYNX

by Kris Slokum

=o=o=o=o=o=o=o=o=
=o=o=o=o=o=o=o=
=o=o=o=o=o=o=
=o=o=o=o=
=o=o=

*This book is dedicated to scientists and researchers striving
to save the endangered Iberian Lynx and the
natural landscapes upon which
it depends*

Published in Great Britain in 2016 by GreenVineBooks, 28 Green
Lane, Blackwater, Camberley. GU17 9DH

A CIP catalogue record for this book
is available from the British Library

ISBN 978-0-9562043-3-2

Printed and bound in the United Kingdom
by Witley Press

=o=o=o=o=o=o=o=o=

COME BACK MY LYNX

FOREWORD

This novel sets 14-year-old Stella Martin against her aged grandfather when she discovers a family of Iberian, or Spanish, Lynx living near his desolate farmstead in southern Spain. Stella is thrilled by the beauty of this rare Lynx but despairs to learn that the animals are threatened with extinction. She also knows she must keep her discovery secret. If he learns of their existence her grandfather will surely destroy the lynx family to protect his goatherd.

There is also tension with her parents who move to the Mediterranean coast miles away from her grandparents. But while Stella also encounters hostility towards carnivores from townspeople and an antagonistic newspaper, she finds solace in donating her school biology project to a wildlife exhibition which, sadly, is itself vandalised. There are other ugly incidents too, between those wanting to preserve these animals and others who see them as wretched vermin.

The novel is written in a very direct and conversational style, but reflects the real-life tensions between conservationists seeking to protect predators and those who still depend on ancient country products and traditions. Passions run high prompting illegal activities and heated disputes between people with opposing views. But Stella's growing enthusiasm for Spanish wildlife leads her to believe that her attempts to bring together people like her grandparents and wildlife workers will succeed in the end.

In this way the story has contemporary relevance to the problems associated with those against the reintroduction of wild animals anywhere in Britain, in Europe or in the World. It is more than just a novel or a gentle way to learn about the Spanish lynx. It is a very human story and would make good reading for young teenagers who, like Stella, are determined to follow careers in wildlife conservation, and so protect and treasure animals like the beautiful and elusive Iberian Lynx.

Pat Morris (Dr)

ONE

"Just one more time, please," Stella begged her parents, "…. before we leave!"

"We were only there two days ago. What about your school work, what about your packing, what about….?" Her mother cajoled.

Why didn't they understand? Stella anguished. Squirming on her seat, her stomach churning, she cried, "I'll finish the packing Sunday evening, and anyhow I haven't any work. It's a new school. I'll work hard when I'm there. Oh, please…?"

Stella gazed earnestly into her father's forgiving eyes.

"Just this last time before….," she gasped, very close to crying.

But she couldn't tell them could she, about 'Pardito', his mother, the other cubs. How many times had she seen them in the last three months? Three, four perhaps, and always the joy mingling with fear. Fear that had grown until now, it was a palpable thing.

Almost without wanting to Stella conjured up her memory of the first tantalising glimpse she'd had of the lynx family. Now, despite the dull morning light in the Martin's west-facing kitchen, Stella pictured again the bright tawny fur of the mother lynx with her magnificent flashing golden eyes, the three boisterous cubs, especially the largest cub, a male she suspected, that she'd quickly named Pardito for his beautiful tawny coat. Much later she learned that lynx were actually called *Lince pardinus* because of that same rich colour.

Even for southern Spain, the spring weather had been exceptionally hot. That one time Stella hadn't wanted to follow the goats with her grandfather up the dusty trackways that lead to their hillside pastures. Instead she'd walked to a small sandstone cliff she knew and sat within the fragrant pine trees intending to study her school books.

Below the cliff a small stream ran which cooled the air marginally, though the heat was no less overpowering. Stella had been close to sleep when the mother lynx stealthily approached the stream and began to drink. She had watched spell-bound and silent as the hungry cubs, impatient for their own meal constantly jostled their mother until she lay down to let them suckle.

Sighing heavily over the precious and troubling memory Stella came back to the kitchen where her parents continued to tower over her and spluttered, "Oh why is everything so difficult?"

"It's you who's being difficult," her mother burst out angrily.

Stella's father decided to intervene. He had studied his daughter carefully, aware of her anguish, knowing the request was important but unable to decide quite why.

"You'll be back here for tea on Sunday," her father asked. But it wasn't really a question.

"Yes," she answered truthfully.

"...and Grandfather knows you're coming?"

"Yes." This time a deliberate lie.

But through the lies, came the urgent need, almost a pain, to see Pardito again, to make sure he was still....... safe!

She made her father stop the car by the lane leading to her grandparents' home. Their house, Holm Cottage, lay hidden in a sparse woodland of holm oaks and pines. But Stella was heading instead towards the distant exposed hillside that stretched into the foothills of the Tejeda mountain range. As she'd planned, neither farm nor hillside were visible from where she'd insisted Jorge stop the car.

"If you drop me here I'll take the track and find grandfather on the hillside," she asked.

"But your grandmother will have your tea ready?"

"I'll go back down with grandfather, I want to find him first," she insisted, "....and Lucia fusses so." Implicit in her plea was his daughter's wish see her grandfather alone.

Jorge nodded in understanding. After the family's imminent move to the coastal city of Guaro, Stella probably wouldn't see Gerardo again for many months.

"All right Stella," Jorge sighed.

She got out and he quickly swung the car around. Dust from the tyres lingered around her as he drove away. Walking lightly Stella hurried along the sandy track in case the sound of her footfalls carried uphill. Despite what she'd told her father she didn't want to meet anyone, especially not her grandparents. Deep down she already felt ashamed of the lies she'd told to secure this very, very precious night alone.

Already, in late afternoon, the high mountains in the east were awash with golden evening light which framed the rim of the much closer sierras. Soon the early autumn heat haze would blot out the nearer peaks and the trees would appear to float above the shaded valley. The high piercing calls of the cicadas were claustrophobic, cloaking, oppressing thought. She would be grateful to leave them behind.

She tramped up the track as the fierce heat of the day moderated, the scattered oaks spreading sparse shade across the hot earth. The scent of rosemary was thick in the cooling air. A small cool breeze tossed loose earth into little streams of sand that blew around her feet. Stella felt increasing excitement. She reached the ruined hut as night shadows were falling across the ridge but her little flashlight proved unequal to the task of distinguishing cobbles from tree roots. Feeling rather foolish she stumbled about blindly towards the inner corner of the hut. She expected the stones to be warm with the day's heat, instead they were cold and oily with cooling dew. Already the adventure was losing some of its magic. But she didn't care. Nothing was more important than seeing Pardito again.

She shivered and fumbled at the cotton shoulder bag, pulling out a thick sweater and jeans, and quickly pulling them on over her light dress. Then she took out the bread and salami taken secretly from the fridge and wondered, as she ate, whether her mother would miss the food. With any luck she would blame Andras, her older brother. He was permanently hungry after all, and often 'stole' from their mother's shopping. Stella drank most of the water from her water bottle then she snuggled down into a hollow beside the tumbled-down wall. But the fine dusty soil rather than being dense soft sand as she'd expected, was only a fine dusting over hard angular rock. She pulled her bag towards her to use as a pillow but was surprised by the hard lump under her head.

She'd forgotten about her father's binoculars. He'd used them for bird watching when he was younger but although he'd declared them of little use now, she'd brought them anyhow, as a kind of talisman to bring her luck. Perhaps it would keep other creatures away too. She shivered at the thought and lay back down trying to relax. Instead she became aware of sounds which in the day she would never have noticed - the constant rustling of tree limbs when there seemed to be no wind, and odd intermittent sounds, like footfalls, which somehow invoked dreams of wolves hunting and waiting to pounce on her. She woke several times in panic mistaking the brilliance of the stars in the harsh black sky, for their fearsome eyes. But when the fresh morning light finally woke her, a far more awesome sight met her eyes....

The genet's gaze was fixed, unwavering, as its long sinuous body glided through the meadow towards a gnarled olive tree squeezed into a jumble of boulders. The meadow, formed of gentle sloping terraces, was a place of whispering grasses where a few pines struggled to survive through the summer heat. Sticky, salmon-coloured resin, straining from pores in the tree's bark, evaporated a rich oily fragrance that carried long distances through the still morning air. The genet's mottled fur was lost in dappled shadows. Bright yellow sunlight shafted down on the olive leaves, some already bronzed and crisp in the autumn light, and formed gaudy gold and red rings around the feathers of a pheasant perched low in its branches. The pheasant preened itself quite oblivious of approaching danger. Stella tried to cry out but she found she could make no sound.

Where had the lynx been hiding? It came from nowhere, pouncing with breathtaking speed. A scream and a brief scatter across the hillside, the stunned look and unsteady flight of the pheasant. Then the lynx soaring, as if itself in flight, its slim body stretched out like a elegant missile, leaping towards the branch onto which the terrified genet had fled. The tiny animal was paralysed with fear, it shuddered as the lynx, spiralling in mid-air, stretched out the full expanse of her huge paw. Stella watched the genet's claws etch livid scars in the olive bark as the lynx dragged it down. As they tumbled to the ground, the lynx clamped the genet's neck tightly in her jaws. There was no resistance from the inert body. For a few seconds, the lynx stood over it, panting heavily, occasionally dropping her head to lick at the dark-spotted fur. Then she shook clouds of dust from her own fur. Grasping the body lightly she tossed it casually into the scatter of rocks. Stella lost sight of the lynx as she subsided heavily under a myrtle bush causing its dense fragrance to swamp the already resin-drenched air. The lynx mewed softly and three cubs bounded into view. They were as tall as their mother, almost fully grown. The mother lynx ignored them and began to groom.

Stella watched with awe tinged with horror as the cubs pulled the genet's body from within the rocks and fought boisterously with it until it became a dusty rag. The largest cub eventually grew bored and rushed across to the female thrusting himself beneath her chin demanding to be groomed. The female leant obligingly forwards. For the first time Stella got a good view over the cub's head and recognised the distinctive v-shaped nick in the mother's left ear. 'Pardito'! She breathed the name she'd given the cub, silently she thought. But the female's head came up. She stiffened and without seeming to move slipped effortlessly into the shrubbery from which she had emerged so violently. The three cubs rushed to follow her, disappearing like phantoms into the thick vegetation.

Stunned into silence, Stella stood up slowly, her legs stiff and aching. Although she was tempted to creep down into the valley where the genet had been killed it was already late morning and she was expected for lunch at her grandparents. It would take her almost an hour to get there. In panic although the heat was at its peak Stella picked up her bag and started to run. Soon enough she reached the shadowed lane. The scene she had witnessed replayed powerfully in her mind. She didn't understand what she had seen but someone would be able to tell her wouldn't they - her grandfather, the teachers at the new school, even her parents. She was enjoying the thrill of telling them, how excited they would all be, how .... , Then suddenly her shoes seem to catch on the trackside, she spun around shaking her head.

"But I can't, I can't tell ….. anyone …….," She heard herself cry out. All the joy suddenly left her. She threw herself down on the bare sand and lay sprawled in the shade of the scrub, sobbing until the early excitement ebbed away in a terrible stream of loneliness. Although she was still wearing her sweater a cold sweat bathed her body. She rolled slowly onto her side and tried to stand. The cotton bag hung awkwardly from her shoulder. In a fit of fury she threw it high into the air. It fell somewhere in the scrub. Her father's binoculars would have fallen there too, tumbling into the spiny bushes where she would never find them − but what use were they to her now, what use was anything?

"I hate you," Stella yelled: at the bag, at the scrub, at the dusty sun-freckled trackway.

TWO

In the late afternoon three days after the Martin family had moved to the city of Guaro on the Mediterranean coast, Andras burst into their new apartment. Despite his slight limp he had run all the way from his new school. Slamming his school bags carelessly down on the kitchen table where Stella was studying a book, he announced, "I'm going to be a hydro …a hydro ....hydrologist!"

Stella squealed, half sneering that he couldn't say the word, half in outrage at his disregard of her books. Andras ignored her.

"What do you want to be?" Anna exclaimed, turning from the work surface on which she was preparing vegetables. Then seeing the scowl on Stella's face she cajoled. "Oh, Andras, mind your sister's books."

Stella tried unsuccessfully to push the heavy bags aside. Andras was too excited to respond.

"What is it you want to be?" His mother asked again.

" A hydro…." Stella mimicked her brother's earlier stammer.

"Shush Stella," Anna barked trying to keep peace between them.

"A water engineer, I'm going to build dams and aqueducts, irrigate the village farms, even grandfather's." He beamed with pleasure as he continued. "The teachers say my maths and drawing are so good I could go to the technical institute next year. Justin's there too, he'll be able to help."

"Calm down Andras. Who's Justin?"

"His parents lived in Triana, don't you remember? I used to visit him - he's always helped me." Andras rubbed his leg as he always did unconsciously when discussing his crippled leg. Anna remembered that Justin befriended her son at junior school when the other children were cruelly mocking him about his 'wonky' leg. She sighed. Did Andras really have a vocation for this *hydrologist* career, or did he just want to emulate Justin. The older boy been kind to him certainly but....

"Your father and I will need talk this over with your teachers," she warned.

Just then their father Jorge came into the room. He wouldn't start his new job until next week and had spent the afternoon putting up badly-needed shelving in the bathroom. Rubbing plaster dust from his hands he asked, "Talk over what with your teachers?"

"Andras is going to be a hy ..drolo ....gist," Stella piped up mimicking her brother again, "...And he's going to build dams to flood the valleys and poison and drown all the wildlife."

"Whatever are you saying Stella?" Anna asked astonished. It was Andras' turn to sneer.

"You're only jealous. You'll have to forget your picture books and fluffy animals when it comes to exams." He grasped the limp woollen cat attached to Stella's pencil case and viciously twirled it around her head. She lunged towards him pulling the case roughly from his hand.

"It's true, I've seen posters at school," she declared, slumping down on her chair and again pushed quite uselessly at Andras' bags.

"Enough of this you two. Andras, we'll need to talk when I've more time. If you want to do your homework, I'll come and see you before dinner," Jorge encouraged.

Andras nodded, pulling his bags carelessly from the table he walked very determinedly from the room. Jorge gazed after his son noticing that he hardly limped at all these days, then he glanced down at Stella's bent head.

"It's thirsty work in that little bathroom, I'll have a beer before dinner, want one Anna?"

Anna shook her head.

"I put some cans on that cabinet behind the sofa."

She gestured through an archway into the small lounge. Jorge turned away from the kitchen table, patting Stella's head as he passed. They heard Jorge's beer can opening, then the stereo burst into life with her father's favourite guitar music.

Anna looked down at her daughter saying quietly, "What did you mean just now, Stella?"

Stella looked up, her face a picture of indecision.

"About what?" She replied in a petulant tone.

"About those posters - at school?"

"Oh those - it's what happens - in Brazil and India, the geography teacher says once it starts all the countryside disappears, all the wildlife, like these."

She pointed down at a class book showing a vast quarry where terrace upon terrace had been gouged out of a mountainside. Blood red water spilled from it into a nearby river. Anna looked quickly at the photograph.

"But this couldn't happen here in Spain dear. These countries are undeveloped, they need the industry." She tapped the picture angrily, but a vague doubt entered her mind. "No it couldn't happen in Spain dear, not in Europe either - people wouldn't let it."

Stella was not at all reassured by her mother's confidence.

"Do you want a drink of squash Stella?" Anna somehow felt uneasy, wanted to change the subject.

"No thank you." Stella was already intent on her books again.

"Have you already had a drink - at a school friend's?"

Stella glanced up shaking her head. "Andras has friends, I don't," she cried peevishly.

She bent her head and talked to the table rather than to Anna.

"I told them in class about grandfather and the goats. Now they call me a peasant and a goat girl. They keep saying I smell - I don't smell, do I mum?" Stella begged.

"Oh Stella, they're just teasing you. I went through the same thing at college. You should tease them back, perhaps they're all city kids, they might just be jealous?"

Stella continued to look depressed.

"Don't you remember Joan, Aunty Joan you used to call her, we visited her in Triana when you were quite little?"

"The one who gave me the photo of an eagle? I kept it for ages."

Anna watched excitement spread across her daughter's face. Talk about animals and Stella came alive.

"Well I met her during my first week at college. I was just sixteen, never been away from home, and remember Lucia and Gerardo's cottage *was* my home, I probably did smell of goats, but she never said and she's been a good friend ever since," Anna smiled as her daughter began laughing.

"Goats, goats, goats," yelled Stella getting up and dancing around the table. "I want to be a goat then I won't have to go to school at all." She collapsed into Anna's arms weak with laughter. Its cathartic effect released all the frustration and loneliness she'd experienced during the preceding week. She recalled a girl called Hanna who she had met briefly at school. Only a year ago, she too had come down from a mountain village. For a moment Stella daydreamed about seeking Hanna out, perhaps they would become friends? Then she remembered she had another, far more urgent, hurdle to cross today.

She shook herself free from her mother's arms and sitting down at the table announced quite seriously.

"I want to give up languages, I want to study nature."

Her mother blinked in disbelief.

"But languages are so important - why can't you do both?"

"Because that's the way it works at school," she said provocatively.

She turned her school bag over and took out several books on nature conservation which she'd borrowed from the school library.

"These two are all about foreign animals in Africa and America, but......," she said moving them to one side and pulling a large booklet from beneath them. It had a yellow border and was labelled 'National Geographic'. Stella swiftly thumbed through the pages till she got to the one she wanted. Keeping her hand across the top of the page she cried, "Look!"

Anna looked. The photograph was of a steep limestone cliff on which several wild goats were trooping. They had small delicate hooves and wide curving horns.

"Goats!" Exclaimed Anna, laughing "why you little….,"

"Goats!" Stella shrieked happily. Quickly removing her hand from the top of the page she revealed the title: 'Mountain Goats and Spanish ibex in Torcal de Antequera Reserve, southern Spain'.

"Antequera? But your grandmother Lucia comes from near there."

"I didn't know," Stella cried out.

Anna flipped over several pages of Stella's book. There were many glossy photographs but little text alongside them. Anna sighed as she read.

"They keep mentioning *extinction* - of our own wildlife. Is this why you want to study nature?"

Suddenly serious, Stella nodded.

"But couldn't you just read library books; languages are so important in Spain, in the world, especially English, it's spoken everywhere."

Stella shook her head and looked pointedly at her books.

"Stella can you tell me truly why it's so important, why you want to study this ....this nature, so badly?"

Stella looked into her mother's face, her warm dark brown eyes willing her to speak, to explain about Pardito, about the night she'd spent alone on the hillside, about the genet.... But how *could* she explain the unformed, desperate desire to learn - to possess the knowledge that would help her understand what she'd experienced and perhaps, in some vague way, make her grandfather change his savage attitude to the Lynx. Her eyes filled with tears, on her dry lips the words were forming, were almost spoken. Then, as if he were standing in the room beside her, she heard Gerardo's voice, harsh and vengeful, *'Vermin, they're just vermin'*.

She swallowed hard. Blinking tears away she only shook her head. "I just do...,"

"Stella, since it's so important I'll make a bargain with you. Look at me dear."

Stella raised her head and swept some loose hair off her cheeks, there was no sign of tears as she nodded. Above the sound of the stereo, she heard her father come quietly back into the room. He placed an empty can on the table and moved into the seat beside her. Anna continued looking at her daughter.

"If we let you do this...," she fingered the nature book lightly. "If we let you, will you make a pact with me."

"What pact?" Stella asked suspiciously. Had they guessed, did they somehow know......?

"If you do this..." Anna continued "I want you to learn English at home with me. You know I taught English at junior school, now if I teach you it will be good practice for us both. What do you say?"

But Jorge was unhappy with his wife's proposal.

"But surely Anna..... "

Anna shook her head briefly and continued watching Stella.

"And I can still do this - nature and the biology class next January?"

"Yes as long as you understand that you keep up English."

"Yes, oh yes please." She pushed her chair back from the table ready to leap to her feet but Jorge put a restraining hand on her shoulder.

"Not only English and 'nature'," he emphasised, rather sadly, "…. but maths and Spanish, your own language is more important than anything - eh, Anna?"

Anna nodded. Jorge got up from his seat shaking his head and saying, "Who'd have children, who'd have a little Stellita," he said humorously, using the name her grandfather had given her when she was much younger.

Stellita the goatherd! Holm Cottage already seemed a very long way away.

THREE

"I'm going to be a biologist," Hanna announced.

Both having grown up in the shadow of the Tejeda mountains, and with similar backgrounds, geographically if not socially, it was quite natural for Stella and Hanna to become close friends. Now some weeks into the autumn term the two girls had gone to Hanna's apartment after finishing their geography class. Stella had learned to think of Hanna as a quiet contemplative girl, so her sudden enthusiasms still took her by surprise.

"A biologist," Stella repeated "How?"

"I'm going to study raptors at university."

"What's a rap…a raptor?" Stella stumbled over the word

"I would have thought you'd know," Hanna called imperiously from the kitchenette as she poured their drinks. Stella wriggled awkwardly in the deep folds of the sofa and looked down at her schoolbag perched near her feet. Hanna's manner made Stella curious about whether the rumours that her family once owned a large estate in the sierras, were true. It was also said her grandparents were members of the old aristocracy.

"Well I don't," Stella replied, vastly irritated. "But I know about……," Stella began, then stopped herself, she couldn't disclose her secret encounters with the lynx family. Hanna was her best friend. Even so *best friends* had a habit of breaking confidences.

"You know about what?" Hanna called in the same disparaging tone, but as she entered the room and saw Stella's bemused expression, her attitude softened. "They're eagles and buzzards, all the birds of prey, silly. You've seen them haven't you?"

"Yes of course I have." Stella answered defensively, but her curiosity was aroused.

"Why do you want to study them…?" Stella asked trying to imagine what connection there could be between this quiet young girl and the pictures she had seen of eagles and vultures soaring over the vast African plains.

"Because they are endangered."

"The African ones? Are they in danger then?"

"Some are," Hanna said cryptically. "No, I meant the ones here, our own wildlife."

"But they can't be endangered, no-one would let it happen. Mum said it couldn't happen to any of our wildlife."

"It could, why look at the wolf and lynx, we've already lost most..."

But Stella didn't want to hear any more, her eyes glazed over and she pictured Pardito as she had seen him on that first evening, his eyes golden in the sunset. Despite all the books she'd read she was no nearer to learning any more about the lynx. Only, worryingly, that they *were* endangered. She waited anxiously for the new nature class they would attend in January.

"Stella, what's the matter?" Hanna saw her friend's face blanch.

"Have you caught a chill?" she insisted A dark pall of cloud and heavy rain had settled over the city for the last few weeks causing an abundance of coughs and colds at school. But Stella's only reply was to push her chair violently behind her.

"It isn't true," she shrieked, "It isn't true," she repeated running from the room. Hanna heard the door slam then the sound of Stella's feet rushing down the central stairwell of the apartment block.

"Well," Hanna breathed to herself putting both glasses down on the wooden table."Well!"

For some days the girls' friendship suffered from this slight quarrel but this proved only temporary. Lessons and homework took over, although neither of them ever spoke about the incident again. Soon enough the Christmas break came around and as if relenting the wet pall of rain vanished leaving the city to its usual sunlight. Stella turned fourteen on the sixteenth of December. On that day the family travelled to the town of El Rosal to visit Jorge's parents, Ramon and Consuela, for her birthday celebrations. Because they lived in a tiny house with only two bedrooms, for the three nights the family visited, Jorge and Andras slept on couches in the lounge while Anna and her daughter shared the spare bedroom. It was a unsatisfactory arrangement although the time passed quickly enough with celebrations and family visits.

On the second day, when the press of the family gathering became too much for him, Ramon, now aged 68, encouraged Stella into his garden, a tiny fenced plot bursting with plants. She felt a special rapport with him, more so strangely than with Gerardo, who she knew better. He had as much enthusiasm for plants as she had for animals. Long since retired, he'd been a professional horticulturist for most of his working life and his knowledge of plants always impressed his granddaughter. That day he pottered about the tiny plot. Pausing to hold a plant leaf, he said, "This one ....." he gave a Latin name which Stella did not recognise, "takes a lot of cultivating, a lot of care." Then he shook his head and peered calmly down at his granddaughter. There was a far-away look in his eyes. "They say it's now extinct in the wild."

Stella heard the sadness in his voice.

"Do plants go .. do they go extinct too?" Stella asked surprised. She watched her grandfather's hand lightly touching the pale pink and yellow blossoms as he searched beneath the leaves for signs of disease.

"Yes of course, plants and animals too, they..... " Ramon didn't continue. In recent years he had seen too little of his granddaughter. Now he sensed a worried intensity in her question. Mildly arthritic, he settled himself down on a wooden bench between large flowery bushes, then patted the seat for the girl to join him. Stella sat down thoughtfully.

"Why do you say plants *too*.... ?" He queried

Stella remained silent. Of course, she still couldn't talk about the lynx, or the night alone on the hill, her parents would get to know and there were sure to be recriminations.

"Come on, out with it." The old man looked proudly at his array of plants but when Stella looked up at him he knew something of that pride belonged to her.

"The wolf, and other carnivores. Hanna said they were becoming extinct, right here in Spain."

Ramon, nodded. The girl was probably right, there had been no reports of wolf in the whole of Andalucía for about ten years. As for the other predators he had heard a report not long since of the death of a young lynx on the new roadway into the sierras. Stella sat pensively beside him.

"And who is Hanna?"

"Hanna Garcia de Gonzales, a girl at school, but her family used to live in Chilches, in the sierras." Involuntarily she looked across the garden towards the sweep of snow-clad hills 30 km away. Ramon nodded, he knew the name and the family's history. Some years ago the large Gonzales estate had fallen into debt. When the old hidalgo died his two sons fought for control but in the end it was sold and became a vast hunting estate. Fences excluded the original wildlife, peasant farmers were shifted off the land. It was a sorry business. The elder brother was rumoured to have left Spain, taking the proceeds of the sale. The younger son still lived in the hills above Chilches and appeared not to have benefited from the sale. It was said he lived a frugal life with his family. If Hanna was his daughter she might well know far more about the wildlife in the sierras than his own granddaughter.

"And what else does Hanna say?"

"We were talking, after our geography class. She says our wildlife is - endangered, Mum doesn't agree."

"And what about Gerardo, he knows the hills after all - what does he say?"

Stella looked away.

"I don't know, we haven't been there....since leaving for the city."

"So, - but you go there in a day or so, a Christmas visit?"

"Yes."

"Will you ask him what he thinks?" Stella thought for a moment. She had been looking forward to seeing Gerardo and Lucia. They never left their home so hadn't visited their city apartment. With no phone in the cottage the family's only contact had been through Jorge who called on them regularly to deliver supplies. He'd implied that her grandparents' lives remained unchanged and unchanging. The Christmas visit would be confined to one short winter's day. Part of her wanted to see her grandparents, but Holm Cottage evoked so many, disturbing, memories.

"No I can't, he wouldn't understand."

Ramon shook his head and looked down into Stella's troubled face.

"Well perhaps I can find something in the library for you, but surely your teachers will know more. Won't you ask them too?"

"Yes I'll do that. I'll be starting proper biology classes in January, perhaps they will know." She swept off the seat, glad to free herself from the dangerous topic.

For the next few days the rain returned and beat down on the Tejeda ridges above Gerardo and Lucia's home. Holm Cottage sat dark and isolated within the cloaking frieze of holm oaks. Their evergreen leaves which soaked up the rain had an annoying habit of releasing the water in slow drenching flurries after the clouds folded themselves away. Hemmed in by winter damp, the cottage had an uninviting aspect that day. When the family arrived at eleven o'clock on Christmas day, Jorge and Anna carried stores of food into the cottage. Rain poured fiercely on the slates of the roof and when the family sat down for their meal in the dark smoky house, they ate without enthusiasm. The rain slowly eased to a slight misty drizzle.

Jorge had noticed that the couple's pile of winter firewood was low. Despite Gerardo's protestations he insisted on chopping up logs in the cottage courtyard. Gerardo followed him angrily to the door of the lean-to. He resented Jorge's intrusion. Instead of joining his son-in-law, he took out his pipe and settled down morosely before the hearth in front of the fire which burned sullenly, giving out little heat. Eager to get out of the mournful house, Stella and Andras joined Jorge and began piling the newly cut logs into the barn beside the goat pen. The animals watched curiously from a doorway. Their rain soaked pelts gave off a harsh gamey smell which mingled uneasily with the rich scent of sawdust. Anna remained in the house helping her mother with the kitchen chores.

By the time the three of them returned to the cottage, grimy and exhausted from their tasks, Christmas afternoon was already over, but as they entered Gerardo perversely left his seat and went out alone to milk the goats. Stella followed, asking to help. Gerardo rebuffed her. He wandered across the yard, not even looking towards the newly raised wood pile. Disappearing into the gloom of the goat shed he pulled the lower door half closed behind him. She stood in the barn doorway for half an hour watching him. In the three months since the family had left the village Gerardo had aged markedly, and now walked unusually slowly. His previously supple hands seemed more gnarled than she remembered. He drew off the goats' milk from their small teats with obvious effort sometimes even missing the pail. Spurts of white liquid trickled down to form puddles in the straw at his feet. Stella ached to help. Disappointed by his continued coldness she turned away with tears filming her eyes. When she fell asleep in the back of the car on the journey home, Stella was aware dimly of snatches of her parents' conversation.

" ...cottage ....needs rebuilding..." she heard her mother say.

" ....lean-to roof's leaking....".Jorge countered.

Then Anna's soft tones again, "if only they would come and live with us " was swiftly followed by Jorge's exasperated response.

".....never live in the city... would kill him......" Eventually Stella drifted into sleep.

The winter months passed quickly enough and by March, the rain ceased, leaving the city to wake daily to clear blue skies. Fresh spring greenery covered the Tejedas and even the city trees perked up and began to shade the increasingly overheated streets from the sun. Stella and Hanna having truly forgotten their differences started their new biology class together early in January. The topic proved even more fascinating than either of them could have imagined, but the classroom atmosphere was marred by their teacher, Janni, who also took their geography class. Janni had no patience with topics outside the school curriculum. Stella's early questions about Spain's own wildlife were treated with cynicism. Even Hanna's protestations about threats to the imperial eagle were brushed aside. Janni was adamant no Spanish wildlife could possibly be endangered. Stella couldn't take her grandfather's advice to ask about the lives of her lynx family in the distant Tejeda foothills as she'd never have the courage to risk Janni's wrath.

Then one day, towards the end of the spring term, something happened that changed Janni's attitude. She invited a visitor to talk to the geography and biology classes together, but strangely had not told them the subject of the talk. That Wednesday the biology classroom was packed with children from both groups. Those without desks were seated on chairs all round the walls of the room. The general level of their voices was deafening.

When she heard a knock on the door Janni ran to it shrieking at the children.

"Quiet. Quiet!" She was a tall thin young woman, with fine blond hair styled into a ponytail. She had little control over the children except when she was angry, which was quite often. The children responded almost out of curiosity rather than fear and the noise abated.

Janni pushed the door open to usher in a young man with hair as blond as her own. Taking his arm she ran her hand down until it nestled in the man's palm. The action wasn't lost on the more mature, more observant children.

"This is Doctor David Foster children, he's English but...." and she gave the man a broad smile, "he speaks Spanish just like us."

It was said in a patronising manner and the man's face formed a grimace which was quickly dispelled by Janni's ready smile. David Foster had worked with Andalucian wildlife for four years, was considered an expert on the endangered animal species in Spain. The class knew nothing of this. Carelessly Janni still had mentioned neither the man's profession nor the reason for his visit. So Stella watched with little enthusiasm as the young man carried boxes of equipment and bundles of paper scrolls across the room. Before he reached the table many scrolls dropped to the floor and in spite of Janni's over-zealous help the man managed to get the remaining equipment onto the table. The children laughed and although he smiled, the man appeared temporarily embarrassed.

"Come on children, we need some help here." Janni turned to the young man asking coyly "Don't we Davy?" Visitor and teacher were obviously more than mere colleagues. No-one got up. Stella was seated on a chair at the front of the room, but she was too shy to volunteer. Janni turned, giving her one of her rare smiles.

"Come on, Stella dear, please," she coaxed.

Stella rose hesitantly and bent down to pick up the roll of posters. It wasn't an easy task. As soon as she picked up one scroll another would fall out. Then another. There was a lot of tittering from the children behind her. After struggling for a time she decided to lay them out first on the floor. Suddenly she was aware that Hanna was at her side. The girl grabbed one of the glossy coloured posters from the floor and held it up.

"The imperial eagle," she cried fluttering the poster till she held it high over her head. It was as if the magnificent bird had lifted off the colourful page and swooped into the room. Stella was impressed. For a moment she was left on the floor while other children crowded around Hanna. When she looked down again she was staring into the face of her very own lynx. But of course it couldn't be Pardito. She gulped then struggled upright to lay the posters on the table. Hands reached out from all around her grabbing them.

She held the picture of the lynx to her chest while the pressure of bodies slowly forced her away from the table. There was a lot of noise and confusion with children chattering and shuffling photos of wildlife: wolves, goats and bears, wild sheep and deer took their attention. No-one took any notice of Stella. Janni was struggling to load photos into the computer and having little luck. Stella could see she was attempting to put the memory stick in the wrong slot but said nothing. The man, Davy, was setting up a screen at the back of the table. His fair hair reached to his shoulders. He was probably about thirty years old and had the thin muscular body of a young man. He was quite tall, but not as tall as her father, Stella thought. His skin was tanned and deeply freckled like a peasant's but 'Davy' did not seem at all peasant-like. Stella edged towards him. Still holding the lynx photo, she tried to catch his eye.

"Where did you get these?" she asked quietly.

Davy didn't hear. He grumbled as he slipped the catch awkwardly over the top of the screen then looked round for Janni, instead he saw Stella's face looking earnestly up at him. She was clutching a poster with such intensity that her fingers were creasing the edges.

"What did you say, little one?" and before she answered he continued in a somewhat patronising manner, "You'd like me to take that?" Stella nodded while following him back to the table.

"You seem very interested in that lynx."

"The lynx, yes. Is it Spanish, is it ,. endangered?"

"Well... " The man winked and grinned broadly "that's what I've come to talk about.....,"

"Children, children sit down please ...," Janni's shrill voice cut through the confusion. Chairs were scraped and desks juggled as pupils resumed their seats.

"Children," said Janni when the room was quiet. "I should have introduced Davy properly." She took his arm again and drew him towards the table.

"Davy...that is Doctor David Foster, is a zoologist and wildlife expert, he's studied our own wildlife, particularly here in Andalucía for many years and he's going to tell us about their lives."

Stella gasped. For the next thirty minutes she listened spell-bound to the 'wildlife expert' talking earnestly about his work. His photographs were magnificent showing among other highlights, the Pyrenees covered in snow where wolves were hunting deer; and in Extremadura a red fox hunted in the cork forests. On Doñana's sand dunes in the south-west where hundreds of migrating birds fed in wide lagoons, Stella was surprised to see a lynx. But at the end of the talk, when David volunteered to answer a few questions, she quickly became dispirited. Much of his work involved assessing the threats to Spanish wildlife. So, at last, Stella summoned the courage to ask, " You showed photos of lynx in Doñana, are there.... do you radio-track any lynx here in Andalucía?"

David looked at the girl's face remembering how she had clutched the lynx poster.

"Yes, yes we do." He told them about the female lynx he, and another man called Lamas, had tracked the year before. The children grew quiet when he mentioned the illegal trapping and death of a cub's mother.

"And did you find the cub?" Stella asked almost in a whisper.

"Yes, the zoo managed to entice her into a trap next day with some food, she was famished, but soon recovered," David said. He looked from the girl towards the class, noticing where a child was bored, another scribbling notes, while a few boys at the back of the class were carrying on a conversation of their own.

"It was a little female cub as we thought. After a health check she was taken to Xando Institute, an animal sanctuary in Granados. She recovered so well she'll probably be able to join a breeding group next year."

This time it was Hanna's turn to ask a question.

"Is Xando like the eagle centre at Palofini, then?"

David looked surprised for a moment. Although Palofini had the same aims as Xando, it was a research establishment with no general public access.

"Why yes, have you been there?" Hanna nodded, beaming enthusiastically.

"Yes, something like that. But the young eagle chicks learn very early to capture food for themselves, they don't imprint on humans so much. It's easier to release them into the wild afterwards."

"What's imprinting?" asked one of the boys who seemed less bored than the rest.

"When a young animal is raised by its parents it has to learn who they are, so they can recognise them and beg food off them. Strangers, even their own kind, won't feed them and will often attack a young animal if it comes into their territory." There was a gasp from some of the girls.

"This imprinting, it's like the orphaned goat kids that follow the farmer around?" Another boy suggested.

David nodded little realising that the boy, Pietro, was laughing and pulling faces to his classmates' amusement. Stella guessed that his interest was feigned. It was Pietro who had teased and bullied her in her early days at the school. But Stella had her own questions and time was getting short.

"Why won't the cub be released, why does it have to stay in the zoo?"

"Well…." David began, but Janni had just come up beside him. She seemed agitated and was looking at her watch.

"There are lots of answers to that but ….I think …. ." and he turned to Janni who said

"I'm sorry, we have to end questions here children," she said hurriedly. "It's already half past three. We must tidy the room before we leave." David looked back at the children's expectant faces and was acutely aware of their disappointment. The girl in the front row particularly looked upset at the interruption. He had a brief whispered conversation with Janni. The teacher nodded several times and then turned back to the class very pleased with herself.

" Well, children, you are in for a treat, David is so impressed by your interest he's going to take us on a trip to Xando. I'll let you know when it's arranged." She had another quick word with David who had already begun to pack away his materials. "Of course your parents will have to approve." She gave another of her little nervous laughs. "But David has already agreed to join us on our trip up to Torcal de Antequera in ten days, so you may be able to ask him some questions then. Now quickly please, help roll up the posters."

First at the table, Stella slowly began rolling the precious picture of the lynx into a bundle with the other photos. She'd been desperate to ask the man about the lynx cub, now it was too late. She watched helplessly as Janni and David gathered up his equipment and left the room. All the other pupils, even Hanna, had rushed away leaving Stella saddened and alone in the empty room.

FOUR

The day of the Torcal trip dawned cloudy with dark clouds clustering in the eastern sky where fine mist hung over the range of limestone mountains. But the mist was dissolving as the school bus struggled up the mountain road towards the reserve at 10 o'clock and soon the mountains were shining in a comfortably warm sunlight. When they entered the vehicle park Stella looked around excitedly for David Foster. He was nowhere in sight. As the children tumbled from the bus, Janni's phone rang. After a brief conversation she announced.

"A disappointment children, Doctor Foster's been delayed, he'll get here as soon as he can. But there's plenty to see, come on now."

Stella sagged back in her seat and had to be coaxed out of the bus by Hanna. The other children piled out and began chasing each around the cars. Janni and a female teaching assistant, Laura, had a hard time ushering them towards the information centre. Most seemed more interested in gathering up leaflets from the display boards than in the park itself. Finally they left the leaflet trays in disarray and streamed into the park. Walking down the first trackway Stella turned constantly, searching through the crowd of children and other visitors. David Foster did not appear. Janni gave her charges a brief talk reminding them that the limestone rocks had been formed at the bottom of an ocean. They had been raised up and were now eroding into bizarre shapes and people had given them strange fanciful names. They must also watch for ibex and the wild goats, but many of the youngsters quickly stopped listening and were wandering away, shouting and laughing noisily. Stella guessed they would be lucky to see any animals. Hanna echoed her thoughts.

"They won't hear a single bird." She sighed. "I doubt if even the sight of an eagle would quieten them. Come on Stella, he won't be here yet."

"Who?" Stella replied casually

"Our wildlife expert, Doctor David Foster," Hanna said emphasising each syllable of his name. "Perhaps he's not coming, maybe he's fallen out with Janni." Stella looked at her friend, surprised by her insight.

"Are they...together then?" she asked rather timidly.

"Of course, wasn't it obvious back in class."

Disappointed, Stella could only nod. If this were true David would surely be too absorbed with Janni to answer her questions.

"I'd like to go to that Xando Institute," she said changing the subject.

"So would I, but I'd also like to go back to Palofini. A friend of my father's runs it, he took me and Dad last year, they were rearing three young eagles. Can you believe it, their parents were killed by poisoned bait. Why do people do that, they're such gorgeous birds. I don't think any of the class have gone down here - perhaps we might even see an ibe," she began running down a nearby sloping path empty of people. "Come on, Stella," she called back.

Stella caught up with Hanna and they walked together along the twisting track looking up at the strange formations that the wind and rain had formed from of the pale grey limestone. Hanna scanned through a leaflet. She looked up into the rocks and said.

" Look there's the Molar, and the Wine glass, and there's the eaglet. Not that it's really anything like the living bird." Despite her criticism, Hanna laughed excitedly.

Stella looked at the brochure then peered up into a rock cleft where the eroded rocks appeared twisted around each other. She pointed at the more obvious ones.

"And there's the 'fated lovers' perhaps it's Janni and Dr. Foster." She giggled, slightly ashamed of her thoughts.

"Or perhaps it's Davy and Stella," Hanna teased. Stella blushed and gritted her teeth. "Oh go on, admit it, I saw how you looked at him in class," Hanna said annoyingly. "You've got a crush on him yourself."

"I just want to learn about wildlife." Stella said lamely. But quick to sense her friend's embarrassment. Hanna changed tactics.

"You know where Xando is. Oh, but just look at this," she said bending down suddenly to look at a shrub covered in brilliant blue flowers. Stella looked from the intense blue of the flowers up into the rocks. Plants sprouted from every crevice. The winter rains and sudden spring heat had drawn colour out of every stone and a profusion of early butterflies fluttered about feeding on the flowers.

"No. Where is it...?"

Hanna was admiring another shrub. She pointed to more tiny yellow flowers smothering the rockface.

"See how they follow the light. We had some at home in Chilches. Come back in an hour or two and they'll be facing that way." She pointed to where the thatched roof of the information centre was half hidden behind an outcrop. Several cars were entering from the roadway. It was too far to see if David's was among them.

"Where is it then?" she badgered Hanna, who seemed to have forgotten everything else and was wandering off down the track, her mind on nothing but flowers.

"Hanna!" Stella insisted, running after her.

"Oh the Xando place." Hanna finally relented, "well you'd better ask your friend Jade, she lives near there. I think her uncle is something to do with it."

"Jade. Jade lives near there?

Jade was a girl in the year above Stella. Her father was English and Jade bilingual. This had encouraged Anna to invite the girl to their apartment so Stella could practice the language. But Jade was from a privileged family. So at first Stella had been quite in awe of her, but the girl's warmth and ready humour quickly endeared her to Stella. A kind of respectful friendship had blossomed between them so Stella felt, in Jade, she had gained an older sister.

" I think so. You had better ask her when you see.... oh no, here they come!"

The raucous sounds of children echoed around the limestone cliffs and a group of twenty of their schoolmates came into view. Some were even playing tag among the low pinnacles of rock, their heavy shoes trashing the tender plants. Laura struggled along behind them, she seemed to have even less ability than Janni in controlling them.

"Let's get out of here," Hanna yelled. "That unsurfaced track looks inviting, quickly.."

Pulling Stella by the arm they entered a deep gorge and the noisome children were lost behind them. The girls wandered about for more than an hour gazing up at the rocks and down at the flowers. It was nearly midday when Stella noticed a faint movement high up in the shadowed cleft of the rock. She stopped to shade her eyes against the fierce sunlight.

" Hanna, look," Stella whispered, pointing skywards.

"An eagle?" asked Hanna hopefully

"Birds, it's always birds with you," Stella laughed. " No .....up there in the rock, that sort of brown shape, like a goat, only it's not a goat is it, it looks ....."

" It's an ibex, you won't get that in a farmyard." Hanna teased. "Look at its big horns. It must be a male!"

The two girls watched in awe as first one, then another, of the wild ibex appeared on the topmost pinnacles, their large polished horns nodding, their light brown skin rippling as they moved in and out of the sunlight, finally disappearing behind a broad dark-shadowed cliff.

"Come on, I'm starving," said Hanna suddenly."We'd better get back to the coach. Think how excited the others will be when we tell them we've seen the ibex!"

But when they reached the car park, they were given no time to explain. Children were sprawled beside the bus, their bags and lunch packs appearing like an animated rubbish tip. Laura was nowhere to be seen but when the girls reached the bus doorway Janni was there, apparently deep in conversation with David Foster. Stella smiled shyly at him as Janni spun around exhibiting her usual impatience.

"Well at last," she cried angrily, "no-one knew where you were! You've got to eat up hurriedly, David is only going to be here for an hour. He thinks he knows where the ibex are."

Ignoring Janni's obvious annoyance, both girls chorused.

"We've seen them already?"

"How can you have seen them?" Janni challenged.

"They were high on the rocks!"

Again Janni chose to misunderstand. "You went up on the rocks? But it's too dangerous, what would your parents say..!" She said sharply.

"Not us.... the goats," insisted Hanna.

"Well even so, go and get your lunch and be ready to move off soon." With that Janni turned around, dismissing them.

"Wait Janni,.... a moment girls...." David called after them. He remembered the two girls from the classroom visit and was anxious to encourage rather than blight their interest, as Janni was clearly doing.

"Whereabouts did you see them?" He asked nodding in the direction of the park.

The two friends looked at each other. Stella spoke.

"We were in a valley in the centre, we just followed a narrow track, there was no-one else about."

" You shouldn't have gone off on your own." Janni demanded again, determined to dispel their interest in the ibex. David grimaced.

"But we wouldn't have heard them, with so much noise," Hanna cried, gesturing towards at the rear of the coach where some children were playing football. "Just listen to ....,"

"Well never mind that now, go and eat both of you and be ready to move soon. Isn't that right David?"

The man nodded. Stella thought he looked unhappy.

"I'll see you in a minute girls," he said encouragingly.

Hanna and Stella were keen to be among the first through the park gates. David walked beside Janni, deep in conversation. When they reached a fork in the path David looked back for the two girls and was appalled to see groups of children tramping noisily past him without a word of constraint from the teachers.

"Children!" he called, trying to get their attention. "We must be quiet, please keep on the path behind me." None of them took any notice. He raised his hands and tried to usher them to the side of the track. "Just stop here for a minute!"

Several ran round his back and a football was tossed high in the air to a loud roar from many of the boys. One boy scrambled on a nearby rock pinnacle showering his friends with a scatter of rock debris. David looked on angrily.

"Look Janni," he said in exasperation "this isn't going to work."

Thoroughly unconcerned, Janni had been chatting to Laura. They both stared at him curiously.

"Perhaps we had better separate them into smaller groups," he declared. "If some of them haven't finished their worksheets you and Laura could each take a group and work with them. If we meet back here in twenty minutes I'll take each group in turn to look for the ibex."

With obvious distain Janni broke off her conversation with Laura and looked quite puzzled.

"Worksheets, what do you mean? I didn't see anything like that in the information centre."

"You must have set them some tasks ..... to help them observe the rocks and the wildlife!" Still Janni didn't understand. Hanna and Stella stood quietly in the shadow of David's tall figure. They could see the consternation and embarrassment on Janni's face.

"But I told them what to see!"

David watched as the children continued to stream past without any word from Janni or Laura, none of them carried any school papers. He began to get an inkling of his problem.

"Don't you give them worksheets?" David sounded exasperated. "That's what English schoolchildren do. It helps them learn by observing what they see. All the English schools do it."

"In England," Janni said angrily, conscious of the challenge to her position. But we're not in England, David? We teach in class, we don't bring these … these 'worksheets' out into the Torcal, or to the sea, or the sierras. The children learn by experiencing things themselves, not by..."

She gestured impatiently towards the information centre and turned back to Laura. Stella guessed, soulfully, that the promised trip to Xando might now be in doubt. The two women walked away from David towards the melee of excited children. Only a few remained beside him. With Hanna and Stella were two boys who Stella knew vaguely from the geography class but Stella was surprised to see Pietro loitering in David's shadow as if uncertain where to go. Everyone, including Stella who had several times been the butt of his sarcastic attentions, knew the boy as the class bully.

"Well it looks as if it's just us." David said, looking down at their expectant faces.

"Now, you had better tell me your names." When Jamie, Pablo.......
and even Pietro had complied David looked back at the girls.

"And can you learn to call me David, Doctor Foster sounds so formal." All the children nodded, but it was obvious they were embarrassed. Pietro grinned crazily from behind David's back but when they moved he continued to trail along behind them.

"Well Stella, can you remember where the ibex were?"

"Yes of course," she said, "down this way. She lead them towards the valley and found that the afternoon sun had swung round to shade the narrow gorge. The tall limestone pinnacles, still caught in the yellow sunlight, shimmered eerily above the shadowed rock wall. She pointed toward the clifftops. In the distance a man and two women were walking down the narrow path directly towards them. The man's camera had a long professional-looking lens. He kept pointing it to the cliffs and tinkering with the focus.

"They were up there, on that ledge," Stella gestured towards a sunlit rock.

"And this is just where I should expect to find them." David replied happily. He patted Stella on the shoulder. "You must have good eyesight."

"They disappeared behind those white cliffs where the rock splits, perhaps they're still there." Hanna added.

" I think you'd have to be a mountaineer to walk up there," said a boy named Jamie. "Perhaps that's what I need to be to study wildlife."

"Not necessary." David insisted. He stood watching the cliffs while the other people drew level with them.

"Have you seen the wild ibex?" asked the man with the camera, "been looking all morning and not a sight!" When David answered, "No, not yet..." the man recognised his accent and replied in English. Stella found to her surprise that she could follow much of their conservation.

" English then..." the man asked, "... on a school visit?"

" On a school trip yes," said David. "But a Spanish school, I work here now."

"Ah! What do you teach? I'm at Madrid university myself - English, linguistics." David shook his head.

"I don't teach I'm afraid, I'm a zoologist, just showing these youngsters the wildlife of the area."

"Well I wish you good luck, we've seen nothing worth photographing yet." He waggled his camera in the air. "Except some wonderful flowers of course!"

The man nodded and moved to join his companions.

"Seems you girls have been very lucky today. Well I can't see the ibex now, we had better be getting back to the others, " David said. Hanna and Stella both rolled their eyes. He realised they were no more looking forward to rejoining their classmates than he was.

"Come on boys," he encouraged.

Pietro instantly grabbed Pablo by the arm, and began running with him towards the car park. Stella saw Pietro give the boy a viscous punch when he tried to pull away. She signed and looked back along the gorge where Jamie remained sitting quietly on a rock at the side of the track. He was looking up at the high cliffs, trying to turn them into animals. He looked up forlornly as David called them. Hanna moved to the boy's side.

"They were up there Jamie." She heard her friend describing the scene. Jamie listened enthralled. How really kind she is, Stella thought. Turning she realised she was alone on the track with David Foster.

"Doctor....." " The man shook his head at the word.

"It's David, remember." He chided.

"D.. David." she tried the awkward English name.

"The lynx cub whose mother was killed, is it still in the zoo?"

"It's still at the Xando sanctuary, she's about 10 months old now, you might see her on the school visit." Stella was relieved, the promised trip was still on.

"But why does she have to stay? Is it because of this - this imprinting thing, or ...?" she didn't quite know how to continue. David came to her rescue.

"Not really, no. But it would be difficult to release her into the wild. She has to learn to feed herself with live rabbits. They form ninety percent of lynx food. The only way we could train her to live in the wild would be to build a vast enclosure where the rabbits roam freely. It takes a lot of time and money, and work by sanctuary staff."

"But you mentioned captive breeding, I thought you meant so the animals could be released again."

"It's just not that simple. Not for that little cub Stella nor for any of the other animals at Xando. Many came in as road casualties or are sick. A few schemes are being considered for lynx breeding where there aren't any farms. Predators, large ones like the lynx and wolf just aren't welcome."

Stella looked at the ground and stayed silent. She thought of Pardito as she had last seen him, his fur glistening. He and his family were wild creatures, she couldn't imagine him being in a zoo - or even in David's "vast enclosure". As the man encouraged her forwards she noticed they were entering a more open part of the park. Few people were about in the early afternoon heat. Some adults wandered about looking at plants and in the distance near the park entrance she spotted a swarm of her classmates. Soon they would catch up with them. Almost involuntarily she turned aside into one of the lesser used paths, then sat down on a rock. This surprised the zoologist. He stood looking up at the cliff.

"David....," she pleaded. He turned, looking down at her. "Why do lynx kill other predators?"

It wasn't the sort of question he was expecting. He leaned his foot on another rock opposite the girl and searched her face for meaning.

"Other predators Stella?"

"Genets, and...," Stella's confidence was slipping. She wasn't sure she had the courage to tell him what she had seen.

"Well they do kill them of course. The lynx are so dependent on the rabbit population that anything which also eats them is a threat."

"But why kill them. Why not just chase them off?"

"I suppose because a competitor will just come back again. It's insurance really. But why do you ask, Stella, did you read that in a book?" he asked trying to fathom the reason for the girl's strange query.

Stella remembered the books Ramon had sent her. In one of them she'd seen a photo of a lion attacking a cheetah.

"Yes in a book." She looked up at David sensing his disbelief.

"And what book was that?" He asked patiently.

Stella only shook her head. The man sensed her anxiety.

"Stella...... " He formed her name quite quietly making it sound attractive.

"It wasn't in a book was it?" Stella only shook her head and looked up the path where Hanna and Jamie were walking slowly side by side. She noticed that Hanna's head was bowed towards the boy as she listened to him. First Janni and David, now Hanna and Jamie, she thought.

" I'm a zoologist Stella." David encouraged, "I'm interested in all wildlife, if there's something you've seen, something you want to tell me.... ?"

"I can't.. tell you," was all she could manage.

" Stella, if you're afraid of .... of someone ? If you want to tell me something important." He let the words linger hoping they could give her courage. "I won't tell anyone - unless you want me to!"

Stella looked up, wondering whether to trust him.

"Not anyone...?" she asked. She had wanted so often to tell her parents about the lynx, how strange she should be discussing them now with this stranger.

"Not anyone," David thought he could guess the cause of her concern. "Is it something your parents don't know about, something they wouldn't like."

Stella looked back at the ground and nodded. Wisps of pale hair caught in the fluttering breeze and played about her face, hiding her eyes.

"You live in the city don't you Stella?"

Again the head of wispy blond hair nodded.

"But you didn't always live there?"

Stella raised her head, her eyes were bright but her body tense.

"We lived in the Valdes valley, but my father got a job in the city, last September, we had to move."

"And you lived on a farm? Is that where you saw the genet ...... and the lynx?"

"My grandfather's farm, but...."

David was finding it hard to curb his professional interest in the face of girl's obvious fear.

"But I can't...." Stella spluttered, trying to get up off the seat but finding her legs wouldn't support her. David eased her back on the rock and came to sit beside her.

"Is it because they're predators - couldn't you tell your parents what you had seen."

"Not just my parents, my grandfather he....."

"He what? Please, I want to help Stella? Remember what I told the class about how all predators are declining. All I want to do is help them, even though they're protected, they are still...... "

"That's why I can't tell you....," Stella was close to sobbing now.

"Stella, please listen." David cajoled, thinking he was at last close to the source of Stella's problem.

"I told you I won't tell anyone. But do you know someone who hunts these animals... your grandfather.....?"

Stella's bravado collapsed. Weeping softly she nodded into her chest and at last declared,

"I've seen the lynx lots of times, but I …..I couldn't tell anyone. My grandfather, he said they were vermin, he sets traps. I was about eight when.........when....."

She couldn't continue. She was crying in earnest, tears pouring down her cheeks. The zoologist leant forward, placing his hand on the girl's shoulder to comfort her. Stella shrugged him off then somehow the words poured out of her as the memory, etched so savagely, so indelibly, on her mind imposed itself before her eyes: The lynx writhing in the trap. The rifle shot as Gerardo killed it. Seeing him swing round angrily at her gasp of horror, his lined peasant face distorted by dismay and ...perhaps...guilt.

She shouldn't have been there. 'Hadn't he told her to stay away,' He'd bellowed viciously at her.

"You see... I shouldn't have followed him....I didn't know how awful….." She wept again, but suddenly lifted her head and smiled through the tears.

"And then, last year ......in spring, I saw Pardito and his family the first time."

"A family, and who's Pardito?" David questioned incredulously.

The girl gazed up at him, her eyes sore and reddened.

"A lynx family, a mother with three cubs. The cubs were so beautiful…so beautiful. I called the largest cub Pardito, I think it's a male."

"Why d'you call him that?" he asked

"He's a kind of sandy brown, isn't that what pardo means?"

Lince pardinus, David recalled the Latin name for the Iberian lynx.

"Before we left the city, I had to see them again so badly that I……that I….." The girl couldn't continue. She wasn't crying any more although tears lay wet on her flushed cheeks.

"What happened, Stella?" He asked quietly. The girl looked up watching the sunlight play on his blond hair noticing the way his eyes softened as he spoke to her. It gave her confidence to continue.

"I spent the night on the hill alone ….in a ruined hut. It was exciting at first, but as it got dark I grew frightened. I slept badly, but when I awoke, in the morning…. I saw…saw the genet. It was stalking a pheasant then quite suddenly the lynx appeared from nowhere. It chased the genet …chased and killed it."

"I know you must have been very frightened Stella."

"No I wasn't … I wasn't frightened at all," she gasped, wiping the tears hurriedly from her wet cheeks and trying to smile.

"Well I'm glad. You know Stella, you've seen something amazing, something very few zoologists, myself included, have ever seen!"

"I think I'd like to be a biologist like you." She said shyly, looking up at him. "When I saw the lynx chasing the genet I wanted to tell people, wanted to ask so many questions but I couldn't, everybody says they're vermin, they'd be hunted down. And I couldn't tell them I'd lied."

"Lied?" David repeated softly.

"I wasn't supposed to be there. I lied to my parents, to…….everyone!" She gulped and bit her lip, suddenly frightened by her confession.

David sat on the rock beside the girl. For a long while he didn't speak and his silence made Stella even more anxious.

"Stella," he said as if coming to a decision. "I want to ask you something. Well two things actually."

Stella nodded apprehensively without looking up.

"Firstly, promise me that you'll never go out alone at night again. Suppose you'd been injured. Your parents would have been out of their minds with worry."

She nodded, fearful his next request would be to tell them what she'd done. Instead, David himself was full of surprises.

"Stella..," he began "This is something important to me and.... perhaps to you." She sensed he was talking to her as he would an adult.

"Janni tells me that everyone in your biology class has do a project next term." She nodded restlessly.

"I'd like to invite a few of her class down to the museum and help with their projects and our work if they'd like to come. Hanna and Jamie perhaps and maybe the other boys." He nodded towards the path where her friends had already disappeared into the mass of schoolchildren. "... and you of course."

Stella nodded, the museum didn't sound very exciting, not half as exciting as the Xando trip.

"You see, I think from what you told me, you might be able to help the conservation team, particularly the lynx project."

" But how can I help?" This 'conservation' team sounded rather daunting and very different from her experiences on her grandfather's farm.

"You could tell them what you've told me. There aren't many people, even scientists like myself who have been able to observe the lynx in their natural habitat as you have."

"But my parents......I'd have to tell them too and..."

"Stella that's why I thought of your summer projects. You could study the local wildlife and the threats to them, it needn't just be about the lynx. You'd have to come to the museum for research and while you're there you can tell my colleagues more about what you've seen. No-one else would need to know about your lynx family."

Stella nodded thoughtfully.

"The lynx ... are they, are they endangered David?

"Well the lynx especially. We only know of a few very small populations in the wild - even those in Doñana park, and in Sierra Morena are tiny. The more we learn about your lynx the more we can prevent them becoming extinct. So you see how important this would be for us - and for the lynx."

Stella nodded but she still couldn't understand quite how she could help.

"Listen I probably shouldn't tell you this but the team are hoping to buy some land to set up a captive breeding unit, by the end of the summer. I can't tell you where but ...." and here David put his finger to his lips. "This is our secret, you mustn't tell anyone!"

A lynx reserve, it sounded too wonderful. Stella looked down at her hands.

"My parents?" Stella asked anxiously and so quietly that David had to bend down to hear her. "And my grandfather, they wouldn't have to know?"

"Not about the lynx no. I could arrange with Janni to act as your mentor for the project so it would be easy to see the team. Janni will have to agree it with your parents, or course, and we'll just have small group."

"And I would really be able to help them - Pardito, his family?"

David nodded.

"I don't know what to say, it's what I've always wanted." Stella laughed in excitement and quickly hugged him.

"Just yes will be enough!"

After the tears, her laughter was infectious. David was soon laughing himself. Suddenly they were aware of a whistle shrilling from the car park. Stella's schoolmates were converging on the school bus, she ran on ahead anxious to catch them up. At the side of the coach she turned, waved enthusiastically, then shot up the steps and disappeared from his sight. Stella hurried towards the seat she and Hanna had shared on the outward journey. Jamie was sitting beside the girl talking animatedly. He shifted when Stella approached and sidled to the other side of the bus. She hardly looked at him, just knelt conspiratorially beside her friend.

"I've got some news," she tried to talk quietly but her voice rose excitedly.

"I can see that," Hanna smirked. "I knew you had a crush on him."

"Hanna, you don't understand." Even Hanna's reproach could not dim Stella's excitement.

"Listen." She twisted in her seat so that her back blocked the view to the other children, including Jamie. Raising her finger to her lips, she whispered, "David's going to invite some of us, just you and me and a few of the boys to do our summer project at the museum."

"The City museum?" Hanna cried out, rather too loudly.

Stella felt a thrill of achievement. A huge grin spread over Hanna's face and her eyes shone magnificently.

"However did you manage that, you angel?" Hanna asked, but she didn't wait for an answer. "This will be wonderful, there's so much research being done there, we'll be in the middle of it all and ...," She hugged Stella violently. Watching them both from across the central aisle of the bus, Jamie felt a sudden pang of jealousy.

FIVE

Later in the week, while rushing down one of the school corridors, Stella heard her name called. Her friend Jade was standing in a classroom doorway.

"Where are you going in such a hurry?" she laughed as Stella juggled the books she was clutching.

"I haven't finished the Maths homework, I just ..."

"Perhaps I'll see you later then." Jade nodded unconcerned and moved back into the classroom.

"Oh, the homework can wait," Stella said hurriedly, following her into the room. She dumped her books on the nearest bench. Jade laughed, she began to clean the whiteboard with a soft rubber. She was class monitor for the week.

"I haven't seen you for some time. Do you wanted another English session soon?" Jade asked as if she were actually Stella's tutor.

"Of course, I'd love to but I've been busy." Rushing on with her news, she told Jade about the Torcal trip and the English biologist.

"So, I suppose you won't need my help with your English any more."

"Oh no Jade, of course I do. I don't want to give up our sessions, rather the opposite, but....,"

"But... " said Jade, obviously amused "there's something else you want to do instead."

"No, I just wondered...... well we're going to visit the Xando Sanctuary after Easter, and Hanna said you lived near there. I didn't know."

"Xando?" Jade turned back from the board. She put the cloth down on the teacher's desk.

"Yes of course it is. My uncle's an administrator and my cousin, Emilio, tends the animals. But it's just a little zoo you know!" Jade's face had clouded momentarily. She thought of the few times she had been inside Xando. To her the animals, victims of accidents or orphans, always seemed rather forlorn. But she thought it best not to dampen her friend's enthusiasm.

"Zoo, I thought it was an animal sanctuary?" Stella said still excited.

"When's the visit?" Jade asked, ignoring Stella's comment.

"The 25th, at the end of April."

"But that's my birthday Stella! Look why don't you come to the party after your visit, I'm sure I can arrange with mother for you to stay. It's a Thursday and we could come to school together next day."

"Oh, heavens, that would be marvellous Jade, and we could speak English, all evening."

"Well I'm not sure mother would like that, you see she never learnt the language," Jade gave a small private smile.

Their first museum trip was arranged for the following Thursday afternoon, the week before the trip to Xando. Only three children, Stella and Hanna and the boy Jamie, joined Janni in the school minibus for the short trip to the city centre. David's invitation had been narrowed down to the five pupils who had accompanied him at Torcal, although Pablo had declined the offer saying he was going to concentrate instead on his technical studies.

Surprisingly, Pietro was expected to join them, though there was no sign of him as Jamie and the two girls entered the minibus. After a few minutes Janni tapped the wheel, becoming irritable. "Where's Pietro, we'll be late if we leave it much longer!"

At the back of the minibus noticing that Hanna and Jamie were deep in conversation, Janni stared accusingly at Stella.

"Go and find him," she shouted as if the boy's absence was Stella's fault.

Stella clambered down from the bus and hurried around the back only to see Pietro loitering in a doorway not two metres away. His face bore a semi-quizzical, semi amused look. Stella had the uncomfortable feeling he had purposely delayed his arrival.

"Aren't you coming, Janni's getting upset," she asked awkwardly, gesturing towards the minibus.

"Doesn't take much to upset her," Pietro said. He slouched against the wooden upright of the doorway. Stella turned to look back towards the bus checking that Janni wasn't listening.

"Well come on." Her mouth was dry.

"No, I don't think I will."

"What do you mean, what about your project?

"Project..." The boy sneered, "....Lost interest "

"But I thought you were interested in wildlife!"

"Well you were wrong. Do you think I want to be lectured by some busy-body academic. It's bad enough when she starts." He nodded towards the bus where Janni had just caught sight of him through the side mirror. The engine revved.

"Come on," Janni insisted.

Stella rushed to the doorway. Janni waved angrily at Pietro who had followed her and now stood by the door.

"He's not coming," Stella gasped entering the bus.

Pietro stared at her but said nothing. His strong hands fastened around the door handle then thrust the sliding door closed with a bang. He remained staring through the open window.

"As you wish, but I shall have to apologise to the museum staff for you," Janni barked, slipping the vehicle into first gear and heading towards the schoolyard exit.

David lead Stella along a corridor in the academic block of the museum. Jamie and Hanna had been met a few minutes before by two museum staff and had already disappeared into the research block. As she walked at David's side Stella became increasingly awed over the approaching interview. She clutched at her biology workbook for support. David came to a halt in front of a door. There was a white sign near the top.

"It says Director's office," Stella queried, feeling even more uneasy.

"Yes that's right." David bent to turn the handle

"But I thought it was just the conservation people - like you."

David hesitated before opening the door

"Don't worry, Doctor Mansera is part of the team too. He's worked in the Austrian Alps studying the European Lynx, it's a cousin of our own lynx. He's really looking forward to meeting you." Stella felt her stomach churn but David smiled, opening the door and giving her no chance to withdraw. The room was large with tall windows through which the afternoon sunlight poured illuminating polished wood furniture. Stella blinked and could not see anyone seated at the pine desk in the middle of the room. Then she realised that a man was walking towards her from a side alcove furnished with easy chairs and a table. The man wasn't very tall and had a thatch of grey hair framing eyes that seemed friendly and warm. It also helped that the man reminded her a little of Grandfather Ramon.

"Hello," the man said rather softly. "You must be Stella." He had taken her hand like an adult and given it a warm squeeze.

"This is Doctor Abra Mansera," David said. Stella nodded shyly.

"Would you like a drink Stella. It's thirsty work looking at all our cases isn't it." He nodded to David.

"What would you like Stella?"

"Eh.. lemonade... please." Stella said looking up at the man rather than at David.

Doctor Mansera ushered her around to the upholstered chairs.

"I think we'll be more comfortable here."

Stella saw that two more people, a man and woman, were seated on easy chairs behind the low coffee table. Both got up to greet her.

"Stella, this is Doctor Liz Delgado, she's leading biologist of the conservation team." The woman was dressed in a colourful summer top and fashionably tight jeans. She wasn't at all Stella's image of a museum researcher.

"David's told us to expect great things from you Stella!" The girl felt shocked and glanced at David before giving her hand timidly to the woman.

"Don't frighten the girl Liz." David brought the lemonade across. The liquid was cold and bubbly. She took a deep swallow before looking at the other man in the room.

"And this is Doctor Bernard van Hertan, Stella. His speciality is ecology, so he'll be able to fill us in on the landscape aspects." Doctor Hertan looked bored, he reached up and took her hand somewhat hesitantly before settling back into his chair. Stella's uneasiness increased. This time David did not seem to notice. He settled himself quite casually on the side arm of one of the chairs.

"Won't you sit down Stella." Doctor Mansera encouraged. "As you can see we are very cosmopolitan here, Dr Hertan is from Holland and of course you know Doctor Foster is from England." Stella didn't really know what the word cosmopolitan meant so just nodded. She sat down and quickly drained the lemonade so that she didn't have to look up at all their faces.

"David tells me that we are going to help with your biology project this summer. Is that your school book, may I see?"

Doctor Mansera gave her a winning smile which helped Stella willingly give up the loose folder. As he reached into it pulling out her notes together with photos she had cut from magazines and information from websites. He had the same determined look and casual air as David himself, perhaps that was how biologists look she thought. Then she caught sight of Liz Delgado watching her intently from the depths of her chair.

"And in return ...," the woman began, "David says you're going to help us."

"Take no notice of any of them Stella." Dr Mansera chided. The others laughed. Stella managed a weak flustered smile. She looked down at the floor, some of the papers from her folder had slipped to the floor and

Liz was picking them up and looking at each page, she nodded over them and carefully tucked them back into the folder which Doctor Mansera placed on the table.

"Stella," Dr Mansera began. "I think David has told you that anything you might tell us will be in confidence. I can promise you that for us all."

"Stella do you want to tell Doctor Mansera about Pardito?" David coerced.

"Pardito?" Queried Doctor Mansera. He gave Stella a knowing smile. "Is he your lynx friend, the one David told us about?"

Stella nodded. Doctor Mansera looked down at her with his kindly eyes. She began speaking, feeling as though she was talking to him alone. It was easy to talk about the goat-herding - far easier than it had been with the children at school. It was very much harder to describe the day her grandfather killed the trapped lynx right before her eyes. Her voice wavered. To the group around the table, it seemed as if she was close to weeping. Then, inexplicably, as she described the first time she'd seen the small cub Pardito with his mother and siblings, her eyes had brightened, then dimmed again sorrowfully as she described her own fears for those same cubs. Finally she came to the morning when the mother lynx had killed the genet. She looked at David for support.

"She simply leapt up and brushed the genet off the branch. I'm sure it was already dead as they hit the ground." She concluded and sighed deeply.

Stella heard Liz gasp from her seat in the corner.

"You really saw that Stella, really....?"

Stella didn't know how to counter the doubt visible on Liz's face.

David spoke for her.

"I believe Stella's telling us the truth."

"But you must have been very close, how did you manage it - if you were out with the goats, they're such noisy beasts."

"Don't say if you don't want to Stella." David advised, but Stella couldn't accept the look of disbelief in the woman's eyes.

"I wasn't with the goats, I went up on the hillside alone, the last day before we left for the city - I slept in a ruined hut - alone."

"Curiouser, and curiouser," Liz intoned. "But wasn't that dangerous, what did your parents say?"

"I think we've heard enough from Stella today, Liz....." Doctor Mansera interrupted.

He nodded to his colleagues. David had told him the full story of Stella's night-time vigil but he had no intention of asking her to discuss any details.

"Remember Stella, nothing you tell us here will go beyond this room. We are just grateful that you have shared this with us."

"Now Liz, it's our turn. Why don't you tell Stella about the work at Xando and our plans for the future."

"The new project too doctor...?" Liz queried

Dr Mansera nodded noting Liz's obvious reluctance. "Just a brief outline at the moment so that Stella knows why Xando's work is so important."

"Well yes. Xando is very special.... " Liz looked directly at Stella, "not just for your lynx friend but for all our endangered animals. If they recover sufficiently then ideally we try to return them to their original habitat - if it's possible."

"Why wouldn't it be possible?"

Liz sighed clearly trying to disguise her impatience.

"Because often new development in the area means it's no longer suitable for them, Stella."

David nodded in agreement.

"We have to make the decision whether to release it somewhere else. It's not always possible. There's one wolf at Xando that was brought in by a tourist as a road casualty. It had a broken leg but although it got better quickly there wasn't anywhere in Andalucía with good wolf habitat. He's been there six years now."

"But where did the wolf come from?" asked Stella puzzled

"He was found east of Granados, Stella, but the nearest known wolf colony is hundreds of kilometres to the east. He was a young male, so he may have been dispersing," David explained.

"Dispersing?" Stella queried again

"When there are too many animals in a territory there may not be enough food for all of them, so some of the young animals have to leave. Often they're driven out by their own parents."

"I ....I think I understand."

Liz leant forwards in her seat, her attitude mellowing slightly.

"It's the same with many young animals Stella."

"Will that happen to Pardito?"

"Your lynx.....probably," Liz replied rather brusquely. "But Stella. just looking after sick animals and returning them to the wild isn't really enough. We want... we have to do something more."

She glanced quickly over at Dr. Mansera, who nodded and gave a slow whistle between his teeth.

"We want to start a captive breeding project for the lynx, Stella. It's the most endangered of all the animals in Spain. We can't let the Iberian lynx die out in the wild, it's just too important for Spain ...... for Europe even."

Stella recalled her earlier conversation with David.

"Will you be able to release all the young animals?"

"Perhaps not right away Stella. Xando is not appropriate for breeding the lynx. In a couple of months we will know if the first part of our plan is to go ahead."

"The first part?" Stella move to the edge of her seat, trying to curb her growing enthusiasm.

Liz hesitated again but was encouraged by Dr Mansera's smile.

"Many people won't understand. We need to educate them about the lynx. Perhaps you can help too - with this project of yours."

She tapped Stella's folder.

"But how?" Stella asked, now quite overawed by the proposal.

"Well, you won't be able to tell people about our project yet, but if we show you our research into the lynx you could use it in your school project, show your family and school friends that the lynx is not to be feared because you see ...," here Liz sighed. "The second part of our project is almost as important. You asked if the young animals will be released. Well there wouldn't be any point if they couldn't be, but their habitat is being lost all the time, through development or road building."

Stella was caught up in the argument

"And David said even the rabbit is de- declining too, and the lynx only eat rabbit?"

"You're right Stella. We can't release the lynx until there are more rabbits."

"What will you do then?" Stella asked rather forlornly

"Work slowly and steadily Stella - to educate people."

"To save the rabbit...?" she asked, incredulous.

"And the habitat," said David

"And the lynx," Liz chorused.

"Well I think we are all agreed on that," concluded Dr. Mansera laughing quietly to himself. "How about you Bernard, have you anything else to offer."

Stella had sensed the man's indifference throughout the discussion. Slowly he leaned forwards and spoke to Dr. Mansera rather than Stella.

"Just that it won't be easy to change people's ways - neither the hunters and farmers, nor the road-builders, and that's what we have to do."

"Well Bernard's right of course, but if our research is thorough enough we should have sufficient evidence to convince people."

Dr Mansera turned in his seat and smiled down at Stella.

"Now Stella, do you think you could come back and see us again, there are some more questions we would like to ask. About where you saw the lynx, how many times you saw them, that sort of thing. It will be terribly useful for our research if you could?"

Dr. Mansera's resemblance to Ramon was very strong. Stella felt as if she were talking to him in his flower-filled garden.

"I'd like to come. For Pardito's sake."

"For Pardito's sake then Stella. I'll look forward to it."

David opened the door and escorted her along the corridor. Stella heard mumbled voices from the room behind them.

"You did really well, I'm very proud of you," David squeezed her shoulder and realised for the first time that the girl was trembling.

"Remember Stella - it's for Pardito, just like you said," he urged. In the darkly lit corridor he thought he saw the girl smile.

The coach speeded into Xando's small gravel car park and had to stop abruptly beside a metal fence. As the coach door opened, the odours from the animal compound quickly became apparent. The musky smell of faeces and stale food mingling with rich animal smells, closed around the children as they disembarked.

"Come on children, " Janni called, stepping down from the coach. "Dr. Foster will be waiting for us."

"Phew, how long are we staying here, that smell's disgusting?" Pietro halted just outside the coach door unwilling to go any further. Several children gathered around him, a few held their noses and pretended to cough.

"Now come on…," said Janni "We'll only be here an hour, I thought everyone was interested in the animals at Xando. How many of you have actually seen a wolf or an eagle in the wild."

"I have," called Hanna defiantly. "I've seen lots of eagles and vultures too." She marched away from the coach towards Stella who was standing beside the tall wooden gates and gazing towards a distant glade of trees. Intriguing noises came from within: tiny squeaks and bubbling sounds that could have come from mammal or bird, and once a slow subdued grunt.

Not wanting to be left out, most of the other children followed Hanna and Stella through the entrance and into the wide compound.

When Stella looked back she could see Janni standing by the bus where Pietro remained leaning against its side. The boy shook his head a couple of times then shrugged and with Janni's hand on his shoulder allowed himself to be guided towards the centre. Stella felt sympathy with many of the other children, unlike her they hadn't grown up with domestic animals or got used to their scent. What she couldn't understand was Pietro's growing resentment. Suddenly David Foster's voice called from inside the building.

"Come on Janni, bring the children in."

David Foster appeared in the doorway, dressed in a bleached blue shirt and faded working jeans. He waved the children forwards and gave Stella a special nod as she passed him in the throng alongside Hanna and Jamie.

"Well Stella are you looking forward to the tour?" She nodded hurriedly.

"We're just going to start the introductory talk, but first have you decided when you're coming to the museum again?"

"It depends on Janni, she has to bring us in the bus, but I think she said a week on Thursday."

"OK, I'll have a word with her. Are Hanna and Jamie coming, they seem to be getting on well together don't they?" Stella wasn't sure he was referring to her friends' projects or their growing relationship. Stella just nodded and was almost glad when Janni called from the end of the room.

"Children, Doctor Farenzo will give us an introduction to Xando Institute or Animal Sanctuary as it is sometimes called. Then you can go round the animal cages - or as he likes to say, animal houses, but remember we have to be back at the coach by 3.30."

Doctor Farenzo was a tall man of about fifty. Like David, he was dressed casually in a light cream shirt tucked into faded jeans and when he spoke he had that rare capacity of seeming to address each child in turn so warming them to his topic. He described each of the sanctuary's animals, their history and health. Stella listened intently about the wolf which had been brought in six years ago. Then a genet cub which had been found by a hunter apparently orphaned only six months before, it had a crippled foot and could never be released. Many of the children appeared deeply concerned but she noticed that one boy wasn't paying attention. Pietro of course. Standing at the back of the class, blowing bubbles against the glass pane with his gum and making his friends laugh.

"But it's not all sad. We've had many successes, many animals, and birds, have been released from here, and we have plans to expand our work to help more animals. Now are there any questions?"

"Why can't they go to another zoo or be let free?" a boy called Soli asked. The room had grown so quiet that everyone heard Pietro's sarcastic snigger.

Doctor Farenzo ignored him and spoke directly to Soli.

"Well, animal society is just as complex as human society, you can't be sure they will get on together and if you release inexperienced animals they won't be able to fend for themselves. We have a young female lynx that was brought here in August last year as an orphan." And here he glanced towards David who nodded. Stella's ears pricked up, sure it was the same cub David mentioned in class,

"David had been tracking her mother, over near the Tejedas, but I'm sorry to say he found the female had been killed." Several of the girls gave woeful sighs.

"We knew she had a small cub. It wouldn't have survived in the wild and we managed to trap her next day. She has never lived independently. Rabbits are a lynx staple food but she hasn't learnt how to catch them here at Xando."

"Well why don't you train her to catch them, is it difficult?" asked Jamie

"Yes I'm afraid it is young man. We would need to build a very large enclosure and.."

"Well can't you do that?...If you're all so clever?" Pietro mocked sarcastically from the rear of the hall.

Doctor Farenzo glanced towards Pietro not seeming at all annoyed by the interruption. Turning his attention back to the whole class he continued patiently.

"I'm sure you understand children, that no matter how *clever* we are, it takes a lot of resources and time, but it is something we are considering - for the future. Now I think I had better let you go on your walk around the site, or there will not be time for you to see everything. David here, and some of the other staff will accompany you."

Stella's first impression of the sanctuary grounds as she walked around the corner of the first animal 'house' reminded her of Jade's description of the institute - a tiny suburban zoo. But this 'zoo' wasn't intended as a public showcase. It was a sanctuary for animals. But she had to agree, it was very small with many of the cages clustering around a central courtyard. Only thirty metres away Stella could make out the high wire fence that bordered the compound. Isolated to one side were some cages screened by high boards. From them subtle animals odours wafted across the site. Stella walked around the courtyard where she found Hanna and Jamie. Hanna was gesturing up into the boughs of a tree in the centre of a pen.

"There, two birds perched at the top."

"Oh, I see them They're well camouflaged aren't they," James yelped excitedly.

"You've found your eagles then," Stella commented, coming up behind them. Hanna swung round to face her looking buoyant.

"Oh yes, Stella, aren't they magnificent? Jamie wishes he had studied them instead of the ibex!" Hanna said hopefully. "But it's not as good as Palofini, the cages are larger there and they're doing such important work and....."

Here Stella interrupted. "But they're doing a lot of work here too, why they're going to... " then she remembered she wasn't supposed to know about the new breeding programme..."to extend the site, that's what Doctor Farenzo said?"

"So he said, but you have to admit it's rather small," said Jamie taking Hanna's side.

"Look Hanna I'd better look at the ibex and the wild goats, I need to do some work on my project."

"OK I'll wait here then, I want to take some photos, mother's given me her camera."

Jamie turned to go and then looked back at Stella

"Have you found the wolf and your lynx yet?" he asked

"My lynx?" replied Stella rather startled,

"Yes, aren't you doing a project on carnivores? I bet you've never even seen a live lynx before have you?"

Stella stared back at him and shook her head.

"Well, I saw a notice when we came in, they're in a separate compound at the back, it's beyond the ibex pens. Shall I show you?" Without waiting for an answer, he lead off down a corridor between the deer pens.

Several groups of children were already clustered around the wolf pen, which was enclosed on two sides by high wooden fences. The other two wire-meshed sides looked out through the boundary fence to an abandoned orchard where fruit trees and olives grew amid ragged scrubland. A pile of large stones and brushwood formed a central lair where the animal could retreat from the sun and the eyes of visitors. The creature was clearly much used to people.

There was nothing aggressive in the listless way it moved about its dusty pen, simply pacing back and forth alongside a low metal barrier. Occasionally swinging up as if to get a better view the wolf would then drop back to begin its pacing once more. This was classic repetitive behaviour known in zoo animals the world over, their innate response to any fence. Stella found the wolf's listless pacing distressing. She noticed too how the wolf's paws grew dusty from the compound soil. The fur on its chin had also worn thin from continually brushing along the fence. Suddenly, as if becoming aware that the noisy stimulus of the children had ceased, the wolf stopped pacing and appeared about to turn, instead it sloped off towards its lair with its grey tail hanging down. He crouched down in the shade of the shrub and slept instantly.

Stella no longer felt any desire to see the lynx pen. The very thought of seeing a wild animal like Pardito pacing in the same way as the wolf had, depressed her. She walked slowly around the back of the wolf pen towards the perimeter fence, and reached another enclosure. It was half the size of the wolf pen with a similar central pile of stones and earth. Stella was almost relieved to read a sign declaring its incumbent, a young genet, to be a secretive animal. Visitors were unlikely to see it. She walked on uncaring past the empty pen, then unexpectedly came face to face with David and three other children.

"Stella we've been looking for you."

"Is it time to go?" She asked half-heartedly.

"No, I thought you'd want to see the lynx pen, we're just going there, isn't that right children?"

Stella could hardly refuse to join them. Two boys and a girl named Susie, fell into step beside Stella. David lead the way down a passage at the side of the genet enclosure. They came out opposite a wide wire-fence facing the abandoned orchard that offered glimpses of the distant sierras. Even, in April, long white swathes of snow cloaked the summits and the dark conifers of the high forest stood out starkly on the foothills. The two boys were chattering and laughing among themselves and the other girl, Susie, who didn't know Stella, smiled at her shyly. The boys went ahead rushing to the next fence. They spotted the notice *Lynx pardinus* with its accompanying photograph of a lynx but within seconds the first boy said.

"I can't see anything, there's nothing there at all. Mr David has the lynx been moved do you think?"

"Well Doctor Farenzo didn't say so. Do you want to go and ask?"

The two boys streamed away up the path alongside the boundary fence leaving Susie to follow slowly in their wake. For a moment the girl looked back at her, but Stella was too obsessed to notice. She stood beside the biologist and looked out across the lynx enclosure. This was so very different from the others that Stella's heart leapt with anticipation. At the bottom of the fence, instead of the metal shields was an extra cordon of wood and wire. Shrubby vegetation with strange grey-green leaves competed for space among last summer's dried grasses crowded on a raised area near the centre. They jostled each other in the faint breeze giving an aromatic tang to the overheated air that reached Stella's nostrils. On the flatter ground a variety of small trees, juniper and myrtle, were growing so closely together that half the enclosure was in shadow.

Stella turned to David in amazement.

"But it's so different," she exclaimed.

"Yes, Stella. It's a new idea, much more natural because we know so much more about the lynx now. They have their dens in thick undergrowth and hunt in the open where the rabbits are. This was built specially for the female lynx. Doctor Mansera realised we wouldn't be able to release her quickly. He must have been thinking ahead to the new project even then."

Stella peered into the pen, sunlight was bathing the scented shrubs and the little breeze had dropped. She could no longer detect their acrid scent. The shade in the centre of the pen was a dark contrast.

"Do you really think they've moved the lynx?" she asked anxiously.

"Probably not Stella, you might never see her in all that vegetation, they're very secretive, but you know that of course! - Do you want me to ask?" he added.

Stella raised her head and gave him an imploring look.

"I'll be back in a few minutes."

Stella didn't bother to watch him go. She walked slowly down the length of the fence until she was standing almost opposite the low mound. In the close-by orchard the wind was rustling the almonds' new green leaves. There were no other sounds as most of the other children were in distant corners of the reserve. Stella placed her hand lightly on a fence post and stood very still looking into the compound. For long moments nothing stirred, the breeze was fickle, blowing idly then stopping again. Beneath the junipers it would be much cooler. At first she thought it was only the grass stems moving, then the herbs parted briefly. She held the gaze of the lynx, not wanting to move or even breath. The sun beat down on her head and a heat haze shimmered on the blanched grasses. After a few seconds, the young lynx edged through the shrubs and settled down on a bare patch of soil bathed in sunlight. It was quite a small animal with pale fur, much lighter than Pardito's, and had round yellow eyes that peered out of an almost white face surrounded by a darker ruff.

Looking deep into the animal's eyes Stella felt a sudden pang of excitement. It was as if some ancient channel had opened between her and the lynx. Still carrying its image in her mind she looked above the almonds towards the jagged peaks of the sierras. Despite the fierce morning heat, she revived her own memories of Holm Cottage: the chill of the mountain tops, the cool smell of pine resin and heard water thawing from snow laden peaks. From lower down the slopes where the great holm oaks stood, came the rich scent of damp earth and the autumn harvest of acorns. She looked back at the lynx sleeping lazily in the sunshine. Long moments passed.

The girl's wondering expression made David hesitate from walking towards her. He looked into the pen and saw the lynx dozing on its raised knoll, but the animal quickly sensed his presence. Almost without moving it melted into the undergrowth and was no longer there. Had he really seen it? He wanted to call out to the girl - did you see the lynx? But he knew she had. He watched her moving slowly as if in a trance alongside the fence. Looking up only when she reached the tarmacked pathway, Stella welcomed David with a sunny smile and came running towards him. "I'm going to be a wildlife zoologist," she gasped.

"I know," David said. "I know."

They both laughed.

Beyond the boundary fence, a figure moved beneath the almond trees. Pietro stood in the shadows listening to their laughter. He was frowning deeply.

SIX

Jade was waiting for her at Xando's gates. Stella collected her overnight bag from the coach and walked with her friend down the long tree-lined avenue which bordered the sanctuary. The smells from the enclosures still lingered in the air and Stella wondered how Jade, with her aversion to the zoo, lived so nearby.

"Well?" Jade asked. "What did you think of Xando, was it what you expected?"

"Well Doctor Farenzo gave a talk before we looked around. I know you said it's just a little zoo - but really it's much more than that isn't it. They take in so many wounded animals and they have plans to expand."

"There isn't much land left around here. They've been trying for ages to buy that abandoned orchard at the back. An old man owns it but his family won't let him sell, I think they want to develop it once he dies."

"That's an awful thing to say," Stella said thinking Jade must be wrong.

"It's what everyone's saying. The orchard would make an ideal extension. But it'll be expensive and people don't want to sponsor an animal centre."

Stella wanted to protest, but didn't feel she could argue with Jade on this her birthday.

"Did you meet Emilio, my cousin?"

"I don't think so, there were so many people."

"Well, he should be at the party so I'll introduce you. He's so good with the animals. At twenty-two he hasn't any formal qualifications. My uncle Estaban is always nagging him to go to college, but Emilio says he wouldn't learn anything from books that the animals themselves can't teach him."

"I…. I'd like to meet him," Stella said tentatively, not quite sure what this implied about Emilio.

Jade had reached the end of the road, now she turned aside towards a copse of trees that appeared to bar their way. Stella couldn't see through the greenery. There was no sign of an entranceway.

"Trouble is…" Jade was saying. "The house will be bursting tonight. Did I tell you you're going to share my room after all. Old Aunt Hilarie and her husband will be too tired to go back to town tonight so they are staying in the guest bedroom you were going to have. My two older brothers are also here with their wives and children - all four under ten!" Jade rattled on as they reached the thick yew hedge.

Without pausing she lead Stella through a narrow archway within the trees. Suddenly they were in a wide spread of garden sloping down across flowerbeds and grass borders towards a tall building set within a complex of low walled parterres. Close to the house ran a broad crescent-shaped bed planted up with a colourful roses. Stella had never before seen such an opulent display. The house was built of solid grey stone and looked imposing with three storeys and eight sets of windows spanning each storey. To Stella it seemed a palace. She looked up and gasped.

"Is that really your house?"

"Yes, it's too big isn't it. It was built last century for mum's parents. When we took it over they moved into an apartment at the back. You'll meet them later. The house will be so full, although it'll be lovely to see everyone of course but so noisy. Do your parents have parties like this?"

"Sometimes, but we don't have such a big family as you."

"I know Dad thinks we're crazy sometimes. He says the Spanish overdo things."

"Doesn't he have any family - in England?"

"He's got one sister we hardly every see, - Gillian, or Gilly as he calls her. She's older than him. She travels a lot. Sometimes she comes to Spain in the spring, but never stays with us for long. You know I have five brothers, all older than me so Gilly hardly remembers any birthdays. Occasionally I get a card and sometimes a present. When I was twelve, long after my actual birthday, a parcel arrived from Australia with a cuddly kangaroo in it - I don't think I even knew what a kangaroo was then, and she can't have had any idea of my age," Jade said vastly amused.

"She won't be here tonight then?"

"Unlikely. Look there's mother now. I'll introduce you first, then take you to my room before all the fun starts. "

The studded wooden doorway of the mansion had opened and in the entranceway stood a tall woman wearing a long dress of elegant turquoise silk which shimmered in the light breeze. Jade's mother beckoned to the girls The woman's obvious sophistication was daunting, Stella held back as Jade introduced her.

"Hello Stella." The women said leaning down to take Stella's hand in both her own. Her voice was gentle.

"I'm afraid, you'll have to introduce Stella to the family, Jade. I've got to help Aunt Hilarie settle in and your brothers' children are already playing havoc in the garden."

Eventually she let go of Stella's hand saying, "I want you to enjoy yourself dear, but I'll have to leave Jade to look after you." With that she disappeared into the shadowed hallway.

"Quickly," Jade said. "Let's get you organised, then we can join the fray."

She lead a rather hesitant Stella through the dark wood-panelled hallway, then ran along a corridor and up two flights of stairs. Jade pushed open a doorway into a bedroom and lead Stella to a bed under one of the tall windows.

"This is your bed," she announced. Stella gazed round the

sumptuously furnished room feeling overawed. She couldn't remember ever seeing such elegance. The room was at the front of the house facing back across the gardens. Through the open windows came the mingled scent of roses and conifers. There was no hint of the animal smells from Xando, only several hundred metres away beyond the tall trees.

"It's lovely," said Stella breathing in the scented air.

"Well we can't stop. See if you can find your way back, then I'll introduce you to whoever's around. Come on."

Stella lead the way to the top of the stairs. A pair of corridors ran towards the back of the house. She glanced quickly at each to ensure she could identify them again, then at Jade's goading ran down to the hallway.

"This way," Jade called from behind her.

Several rooms lead off to the right. From many of them came the sounds of conversation and laughter, but Jade rushed towards the rear of the house and came out eventually into a large salon running the whole width of the house. The room was decorated in soft pinks and greens and furnished with more easy chairs and settees than Stella had seen in any department store. Windows ran the whole length of the room, their span broken only by wide conservatory doors standing open to rich lawns bathed in evening sunlight. It was full of people, conversation bubbled over them in waves. More comforting, laughter rang from the shrubbery where flashes of sunlight caught the colours in the children's clothing. A child shrieked. Two boys about six years old, burst from the bushes and tumbled giggling to the ground.

"Oh that'll be the twins, Ingles and Jose," Jade said noticing Stella's gaze. "They're just like their father - my bother Felipe," she explained. "He's always teasing me. Now you must meet everyone, then I'll have to help mother, you won't mind being left for a while?"

Stella looked around the room full of people feeling a pang of fear, noticing the shimmer of silk and soft ripple of the women's dresses and smart suits of the men.

"Just for the moment Stella," Jade added, noticing her friend's reaction. She nodded towards the open doorway. "Do you think you'd be happier out there?" Stella nodded, grateful to leave the busy room.

" We'll be eating soon, I'll come back and find you."

Jade turned and ran back across the room. Stella waited on the threshold of the garden looking back at the people in the room and making a new assessment of her friend's affluence. She walked thoughtfully towards the shrubbery where children were playing.

"Hello, who are you?" said a voice beside her. She looked down to see two pairs of bright eyes staring up at her.

"I'm Stella," she said quietly to the two excited boys. " And I know you're the twins." The boys giggled, their faces creasing in identical smiles.

"Want to play 'ring-a-roses' Stella?" asked one boy. Before she could answer he called out and she found herself in the centre of a circle of excited children. Then someone called: "Come and eat. Come on everyone!"

Like children everywhere Stella's young companions scattered towards the conservatory door where Jade was also watching her.

"You seem to be having fun."

Stella nodded, blushing slightly without answering.

"The food's through here, quickly or these vultures will eat all the good things," Jade laughed leading the way towards three large tables groaning under a vast array of food where people were already crowding round with half-filled plates.

"We decided to make it a buffet." Jade laughed. "It's easier this way. Look there's Timothy, my youngest brother, he's just got back from technical school in El Rosal. Just push through there and I'll introduce you."

Timothy was very tall but otherwise he was the image of Jade and had the same knowing confidence. Stella didn't feel so shy with him and asked,

"You're at the technical college? My brother Andras is hoping to go there, what are you studying?"

"Mathematics and technical design, I want to be a surveyor. What does Andras want to do?"

A little embarrassed by his interest she answered quietly

"He wants to build dams and canals... I don't remember what he calls it."

"Hydrologist, that'll be it. How old is he?"

"He's only fifteen but he's hoping to transfer to college next year."

"Well I'll still be there then, perhaps we'll meet up. Look I'd better go, I'm supposed to be helping mother."

With that he was gone and Stella was lost within the moving crowd. She hurriedly gathered some tiny canapés and one thick wedge of Spanish omelette then headed through the throng towards the salon. Feeling completely overawed she perched on a small wooden seat beside the window and began picking at the food. She'd eaten very little when Jade came to find her.

"Are you all right Stella, have you got enough food?" Stella nodded gesturing at the plate.

"It's lovely."

"Oh good, I've brought someone to meet you." Jade announced turning slightly to her left where a young man stood."This is Emilio."

The man smiled down at her but remained silent. He was a little shorter than Timothy and very thin. He wore a startling blue shirt over thin light jeans and soft white trainers and seemed totally out of place among his relations' finery.

"What will you have to drink Emilio?" Jade asked.

"Beer please," he said. As he inclined his head Stella caught a faint glimpse of a thin gold chain at his neck.

"Stella, another drink?" asked Jade picking up Stella's empty glass.

"Some more lemonade please." She looked briefly up at Emilio. He looked younger than his years and had dark wavy hair which he wore down below his ears. He seemed rather an intense young man and disinclined to talk. When Jade returned with their drinks she lingered for a moment nodding quickly to Emilio.

"Well I expect you two have lots to talk about," she said, looking expectantly from one to the other of them. "Well, I'd better mingle." With a sigh Stella watched her friend disappear into the crowd. Emilio remained standing near her. Finding his silence intimidating Stella sipped her drink. She felt rather than saw Emilio place his full plate on the small table beside her. Carelessly he knelt down and stretched out his long legs on the floor.

"David has told me a lot about you Stella."

Stella was so surprised that she looked straight up into the man's face. His dark eyes held her gaze and the tight lips softened into a gentle smile.

"David?" Stella spluttered...."The.. the... zoologist?"

"At Xando, who else. He speaks highly of you."

"But what about....?"

"He says you are good with the animals. You are doing a project on our carnivores, yes?"

Stella could only nod.

"It is a good thing - to work with animals. David says you will be a biologist too, just like him." Stella felt herself blush violently and leant over her plate in embarrassment. But Emilio noticed and was quite forthright.

"You must not be embarrassed Stella. It is a good thing, to work, to be, with animals." Emilio looked away as a sudden burst of laughter broke through the crowd."... and quieter too."

He looked at Stella and winked knowingly. She found herself smiling. She wasn't the only person who found the loud throng intimidating.

"It is more peaceful to be with animals, out in the sanctuary. But sometimes there is sadness too. We do not manage to save all the animals that are brought to us, and some like Malo the wolf, can never be released."

"Why do you call him Malo - he's not bad surely."

"No, but a bad thing happened to him - the accident was a bad thing. And perhaps he had been driven from his home - probably by his own parents. Too many of them and too little food. Not like here." He nodded towards three rather portly women, his own cousins, whose plates were loaded with food.

Discovering it was too easy to follow Emilio's thoughts, Stella found herself laughing inwardly. At the same time she sensed strong emotions playing beneath his calm exterior.

"David said he watched you with the lynx, little Marmit."

"I... I didn't know David was there." She exclaimed rushing on to cover her confusion. "Did he see the lynx too?"

"He said she just melted away as he arrived. He was really surprised to see Marmit with you."

"I .... ," Stella didn't quite know what to say. "I only waited beside the fence and then she appeared. I stayed very still."

"But not everyone would know what to do Stella. And little Marmit is wary of everyone. You were either very lucky, or very clever, I think it is the latter!"

Unused to such praise Stella took a small mouthful of food, all the time feeling Emilio's eyes on her.

"She's been on her own all the time she's been here?"

"Yes, Marmit has been alone for nearly a year now. Perhaps one day we will be able to find her a mate."

"Is that likely, will she accept him if you do?"

"I don't know the answers Stella. All these researchers tell you many things, even David, and ask you to believe them, but animals are individuals with their own experiences and their own natures, you have to consider these too." Stella remained silent mulling over his words. Emilio began eating. Rapidly emptying his plate, he got up.

"That was delicious. I'll get some more. Do you want anything Stella?"

"No ... no thank you. I'll just pour myself some lemonade."

"But you must let me!" Emilio said reaching across the table to pour her drink. Then he disappeared into the dining room. Stella wondered if this enigmatic young man would return. Picking up her drink she squeezed through the bustling crowd but as she reached the doorway Emilio was again beside her.

"You are going to sit on the lawn Stella, I will join you," Emilio announced and preceded her down the steps. "You see how green this lawn is. So very different from the dry pastures - it's such a waste."

Stella decided Emilio was unlike anyone she had ever met. He had an independent train of thought which she found difficult to follow.

"Why a waste?" She asked, the gardens looked particularly beautiful to her compared to the sunburnt hillsides she was used to.

"The water, it's such a waste," he said while tucking into a large slice of potato and onion omelette. "We are draining our landscape dry, there'll be nothing left for the plants, nothing for the animals." He finished the omelette and plucked some grapes from a small bunch in his hand. He offered some to Stella. Too shy to refuse, she took two grapes.

"We feed these to the birds sometimes." He began munching through the remaining grapes.

"To the eagles?"

"Oh yes, they like fruit. Of course we give meat to all the carnivores. We have fairly strict diet sheets for them. People like David prepare them but when you work with them you quickly find out what they like."

"Do you prepare all Xando's food here then?"

"Why of course, I help prepare all the morning feeds and take them round to the pens."

"I'd like to see that, what time do you go round?"

"Before the place is open. But Stella you know we are not an ordinary zoo, people have to phone up and ask to see us. That way disturbance to the animals is kept to a minimum."

Stella lowered her head, suddenly disappointed.

"But ...." Emilio mused to himself, "If you would really like to come, I could perhaps arrange something...,"

"Oh please....,"

"Sometimes we invite children from the local junior school. In fact a visit is planned in a couple of weeks, would you like to join them?"

"Oh Emilio I would love to," Stella cried, realising her shyness of Emilio had completely vanished.

"Then we will try to arrange it, but you shouldn't get too excited Stella. Remember the children are very young, so the visit is quite short. Would you mind?"

"No of course not, perhaps Jade could come with me."

Emilio shrugged. "Yes, Jade is not so interested in our work, but if she will accompany you then that will be for the best. I will ask my aunt to let you know when the arrangements are made. And now I think I must be getting back to Xando." He stood up, suddenly all businesslike.

"You're going back tonight?" Stella asked rather surprised. Shadows had already fallen across the garden. "I thought it was closed up for the night."

She stood up quickly. Emilio was between her and the house. With the lighted windows behind him she again noticed how thin he was.

"It is Stella, but the animals don't know that. We always have someone on site in case there are any problems and Doctor Farenzo or another vet are on standby too. Mostly nothing happens though and we have a little cot to sleep in. It's quite comfortable." He didn't add that the cot was in a room housing a locked case of special guns with anaesthetic darts in case of emergencies.

It was past midnight before Stella and Jade got to bed. The crowded household took a long time to quieten, even so the girls were too excited to sleep. In the cosy darkness of the room, Jade began talking over the events of the evening, then quite casually and without the least suggestion of boasting recited her list of presents. Somehow this lack of pride made Stella respect Jade much more.

"I even received one from Aunty Gilly. Mother said it arrived from Switzerland two months ago but she kept it hidden. Can you guess what it was?"

"I can't possibly guess Jade, at least it can't be a kangaroo," Stella smothered her laughter in her pillow. Jade chuckled but remained silent.

"What was it then?" Stella chivvied.

"It was a beautiful little wooden statuette, exquisitely carved - of a European lynx."

"Oh, do they have lynx in Switzerland?" Stella asked, remembering that Dr Mansera had worked in many European countries.

"I guess so. But you know I thought of someone else who might like it. I've so many other presents and I've already spoken to mother and she says it will be all right. I'll show you it in the morning, but I'd like you to have it ...... if you want that is."

"Oh but, it's yours Jade, I couldn't."

"Well we'll see," Jade swiftly changed the subject. "How did you like

Emilio? Isn't he a remarkable young man?"

Stella considered her answer for so long that Jade must have thought she'd dropped off to sleep.

"Yes, I liked him very much, he seems so dedicated...to the animals," said Stella at last, stifling a deep yawn. "He says I could join a school group visit for the morning feeds. It'll just be little children so I wondered... I wondered whether you could come too - for company?"

"Hum...," Jade murmured into her pillow not knowing what to think of this surprising news. "We'll see, she said at last. "Emilio is very frugal with his invitations, he must have thought you quite special." Stella shifted in her bed and yawned. Enveloped in darkness she tried to picture Emilio asleep in his lonely cot at the Sanctuary, the thought made her shiver. Eventually she too slept.

The following Wednesday a small damp rain worked its way down from the mountains and enveloped the city. The school children had been driven indoors. Stella was pouring over a book in the school library where Jade found her.

"Ecology for schools," she said, reading the title upside-down. "Hola," she said brightly as Stella looked up.

"Have you heard from Emilio?" she asked excitedly, slamming the book closed.

"I might have, but shouldn't you be more concerned with your studies?" Jade teased.

"I am studying - very hard, but...."

Jade relented. "Emilio says it will be O.K. to visit on Saturday week. I'll come in with you if you like, but I have to visit a relation with mother that afternoon. Do you think your parents will be able to bring you?"

"Oh I hope so, Dad says he would probably bring me but I don't think he really wants to visit Xando. So it would be nice if you could come and introduce him to Emilio." Jade looked down at Stella's slightly troubled face, parents were so protective these days.

"O.K. Emilio will be starting work at 8 am. It can't be any later because it takes time to go around all the pens."

"I'll have to check with Dad that it's O.K. Shall I let you know by tomorrow."

"That's fine then. You can get on with your studies now," she said slyly. At that moment the school bell rang.

Next morning the weather had reverted to its normal intense heat. By the end of the school day the classrooms were sweltering and unbearable. The school bell rang at three and most of the children raced for the doorway heading for swimming pools or the beach, but Stella remained expectantly beside Janni's desk alongside Hanna and Jamie.

" Well, it's rather hot children." Janni gathered up her books. "Do you really want to go to the museum? I'll take you in the bus but..."

Hanna's reply was predictable. "Of course, it's all arranged isn't it?" She said, as if there wasn't any doubt.

Although Stella imagined the deliciously cold water of the sea, she knew David and Liz would be expecting her, but in reality she didn't know what more she could tell them about Pardito and his family. She reached into her bag to fondle the small wooden statuette Jade had insisted on giving her. It was made of a rich dark wood with some pale streaks that the craftsman had cleverly sculpted to highlight the lynx's ruff and mottled fur. Jade had seen the sudden light in Stella's eyes when she pressed the gift into her hand. But Stella knew if she told parents about the statuette, they would insist she returned the birthday gift, so she kept it hidden in her schoolbag.

Janni parked the minibus in the temporary bay at the museum and rushed the three children into the entrance hall. There, rather brusquely, she left them in the care of the receptionist, saying:

"I'll come back in an hour and a half." She turned and left without giving the woman a chance to respond.

"Well you had better all tell me who you are visiting. First you little girl?" she said directing herself to Hanna. Stella was amused as Hanna bristled under this title.

"Josie Xavier, the avian curator is expecting me, but I know where her office is, I can easily find her."

"Well I think I'd better telephone Doctor Xavier first?" The receptionist insisted. "She may not be in her office."

She made the call and announced, "She'll be out in about 5 minutes, if you could wait."

"Now," she said turning to Stella "who is it you are visiting?"

"Dr. Mansera and Liz..."

The woman gave Stella a studious look.

"The Director?"

"Yes." Stella replied timidly, aware of the woman's hesitation before she decided to pick up the phone. After a brief conversation the woman's haughty attitude had dissipated.

"I'm afraid they're in the laboratory across the road. It will be about fifteen minutes before they can get here, but Dr. Delgado wants to see you. Perhaps you could go with your friend to the avian section, that way I'll know where to find you."

"Oh O.K. Hanna do you mind?"

At that moment one of the mammal technicians was passing. He recognised Jamie and offered to look after him. The two girls were left to wander around the museum hall where they saw a glass case housing a giant anteater that had once inhabited the hills of Andalucía.

"Two hundred thousand years old, that's unbelievable, isn't it Hanna?"

The girls moved round a bay and looked at another case housing an extinct eagle twice the size of Spain's imperial eagle.

"Now that's what I call an eagle," Hanna said joyously. "Wouldn't it be wonderful to see it flying," she looked longingly at the bird. "Why did it disappear I wonder?" Hanna couldn't take her eyes off the case.

"Probably human influence." Stella ventured.

"But talking of disappearances....." Hanna looked back at Stella, quickly grabbing her by the arm, then uncharacteristically sidled into the wood-panelled corner. "Have you heard anything about Pietro?"

"Pietro?" asked Stella, surprised at the sudden change in Hanna's thoughts.

"I thought you might have heard, he's still in our class you know."

"Well yes, I think he's been away sick, if that's what you mean."

"That's what they like you to think, he's been away all week and there have been other times when he's just not appeared. I heard ..." . and here Hanna looked around conspiratorially, "I heard that his parents are being pursued for his truancy."

"He's got two older brothers as well hasn't he?"

"That's right. They're older and have both left school, but they were always playing truant too."

"It's such a shame," said Stella thoughtfully. "When he joined the nature classes I thought he must really be interested."

"Well I think your concern's misplaced young lady. My father says the family's a bad lot."

"I don't know about that, but I *was* surprised when he came on the Xando trip. He tried to ruin it for everyone else."

"I wouldn't worry about...." but she stopped as a woman in a white laboratory coat walked around the eagle case.

"Hanna," the woman called, "I thought I heard your voice. Doctor Xavier said to bring you along to the lab, she's ready for you now. I told the receptionist your friend would be with us too."

She lead the way back through the maze of offices to the avian department, where Stella sat watching Hanna and the researcher pouring over research papers. Thirty minutes later, just when she began to think Liz had forgotten her a secretary called her away to the office. Liz Delgado was the only person in the room. She wore a lab. coat and was jostling papers on the low coffee table.

"There you are Stella." She stood up hurriedly waving the girl towards her.

"Sit down, sit down. Look I'm sorry but we're rather busy at the moment. Dr. Mansera sends his apologies and.."

"And .... David?" asked Stella feeling rather lost in the big room.

"Oh, Dr Foster wasn't due to be here was he?" Liz asked, surprised. "I thought he was radio- tracking in the sierras. Oh here it is." She handed a small file of papers across to Stella saying.

"I've put all the recent reports of lynx and wolf sightings in Andalucía over the last ten years in there, I thought it might be useful for your project."

Stella thumbed excitedly through more than a dozen pages. The text was closely printed, the information supplemented by graphs and tables. It would take her a long time to sort through them. She started thanking the woman but Liz hurried on.

"Look, I'll be honest Stella." She looked at the girl's eager face. "I haven't got a lot of time to spare at the moment but Doctor Mansera's is keen to get your information down on paper." She paused, sensing the girl's anxiety.

"It is very important Stella, you know that don't you?"

Stella nodded.

"Well I'll try not to rush you but I have a sort of check list here, do you think we could go through it together. What time does your bus go back."

"In an hour." Stella looked forlornly down at the sheets, they were covered in close text.

"Look it won't take long. Let's work down the list together shall we?"

Liz edged around the coffee table and settled herself down beside Stella.

"There's a page for every sighting. The first question is the day and time - you can just estimate the time of year if you can't remember. Then we need to know the weather - again don't worry if you can't remember.

And the place of course. I've got a map here to help us...., and finally the number of animals and relationship if known - and lastly, what they were doing."

After fifty minutes pouring over the charts, Liz looked up and studied her watch.

"Heavens it's already time for you to go Stella. I'll get this typed up and let you have a copy, then if...." She looked quickly down at the girl. "My you look shattered child, and I didn't even offer you a drink."

"It's all right Liz... eh Doctor Delgado."

Stella was so tired that she could hardly think straight.

"Liz will do well enough." The woman had rung from Stella all the information she could remember, so many dates, times, places that it hardly seemed to be about living animals at all. She wondered if this was what being a biologist was really like. She would ask David.

"Is David going to be back here soon?" she asked hopefully.

"Well I don't know Stella." The woman said, quickly gathering her papers into a slim briefcase.

"They're investigating the sighting of a lynx over in the sierra foothills. Lynx haven't been seen there for almost a decade, so it could be quite exciting if they are there." She didn't add that both reports were from traffic accidents.

"When will he know?"

"Well, tracking is a chancy business Stella, you have to study the area for weeks, even months before you can be really be sure there are lynx in the area."

Stella sighed deeply and left.

SEVEN

Stella and Hanna had finished their last class of the day. At the top of the stairwell that lead down to street level Stella gave her friend a worried look. She reached into her school bag and pulled out some computer sheets.

"Hanna, I don't know what I am going to do with all this material Liz gave me."

"I expect you'll manage."

"Well isn't this nice?" The girls hadn't been aware of anyone following them. Stella turned and came face to face with Pietro. The boy greeted her with a sly smile. Instinctively she pushed the loose sheets back into the bag.

"I saw you were back, in the class yesterday. Have you been ill?" She asked, trying to sound friendly.

"Oh yes, I've been ill," Pietro said, emphasising the last word. Then he laughed.

"That's not what I heard," said Hanna always ready with a challenge. Stella sighed, wishing her friend would not be so forthright, she wanted to understand Pietro's actions.

"Oh, and what did you hear Miss Prim?" Pietro blustered sourly. He dropped his schoolbag on the corridor floor and edged nearer to Hanna. At nearly fourteen he was almost as tall as the boys in the class above his. His action was designed to be intimidating.

"Don't come any nearer," Hanna bravely challenged.

"Why not?" chided Pietro. "I thought you wanted to talk."

"We were all worried about you Pietro," interrupted Stella, hastily.

Pietro turned from Hanna who stood defensively against the corridor wall.

"But not as worried as you are about your project Stella, I'll bet. Here let me look." He reached for Stella's schoolbag.

"No it's not," but Pietro had already torn the bag from her grasp.

"Please give it back!" Both the girls chorused as he backed away.

Pietro pulled out several of the books and idly dropped them on the floor, now he was fumbling with the sheets Liz had given to Stella.

"Well what's all this," he said marvelling over the data. "Why it's all about your filthy carnivores." There was definite venom in his words.

"Wolves, lynx, genets - they're all vermin. These sheets say there's hundreds of them."

"They're not....not vermin!" Stella protested and again reached out for the sheets. Pietro laughed. He pushed her so savagely that her elbow crashed against the wall.

"Ouch," Stella gasped.

"Can't you just leave us alone," yelled Hanna trying to push herself between Pietro and Stella. Pietro's response was predictable, he caught Hanna's arm and twisted her round pushing her towards the top of the stairs. Stella screamed. She clawed at the boy's back, but he continued to force Hanna forward, cleverly releasing her just as she tumbled down the first steps. Hanna clawed at the banister, just stopping her fall on the third step. She sat down breathlessly glaring up at him.

"Your friend should be more careful Stella." The boy laughed and stretched out his hand. Hanna shrank back.

"Are you all right Hanna?" Stella gasped, pushing past him.

"Just," said Hanna, "but it's no thanks to him. I told you he was a bad lot," she whispered. Stella tried to ignore the comment. She took hold of her friend's hand and eased Hanna towards the top step where she sat down. Pietro stood over them laughing.

"Do you think you can stand up O.K.?" Stella enquired, crouching beside Hanna whose face had gone incredibly pale.

"Yes, in a minute." Hanna replied and began reaching for her own schoolbag. As Pietro turned away she screamed. "Stella, your bag!"

Stella turned around to see Pietro sorting through her own papers.

"Why don't you just leave us alone," she begged.

Pietro snorted. He opened Stella's biology project and drew out a photo of a wolf.

"It's you should be leaving us alone."

He leaned over and shook the papers in her face.

"You do-gooders don't know a thing, they're vermin, the whole lot of them and they have to be killed!" He screamed into her face. Stella cringed beside Hanna.

"And we're going to do it - do you hear, me and my brothers, it's no good you setting up your reserves or zoos. They should all be shot."

He started tearing up Stella's papers and shoving the tattered remnants into her bag. As he did so the lynx figurine fell onto the floor at his feet. Stella gulped when Pietro lent over and caught hold of the statuette.

"Well what's this?" He asked scornfully.

Something inside Stella rebelled violently.

"Please can't you leave us alone," she cried, lunging at him.

Pietro grabbed her arm and held it tightly as he examined the little ornament. Stella squirmed. His fingernails bit into the skin of her upper arm. However hard she tried she couldn't reach Pietro's other hand.

He turned the sculpture in his hand. Pale flecks in the grain caught the light accentuating the subtlety of the carving. The tiny animal seemed alive. An insane light came into Pietro eyes. Suddenly he clamped it in his fingers and swore in disgust. Stella lunged again.

"Stop it!" He shook her so violently that she felt her head spinning. Hanna tried to stand up behind her, her face now red and enraged.

"No Hanna, wait," Stella stopped struggling and turned back coldly to face Pietro.

"That's better," he said. He loosened his grip on her arm and stood watching as she rubbed the bruised flesh.

"This.... this "lynx"." He could hardly bring himself to say the word.

"You might as well have it, soon it's all you do-gooders will have!"

His words send shivers through Stella. Pietro's grip continued to tighten around the statuette, he leant forwards.

"Here....," he insisted. Stella reached out believing for the moment that the boy was actually about to hand over the tiny statuette. Instead he twisted around, intentionally throwing it down on the corridor floor. The carving bounced, spun several times, then lay still. The pale wood glistened against the cold concrete. When Stella leant over to retrieve it Pietro pushed in front of her wedging his shoe down hard on the lynx and laughing. The wood eased and cracked loudly.

"How unfortunate," Pietro said, removing his foot. The carving had broken into three separate pieces. Stella knelt with tears in her eyes to scoop up the fragments. She sobbed quietly as Pietro turned and without another word, walked down the corridor to disappear around the corner. The girl sensed Hanna beside her as she tried to fit the pieces together.

"What did he mean ... about his brothers, Hanna, - what did he mean?" Stella begged.

"Nothing Stella, it was all talk. I told you his brothers are no good. He's trying to be like them. Forget him."

"How can I?" said Stella looking sorrowfully at the lynx fragments.

Pietro's words had struck terror into her heart. She couldn't forget the look of triumph on his face as he stamped on the statuette.

The call came late on Thursday evening. Stella was in bed with the light switched off. She was already dozing and only dimly aware of the telephone's insistent ringing.

"Stella, are you awake?" It was her father's voice. He stood in her doorway calling softly.

"Just," she replied slightly disoriented. Sleep clouded her mind.

"Can I put the light on?" asked Jorge.

"What's the matter?" Stella asked feeling uneasy. The overhead light flickered on. She searched her father's face. He didn't seem at all worried as he crossed to the bed and seated himself down on a low stool. The bedside clock shown 10.40 p.m. and as he looked down at his daughter's tousled hair and sleepy expression Jorge wondered whether he should have woken her.

"I've just been speaking to Jade's mother ..," he began, but Stella started up from the bed, sleep suddenly banished.

"What's the matter, is Jade ill?" What other reason could cause Jade's mother to ring so late in the evening? She switched on her bedside lamp and threw off the bedclothes.

"No, Stella, no-one's ill, I promise. There's no need to get up."

Stella sank back down sensing that something was dreadfully wrong despite her father's protests.

"What is it then. Oh, no the Xando trip's cancelled isn't it....?"

"No Stella, calm down, it's some good news - in a way." Even Jorge seemed unsure of himself.

"Oh," she sank further down onto the pillow, not able to imagine what type of "good news" would make her father wake her so late on a school day.

"Jade's cousin was there, Mrs Verity put him on the telephone."

"Emilio?"

"Yes, he seems very impressed with you."

Stella was even more puzzled. When she had told her father about the opportunity to attend the feeding round at Xando Jorge had voiced his disapproval, saying she was spending too much time on her biology project at the expense of her other school work. Whatever Emilio had said must have convinced him otherwise.

"But....why did he call?" She continue scanning her father's face for signs of anxiety.

"It seems they have had a special new arrival at Xando."

Now Stella could not contain her imagination and begged, "Is it another lynx, a mate for Marmit?"

"Too fast." Her father exclaimed, ushering her back to the side of her bed.

"It's a lynx yes, but it's just a little orphan cub. Emilio said it was brought into him two days ago by the traffic police. Its mother had been killed on the road."

"Oh, no," Stella cried, tears quickly welling under her eyelids.

"It can't be very old?" she asked sadly.

"Emilio says it's less than six weeks old. He's looking after it himself."

"But it's so sad," Stella said nestling back into her bedclothes, then demanded again.

"But why *did* he phone Dad?"

"Well that's what I was coming to. You see the director Dr Mansera has decided to publicise the plight of the cub and get some sponsorship. There'll be an article in the Monday paper but Emilio wanted you to know beforehand."

"Oh, is that all?" Stella had hoped for something more, a wish she could not voice even to her father. She lay back on the bed. The pillow, already cold, felt chill and unwelcoming against her cheek.

"No it's not all Stella." Her father said, stroking the top of her head. Stella closed her eyes and tried to visualise the lynx, wondering if it was like Pardito.

"Emilio asked me something else." Jorge said. "Tell me Stella, is all your school work up to date?" Stella's eyes flew open, her father was challenging her again.

"Oh yes, Dad, you know it is, I told you...," she declared.

"All right, no need to create. Emilio has asked if you would like to see the cub tomorrow evening before the article is published and the press invade Xando. Mrs Verity has agreed that you can stay with them and I'll collect you on Saturday."

"Oh yes, please, please can I go," Stella shouted ecstatically. She shot out of bed into Jorge's arms.

"Well," said Jorge laughing. "I had better phone Mrs Verity right away then." He struggled free of his daughter's arms.

"Now back into bed with you."

Stella wriggled from his grasp and leapt into the bed. Both of them knew she was now far too excited to sleep. Jorge moved to the door.

"Your mother will call you half an hour early, so you can pack a small bag." He studied his daughter's face, wondering at the excitement in her eyes. She blew him a kiss before he turned off the main light.

"Now go to sleep!" He ordered, closing the door.

As Stella reached over to switch off the bedside lamp she caught sight of the tiny lynx statuette on the shelf near her head. She had finally told her parents about the present from Jade but had lied about the breakage, saying it had dropped on the school floor. Nor had she mentioned Pietro's bullying. 'What's the point?' Hanna had said, 'He's just a nobody. It'll only stir up more trouble.' Stella wasn't so sure but Hanna had been persuasive. Jorge had stuck the figurine back together so it was nearly as good as new, except for some scratching on the polished surface. In the privacy of her bedroom Stella had painstakingly sellotaped together the torn pieces of Liz's material. There was nothing missing. The lynx model was different. It would never look the same as on the day Jade had given it to her, but now the subdued lamplight seemed to breath life into the little creature. Stella gazed at it for a long time before she slept.

Xando's heavy wooden gates were firmly bolted. On the left-hand gatepost a large metal handle was positioned beside a small notice printed in white enamel which read "ring for admittance". Jade stepped back to let Stella pull on the handle. The lingering daytime heat beat back from the car park's bare dusty soil. Wisps of fine dust blew towards them across the empty lot, coating their clothes and hair. It was still light and none of the Institute's windows were illuminated. Minutes passed without any reply. Stella grew concerned.

"Do you think anything has happened to change Emilio's plans?" She queried. Although she'd no appetite earlier, Jade's mother has insisted on giving them a full meal. Stella ate out of politeness but had worried all through the meal that they would be late. Now she felt bloated.

"I'm sure he would have let us know, Stella. He said seven pm and it's only five past. He really is very reliable."

Stella nodded. She reached up to pull on the bell again. Jade switched her torch on and off several times but both girls grew anxious when more minutes passed.

"Perhaps we had better go home and phone, look the sun's starting to go down." She pointed to an area of western sky where the deeper blue of evening showed through the conifers. "I know Dad would want us to."

She was interrupted by a voice calling from deep within the Institute.

"Just coming....coming," Emilio's voice got louder as they heard him running towards the gate. He fumbled with the complex locks, then the gate swung open creaking noisily. Emilio beckoned the two girls inside then turned to secure the gate.

"Is it late, what can you think of me ... Jade?" He bent down and hugged his cousin, but simply took Stella's hand and nodded to her.

"I'm glad you could both come."

"We couldn't see any lights?" Jade queried.

"Of course I am the only one here at the moment, so I have only the office lights on." Emilio gestured the girls to follow him to the rear of the building. The path beside the exhibition area was in shadow, Jade switched on her torch.

"Don't you have security lights," Stella asked. Shadows forced their way beneath the low veranda. Emilio turned a corner to his left and as if in answer a bright light instantly illuminated him and a small doorway at the side of a building. He nodded and motioned to the door with a faint rim of light at its base.

"The food store's in there, I'll just be a second." He disappeared into the room, quickly reappearing carrying what looked like a coolbox.

Emilio hurried along the veranda and stopped before a low building which Stella couldn't remember seeing before. It was made of light metal panels with slim window slits high up on the wall. As Emilio stepped towards the doorway another security light flashed on above his head. He punched a security code into the panel beside the door. The light blinked slightly, before steadying. Emilio didn't notice.

"We must be quiet here girls." They followed Emilio into a wide dimly lit room with another much smaller compartment set against the right hand wall. A warm slightly musty smell hung about the place. Large windows set well up near the ceiling revealed a patch of pale sky. They seemed to cast an aura of gloom rather than light. A much warmer glow shone out from a double glazed panel at the front of smaller inner compartment.

"I will go in to feed the cub, he is still in an incubator you understand. Stella found herself nodding. Emilio looked first at Jade and then at Stella's anxious face.

"It only lost its mother three days ago, but we have got it to take a little meat. He is partially weaned but prefers our special milk formula. You understand Stella." Stella sensed he was trying to convey something more than mere words.

"It is a very difficult time for the little cub so you must look through the window .....for the moment."

Stella watched Emilio enter the side door of the compartment and realised that an incubator lay at its rear attached to a generator which hummed gently providing both warmth and light. The incubator was sited on a sturdy bench half a metre above the floor. It had a glass hatch and two lights, one at either end, which gave out a soft glow. Deep within the mass of fine straw she detected a slight movement. Emilio placed the coolbox gently on the bench and took out several items. One metal container was filled with thin strips of meat and another a minced meat gruel, For the moment he set it to one side. Alongside the incubator stood a small stool where a thick woollen blanket was folded up.

Emilio settled himself on the stool and spread the blanket across his lap. His face bore a intense expression as he reached to open the incubator's lid. Little rustling sounds greeted him which the girls weren't able to hear through the glass partition. Then a small dusty brown shape emerged topped by two furry triangular ears. Emilio felt the rasp of the cub's strong tongue and deep throbbing purr. He transferred the tiny creature to his lap and folded the blanket around it. The cub's insistent purr increased as he offered it the first bowl of gruel, but it rejected the food at first, seeming more interested in pawing at the folds of the blanket. The girls watched mesmerised as Emilio's supple hands patiently coerced the cub towards the food bowl. After a few minutes he was rewarded when the cub took its first lick at the gruel. Then amazingly there was no stopping it. It guzzled at the contents splashing some of the gruel onto the blanket.

When the bowl was almost empty Emilio laid it aside and massaged the cub's back and sides, mimicking an action its mother would have used to aid digestion. Next he reached into the other bowl and offered a few thin strips of meat but the cub only wriggled in his hands and tried to suck his fingers. A gentle fight ensued between them as the cub lunged for Emilio's fingers when he dangled tiny strips of meat over the cub's mouth. Eventually the cub's fine claws grasped two pieces of meat. Tearing them away from Emilio, it snuggled down to chew on them. It took several more pieces then would take no more. Once again Emilio massaged the cub's now fat sides to encourage defecation. Finally he reached into the box and offered a bottle of warm milk to the cub. This time there was no hesitation, the cub latched onto the specially strengthened teat with its tiny teeth and suckled with all its strength. Emilio sensed the cub's deep shuddering purr sweep through its body. For the first time since he'd entered the room the young man looked up from his task and noticed the faces of his audience. His own face broke into a wide self-conscious grin. Stella guessed rightly he'd completely forgotten the girls. He looked down at the contented cub then nodded across to the doorway.

"He wants you to go in Stella," Jade said stepping back from the glass.

"Are you sure, I thought we couldn't."

Jade merely gestured towards the door. Emilio nodded more insistently, grinning encouragement.

"Go on then," Jade urged.

Stella looked at Emilio's eager face then back at Jade.

"Aren't you coming?" she asked naively.

"Not me," Jade insisted, "I don't want milk all over my clothes."

Stella knew the girl only meant to encourage her.

"Quickly, Emilio will have to put it back in the warm soon. It's what you wanted isn't it... well, isn't it?"

It didn't seem possible, suddenly she was inside the room, sensing the warm dry air, the smells of gruel and milk mingling with the sour smell of the cub's faeces and for the first time she heard its deep rhythmic purring.

"Over here," Emilio whispered.

She took two steps then knelt down beside him. Incredibly, Emilio shifted off the stool and was handing her the blanket with its tiny occupant. She shook her head but under Emilio's guidance found herself seated on the stool, the cub nestled deep in the blanket with just the bottle of milk and only a tiny head visible. It was a miniature of Pardito's own. The same sandy-brown fur, the same rounded head, the small ears with thick dark hairs clustering at their tips so characteristic of the lynx he would grow to be. The cub gulped milk greedily. Half hidden in the deep folds of the blanket its body vibrated, sending shivers of excitement through the girl's own body. She beamed her gratitude at Emilio. He smiled knowingly, understanding and great tenderness evident in his gentle expression.

The moment was over all too quickly, the cub never opened its eyes on the stranger and had fallen asleep with its mouth still clasped to the empty bottle. The deep throbbing purr was replaced by steady rhythmical breathing. Emilio leant down, gently lifted the animal from Stella's lap and nestled it back into the bedding. Carefully he closed the incubator hatch, took the blanket from Stella and wrapped it into a ball for cleaning. With Stella gazing blindly at the closed incubator he collected up the containers and ushered her from the room.

EIGHT

Guaro's local newspaper, the *Playa*, that Monday carried the short article by Dr Mansera about the cub and their work at Xando but a shock awaited the readers of the *Playa's* midweek edition. On Tuesday evening, the paper thumped through the apartment's letterbox just after Jorge Martin arrived home. He set the paper aside on the hall table intending to scan it later. It was a free paper usually carrying little that was newsworthy but before setting it down Jorge noticed a small picture of a wolf. He set his briefcase down and wandered into the kitchen turning the pages of the paper. He stopped before the kitchen table with the paper held wide between his hands and exclaimed, "What on earth ....?"

Anna turned from the stove. She saw her husband standing with the paper held in front of him.

"What is it, what's the matter?"

Jorge lowered the paper. He was frowning and extremely angry.

"Has Stella seen this?"

"Seen what?"

"All these letters about Xando."

"About the cub....?" Anna quizzed

"Yes and other things, it's not good."

Jorge set the open paper down on the table.

"Dr. Mansera thought the publicity would help the centre raise awareness of the animals' plight. It looks as if it's backfired. What is the editor thinking. It's almost as if they are inciting opposition."

He sat down heavily. Anna came to the table, leaning over his shoulder she scanned the pages of the paper. In the centre of the right hand page was a long letter from Guaro Region Hunting Brigade and set alongside it were three shorter letters sent in by individual readers. The letter from the Brigade briefly acknowledged Xando's work, but questioned the protection of wolves and lynx (even calling them 'vermin'), simply because they were rare without consideration of the dangers to domestic stock. Two of the readers' letters were written with the same concerns, one came from a peasant farmer in the sierra foothills, another from a nurseryman who raised chickens for the tourist market. Both claimed to have suffered depredations by lynx and wolf. Anna grew more concerned as she read the letters.

"The paper doesn't seem interested in setting the story straight does it. Didn't Stella say there aren't any wolves in the region at all. I can't understand why they didn't talk to Dr. Mansera again."

"I wonder why they even printed the article about the cub in the first place. Maybe they were hoping to stir up just this sort of opposition," Jorge replied cynically.

"Oh I can't believe they'd do that Jorge."

"I don't know so much, look at the letter at the bottom of the page it's even flanked by advertisements for the hunting suppliers. They shouldn't have published it at all!" Jorge shook his head.

Anna sat down beside him to read the letter. It was from someone claiming to own goats along the Visua river. The writer blamed lynx and wolf for countless losses and called for both animals to be eradicated. In the last line was a veiled threat. Without a change in the law it said, people would have to safeguard their flocks 'in the only way they knew how'. The letter was signed by one Juan Delgado (*John Smith*), of Plaka Square, Carlos Boulevard on the outskirts of the city.

"It's outrageous!" Anna rapped her knuckles on the page and rose to her feet. "They've no justification for publishing something like that."

"Indefensible, just indefensible," Jorge agreed. He turned suddenly at the sound of voices from lower in the apartment block.

"When's Stella due home?" He asked, quickly screwing the paper into a tight ball.

"She's with Hanna going over their projects, she'll be home in about half an hour." Anna looked down at the scrunched up bundle of newspaper. "You don't think we should let her see it?"

"No, I'm going to put it straight in the bin downstairs. She shouldn't see such malicious rubbish. Why I've a good mind to write back to the paper myself."

Anna simply shook her head and watched Jorge disappear through the kitchen doorway. He walked thoughtfully down to the courtyard where he stuffed the crumpled newspaper into a garbage bin.

Stella went to school next morning unaware of her father's actions. She had spent an hour and a half on Tuesday evening at Hanna's home working on her project. A final visit to the museum was planned for Thursday and the projects were to be handed to Janni in three weeks time. But Stella hadn't seen David for nearly a month and badly wanted his advice. He might, she hoped, have time to see her on Thursday. Liz remained evasive over David's whereabouts - 'he's out surveying', 'he's working in the sierras' was all she'd say.

The first lesson on Wednesday was chemistry. Stella hadn't finished her chemistry homework so left home twenty minutes earlier than normal, saying she needed to call in on the school library. She reached the chemistry classroom intent on getting the work completed before the class started. As she sat at her desk she noticed a sheet of newspaper lodged against the chemistry books in front of her. At first, she took no notice of it and quickly set to work. When she eventually finished, she clipped the homework pages together, and slipped them into her folder. As she did so, the piece of newspaper tipped sideways and fell open in front of her.

She felt impelled to pick up the two pages of the *Playa*, noting the ragged edges where they had been torn from the newspaper. In disbelief she began reading the first letter from the hunting brigade, her emotions alternating between anger and fear. She continued through the two following letters and down to Juan Delgado's threatening diatribe, hardly pausing for breath as she read. Finally she gasped and thrust the paper down in front of her. The room was filling with pupils. The chemistry teacher was just entering the room. Seeing the expression of outrage on Stella's face the teacher halted in front of her but Stella was looking beyond him towards the corridor.

When he turned to follow her gaze he saw that a young boy was standing a little back from the doorway. A lad, tall for his age, who the tutor knew to be barely fourteen. The boy's face bore a malicious grin. The teacher looked back at Stella, noticing for the first time how her fingers clawed at a shred of newspaper, the text of the Xando letters standing out prominently in the girl's grasp. Pietro stood back, melting quickly into the corridor shadows. Only the memory of his vicious laugh remained to worry the teacher and to haunt Stella for the rest of the day.

"Stella..... Stella," Hanna called as she sat down at the desk beside Stella but her voice could have come from a hundred kilometres away.

"Stella, what's the matter?" The girl didn't even feel her friend's hand on her shoulder.

"Is that the *Playa*, have you read it?"

Stella turned a rather bitter expression towards her friend. She nodded briefly.

"I can't think why they printed that stuff. Why did you bring it in here?" Hanna asked.

"I didn't," said Stella bleakly, looking down at the crumpled sheets.

Hanna reached over and gently eased the pages from her friend's hands. Stella's grip lessened and with the removal of the newspaper she felt a sudden relaxation of tension. She gave one huge sob and fought back the tears welling up in her eyes. She had a sudden watery view of the teacher setting out his papers at the front of the room. He looked at her and shook his head. She turned back to Hanna.

"I didn't .... bring it in..... Pietro did," she stammered

"He gave it to you?"

"No, they were put right here for me to find - I know it was him, he was there in the corridor staring at me and laughing, didn't you see him?"

Involuntarily, Hanna looked up at the closed classroom door. There was no sign of anyone visible through the square window.

"He wants to upset you again."

"I can't think why anyone would write such letters. Why, when I saw the cub at Xando last week...."

"You saw the cub, the one in the original article?" Hanna asked amazed.

Stella's face brightened suddenly and her eyes lost their glazed look. She nodded.

"I told Emilio about my project and he .... he invited me over on Friday evening to see the cub being fed - before the article was published.

Why Hanna, I even held it, it was just a tiny little thing. I don't understand why anyone could want to hurt it."

"But didn't you see the *Playa* yesterday, my father brought it in after you'd gone? "

Stella shook her head.

"It came late evening. Dad said it was disgraceful to print that last letter, why...."

But just then the chemistry teacher started the lesson. The girls had to wait until the class ended to resume their conversation. Stella's mind was not on the work, she frequently looked around the class to see if Pietro had entered by the rear door. Just before they completed a final exercise she whispered to Hanna.

"Stay with me afterwards Hanna ... I don't want to meet Pietro alone again." Hanna nodded.

The teacher, a Mr J Haloran, saw the girls' heads together. He tapped his books to get their attention, frowned and nodded for them to finish their work. But he was not an unsympathetic man. He had noticed that Stella was distracted throughout the class. As the bell sounded for the change of lessons he moved solicitously around her desk and asked quietly:

"Are you all right Stella?"

"Yes," Stella gulped expecting a reprimand.

"Only, I thought you might not be well, you seemed upset."

"No I'm all right, really."

Unwilling to answer further questions, she quickly collected her books and got up, motioning Hanna to follow. The girls hurriedly left the room. As they moved away the crumpled sheets of newspaper fell to the floor. Mr. Haloran moved round the desk and picked up the discarded paper. As he did so another class of children began filing noisily into the room. He returned to his desk and unfolded the pages of the *Playa*. He scanned the letters and noticed the address given below Juan Delgado's letter. He puzzled over this for some time. Every day he drove down Carlos Boulevard from his home in the leafy suburb of Rosas. But the Boulevard was a long avenue in a depressed area of the city . He recalled that Plaka Square contained several warehouses and a large abandoned plot half full of rubbish. He couldn't ever remember seeing any houses on Plaka Square or within half a kilometre of it. Shaking his head he thrust the torn pages into his case and looked up to a sea of expectant and rather amused faces.

Next afternoon, the Thursday of the proposed museum visit, Janni entered the biology class carrying piles of class books which she placed haphazardly on her desk. A few slipped to the edge of the desk and seemed about to fall. Janni didn't notice. She appeared even more disgruntled than normal. Some children sniggered from the back of the class. She ignored them. The biology classroom was full. Stella had already scanned the room twice. No, Pietro was not there, his habitual scowl absent from the sea of eager faces and it was rumoured he'd been absent since Wednesday morning.

Janni began passing around books for the lesson. As she passed Stella she said in a subdued voice.

"I'll need to see you and Hanna, and of course Jamie, right at the end of the lesson."

Stella nodded. It was after all the usual arrangement before their museum trip. Her project folder lay on the desk before her. She opened it, pulled out her work and said.

"I wanted to ask about....?"

"Later!" Janni looked down at Stella and said quite sharply. "Didn't you hear? I'll talk to you later." Even for Janni this was unusually abrupt. Stella replaced the project in her folder. Hanna was sitting in the second row next to Jamie. Stella managed to catch her eye briefly, frowning at the teacher who was already moving to the back to the class. Hanna shook her head and turned back to talk to Jamie. Janni made the class read a text book while she sat lethargically in the front of the class either marking class books or simply gazing out of the window. Once Stella looked up to see Janni's piercing gaze focused on her. When the class bell rang the children filed out of the room, there was none of the enthusiastic discussion so characteristic of Janni's classes. Stella quickly gathered up her books and joined Hanna and Jamie in front of the teacher's desk. Janni was usually very eager to get the children away in the minibus. On this occasion she didn't begin to pack up her books. When the other children had left the room she rose with conscious effort.

"Sit down please children. Here near my desk." She walked towards the door, her head bent. The teacher seemed pensive and rather disturbed. Hanna and Jamie came to sit near Stella. When she had closed the door and assured herself that no-one else was in the room Janni came back but instead of returning to her desk drew up one of the children's chairs to sit near them.

"I'm afraid......" she began, then paused and looked at each of their faces in turn. Stella felt her stomach leap. "I'm afraid we can't go to the museum today." Stella sighed. Even Hanna sensed Janni's mood quelling her inclination to question the decision. Jamie nodded rather more philosophically. None of the children spoke.

"I heard from David, Doctor Foster, on the phone, just before the lesson." She paused and patted Stella's arm. Instead of calming her, this unusual tenderness filled the girl with dread. Janni moved her hand away and began to fiddle briefly with one of her gaudy rings, before looking up at them again. "You'll all be sorry to hear that ... that there's been an attack on Xando."

Hanna gasped. Jamie quickly reached for her hand. Only Stella found her voice, she stood up rapidly, her chair legs screeching on the floor.

"On ... on the lynx?" Stella wailed. Janni placed a retaining hand on her shoulder.

"On the lynx? ....I don't know Stella. David said a wolf had been shot. But it's worse than that!" Stella quailed, her mind so full of the new lynx cub that she couldn't imagine anything worse than an attack on so vulnerable a creature. Janni gently pressed her down into her chair. She sensed the girl's despair and nodded in understanding,

"David was calling from the hospital. One of the keepers, Emilio Mistral was shot and knocked out."

"Emilio.. oh no!" Now Stella slumped back into her chair.

"He's going to be all right children, but ...," and here Janni paused.

Stella couldn't bring herself to speak but Hanna asked quietly.

"But what Janni?"

The teacher shook her head.

"When Emilio was at Xando last night, he heard some noises to the rear of the site." Janni heard Stella's stifled sob, she took the girl's hand between her own.

"Apparently he found a large break in the perimeter fence, then heard a shot. When he ran back to the wolf pen it was sprawled on its side, apparently dead. Someone also shot at him, then he was knocked out. He doesn't remember anything else. The hospital is keeping him in for observation."

The three children were stunned, none of them able to speak.

"I'll run you all home in a minute, then I'm going on to the hospital to see David. He's with Emilio." She rose from her chair.

"Will all your parents be at home?" She quizzed. "Hanna?" Hanna nodded. Her mouth was very dry but she managed to reply.

"My father will be there, he's working from home at the moment."

"Jamie?"

"I'll try to phone, but if there's no-one there perhaps I could go to Hanna's." Hanna nodded encouragingly. Through Stella's grief she felt envious of Jamie's calm assurance of Hanna's friendship. She almost wished she could go home with them.

"Stella?"

"I think my mother will be, but ... couldn't I come to the hospital with you?" she begged.

"Oh Stella, I don't think that would be a good idea. Perhaps I could phone you later at home. Would that be all right do you think?"

Stella nodded unhappily.

"Does David know about the new lynx cub... is it ...?"

"He didn't say Stella, but I'll ask him .... and let you know."

Stella began to rise from her chair. Janni leant over, clasped her arms around the girl and hugged her. Tears brimmed up over the girl's eyelids. Keeping hold of Stella's shoulders, Janni asked very solicitously.

"I heard that you went to Xando last week, is that right?"

Stella looked up through her tears and could only nod.

"And saw the lynx cub?"

"Yes, Emilio let me feed it." The image of the nursing cub cradled in its dark blanket was almost too much to bear. She wept hot tears.

"David didn't mention it Stella, so I expect it's quite all right. I'll ask him and phone you this evening."

When Stella walked into her mother's kitchen the local radio station was repeating one of many reports of the attack on Xando broadcast during the day. Anna turned to see her daughter standing silently in the doorway and moved quickly to switch off the set.

"No don't," Stella demanded, her hand holding tightly to the door handle. Anna came around the table to embrace her. Stella turned away. If she wept now she wouldn't be able to stop.

"I'm all right. Janni told us, at school. She's gone to the hospital, David's there now with Emilio." Stella dropped her schoolbag at the entrance to the hallway instead of tidying it away in her bedroom. She couldn't bear to be embraced, to see the overriding sympathy in her mother's face. The radio presenter rattled on describing the attack: carnivores were the target he emphasised; one wolf had been shot and another animal, a genneti he called it, had been disturbed during the attack and had leapt from the top of its cage falling awkwardly and breaking its back. The animal had been put out of its agony by a Xando vet.

"Stella, you surely don't want to hear all this, I'll turn it off."

"No." Stella yelled. "I want.... I want to hear, to know....." Stella stood upright grasping tightly to the back of a kitchen chair, her body unnaturally tense.

"But..." her mother began. "Why don't you sit down dear."

"In a minute, when they finish!" She was preparing herself for the worst. The radio presenter was again giving a graphic description of the attack on Emilio. Anna stood behind her daughter rubbing her shoulders and trying to ease her obvious strain. The newscast continued: none of the birds or even the deer had been touched. One wolf was dead and a 'genneti' had been destroyed he repeated, the fence around a compound housing a young female lynx, had been cut open.

Anna felt her daughter's body stiffen. The lynx was a secretive creature, the compound filled with dense vegetation. At first, zoo staff couldn't confirm whether the animal, which was not considered a danger to humans, had escaped, but later, during a feeding round, the lynx been spotted under a juniper in its own compound. It was unharmed and later had eaten most of its food. Partly reassured Stella let her mother guide her to a chair. She laid her arms on the table and began to cry silently.

"They still haven't mentioned the cub," she wailed.

Anna had not been concentrating on the latest broadcast, she had heard many others during the day.

"Didn't they?... I thought..."

"Janni said David didn't mention the cub . She thought it must be all right."

"Then it must be, they would have mentioned it otherwise, wouldn't they?"

"Janni's going to ask David. She'll phone us this evening. I don't know when."

Stella spent the next hours slumped on a settee before the television, the remote control clasped fiercely in her hand. Anna had turned the sound down low. Her daughter didn't notice, she seemed in a trance switching stations every few minutes, anxious for the latest reports. Pictures of Xando's animals flashed again and again across the screen. When Jorge returned home at seven o'clock, Stella's dinner lay uneaten on the kitchen table. He'd heard news of the attack and looked anxiously across at his daughter. With a nod from Anna he picked up the plate and took it across to his daughter.

"Try to eat Stella dear, it's not good for you to......"

At that moment Stella gasped. She started up from the settee and gazed intently at the screen. Jorge turned round to see Dr. Mansera being interviewed.

"Turn up the sound." Stella fumbled with the controls and Dr. Mansera's voice boomed from the speakers.   Jorge took the control adjusting the sound level until it became bearable. Dr. Mansera had given his interview earlier in the day. There was no further news about the animals and nothing at all about the lynx cub. Dr. Mansera didn't even mention his article in *Playa*, instead, he fiercely defended the work at Xando condemning the attack as an assault on all Andalucian wildlife, especially those endangered animals like the wolf and lynx. Throughout the interview he retained a calm professional attitude making it impossible to guess at the emotions churning inside him, but he came very close to accusing the *Playa* of inciting the attack. The interview ended abruptly after the reporter asked Dr Mansera whether he wasn't biased against the human inhabitants of Andalucía. He countered with one brief statement "I don't think there's any danger of human beings going extinct - do you?" he challenged the interviewer, abruptly dismissing him.

After the broadcast, Stella tried to eat a small portion of her meal, but after a few mouthfuls she felt sick. She pushed the plate back towards her father, shaking her head and picking up the remote control. Jorge rejoined Anna in the kitchen to eat his meal. His own appetite was dulled. He ate slowly. For a long time neither of them spoke. At about eight-forty their imposed silence was destroyed when Andras bounded into the kitchen. He had been for a meal with friends and spent most of the evening quizzing one boy attending the technical college about college life. When he pushed open the hall doorway he quickly sensed an atmosphere and groaned loudly. His mother smiled briefly. Jorge only nodded. Both looked towards the settee where Stella lay curled up. She looked pale, otherwise he couldn't see much wrong with her. His mother silently shook her head.

"What's the matter with all of you?" Andras demanded morosely. "I've had a wonderful evening and now here you all are as morbid as the grave!"

"Andras, there's been some bad news, haven't you listened to the radio."

"How could I? I've been out with friends, they were a jolly sight more entertaining than you lot!"

"Andras please!"

"All right then you'd better tell me what's happened, but I warn you I want to watch the match, it starts in five minutes."

"Just sit down and listen to your mother for once," Jorge demanded. Andras could tell he was serious. He stood by the table and waited.

"Listen son." His mother began, " you've heard of the Xando animal institute."

"Oh yes, the animal place Stella keeps running off to."

"As you say the one Stella's been to. There was an attack there last night. Emilio, Jade's cousin, was shot and knocked out, some of the animals were killed. I'm surprised you haven't heard it on your walkman?"

"I only listen to sport," said Andras only a little deflated.

"This Emilio, he's O.K.?" he hesitated.

"Yes, he's in hospital with a wound to his arm. They're keeping him in for observation." Andras simply shrugged, his mind on the impending match. He looked across at the kitchen clock.

"Well, I'd like to watch the match now if you don't mind!" He slung his school jacket around the back of a chair, limped quickly across in front of Stella and slumped down at the far end of the settee.

"Well, let's have the remote control madam!" Stella did not move or even indicate she was aware of him. A newsreel channel flashed pictures across the screen of an international plane accident, Stella punched out the code for another channel, then another. The picture changed three times before she looked at her brother, her voice little above a whisper as she begged.

"Can't you watch in your room?"

"No I can't. The screen's too small," Andras said snatching the remote control out of her hand. Stella shrieked and snatched it back. Not to be outdone Andras grabbed both her wrists and pushed her down onto the settee. Only vaguely aware of his parents' pleading to stop, Andras jerked his head away and Stella turned to bite at his ears. He yelled in pain throwing her back against the wooden arm of the settee. Stella gasped, her face deathly white.

"Stop it, you two, stop it I say!"

Andras felt himself pulled off the squirming body of his sister by his shoulders. He clamped his hand to the side of his head.

"She bit my ear, the little animal!"

Jorge pulled him off the settee and made him stand upright. He shook the boy violently, unable to control his own anger.

"And I don't suppose you earned it.. did you? I've never known you so callous Andras, what on earth's got into you?"

"Well I wanted to watch the match, the other boys...."

"So it didn't matter that your sister's had a bad shock, what the other boys do come first does it..? I'm fed up with you Andras, go and watch the match in your room if you can't be civil." Andras shook his head and ambled towards the corridor. Still holding his ear he paused in the doorway and looked back at his father who was standing irately behind the settee. Anna was stroking Stella's bruised arm, the girl looked forlorn and totally subdued.

Comprehension of what he had done began to sink in. His father had called him callous. But he wasn't callous at all, a little thoughtless perhaps but somehow he couldn't think beyond his own aims. He had viewed Stella's little exercise with the animal institute with amusement and constantly teased her about it. He closed his bedroom door quietly behind him and flattened himself on the bed. The small blank TV screen glared back at him but the match no longer had any appeal. He tried not to think of what his mates would say when he told them he hadn't watched it.

"Do you want to go to bed Stella?" her mother asked continuing to stroke her hair.

Stella eased herself up and sat on the edge of the settee. She was shivering.

"You could sleep in my bed, Jorge won't mind sleeping on the couch."

Anna sat beside her, trying to avoid her husband's pained expression.

"No, it's all right, and no I don't want to go to bed - not yet."

Stella knew if she slept in her mother's bed she wouldn't be able to cry for fear of waking her. In her own bed she would probably lie wide awake in the dark thinking of the lynx cub and remembering how he resembled Pardito. She wouldn't sleep and tears would pour down her cheeks all night.

When the doorbell rang it startled everyone. Jorge moved across to the hallway, but Anna continued to stroke soothingly at Stella's hair. Rousing herself, the girl looked towards the hall door. The voices she heard were familiar. As the inner door opened Stella struggled free from her mother and ran towards the couple standing in front of Jorge.

"David, Janni. I thought you'd never call." Instinctively she ran into David's arms. "The cub - is it .....?" She sobbed out a few words but couldn't finish, fearful of what was in her mind. She clung to David. In a glance he saw the tortured expression on her upturned face. He held her away from him and let his face break into a smile.

"It's all right Stella." He spoke slowly, knowing the girl would take time to accept his assurance. "It's all right," he insisted and the girl's body sagged in relief, her eyelids flickered as if in a faint. But she was stronger than he thought. Clasping his sleeves in her hands she begged.

"And Emilio?"

"He's fine too." Janni offered. "It was his request we came."

"Stella, remember your manners. Offer your visitors a seat," Anna said apologetically.

"Oh... I....," was all Stella could manage.

Anna took over. "Please come through to the lounge, Mr. ... Janni...."

Janni nodded to David and lead the way Stella was still clinging to his hand. Janni put her arm around the girls' shoulders encouraging her to join them, acting totally unlike the tyrant Stella was used to from school.

"Thanks Mrs. Martin this is Doctor David Foster."

"Please call me David." As he sat down on the settee, he turned to the girl releasing her hand. "Stella does." The girl blushed.

"Would you like a drink, some coffee." Jorge offered, hesitatingly in the kitchen archway.

"Not for me thanks, we've been drinking coffee all evening at the hospital. What about you Janni?" David reached across and squeezed Janni's hand.

"Could I have a mineral water?"

"Make that two if you could." David added.

"Of course," Jorge agreed. How about you Anna?"

"Some coffee would be fine. Stella will you have your chocolate now, it'll be your bedtime soon?"

The girl was still very keyed up, her eyes wide with tension. She only nodded.

"Emilio asked us to come and see Stella." David looked up at Anna. "I hope you don't mind."

"Of course not. Stella's had been waiting for Janni to call, but I hope you didn't come out of your way."

David waved the comment aside.

"It's been a tiring day of course but Emilio wanted us to come, insisted even."

Jorge brought a tray of drinks into the room. David reached forward, handed Janni her drink then took a sip of his own. He turned back to Stella.

"The lynx cub's fine Stella really. We purposely kept any news about it from the media. It's nonsense of course but Emilio blames himself for what happened in the incubator room." He heard Stella gasp. A look of horror crossed her face.

"Now don't get upset Stella, I told you the cub is all right. We've moved it temporarily to one of the keeper's houses in a new incubator. I phoned just now. He's eating and sleeping as if nothing's happened."

It was Anna's turn to be curious.

"What happened to .... to the incubator room?" She was watching Stella intently.

David nodded slowly.

"We're just lucky that Emilio wasn't hurt more seriously than he was. After he heard noises on the site he loaded up one of the dart, or anaesthetic, guns. It's kind of standard practice in case an animal has escaped you see." He took another sip of water.

"It seems Emilio went round the back following the direction of the noise. He found the hole in the fence, then heard a shot, the one that killed the old wolf probably. He didn't see anyone, but became worried about the incubator house. You see, he had just finished feeding the lynx cub. He didn't have time to lock up."

"Oh no," Stella stood up quickly. "Did they....?"

"Stella, let David finish. He told you the cub's all right." Anna beckoned the girl towards her and settled her onto the arm of her own chair. She gestured to the cup of chocolate steaming untouched on the tray. "Try to drink some."

David continued calmly. "The intruders tried to ransack the incubator room, but they must have been alarmed by Emilio's return. Emilio doesn't remember much about what happened just the shot in his arm, then he was knocked unconscious. He was lucky to be found within half an hour of the attack."

"Was the premises alarmed?" Jorge quizzed.

David sighed and lowered his head briefly.

"I'm sorry to say not. All the funding is spent on the animals. It's hard to get resources for things like security. We never dreamed anyone would want to attack the place."

"A bit of a blinkered view in the circumstances," Jorge commented.

"In hindsight it can't be excused," David nodded.

"How *was* Emilio found then ....." Anna queried but Stella interrupted impatiently

"And what happened to the incubator, to the cub?" She demanded.

"Calm down Stella," Anna insisted.

David nodded to Anna.

"Emilio's uncle, was driving home late and saw a car tearing from the car park without lights. He thought there must be something wrong so he went back with his son to investigate. He has a key to Xando you see. They found Emilio lying unconscious at the entrance to the incubator room." He looked at Stella's anxious face. "They called the ambulance, apparently it came very quickly." Stella sipped at her chocolate waiting impatiently for David to continue.

"After the ambulance had gone Mr Verity stayed behind waiting for Dr. Mansera. Together they went into the incubator room. As I said, the intruders must have been frightened away. The incubator, comes with its own generator, it's quite a heavy piece of equipment and would have been difficult to move. All the wires had been pulled out and the whole thing shifted half a metre across the floor. The important thing is, the chamber hadn't been opened. It needs a special key, and thankfully the glass was still intact. We don't even know if they realised the cub was inside but it was still sleeping peacefully curled up in its litter. Dr Mansera telephoned several of the staff and all of them turned up within half an hour and began clearing up. Julia is one of the keepers, she has her own incubator. Dr. Mansera took the cub straight round to her house. It's there right now, sleeping contentedly."

Relief at the news poured through Stella. Her legs suddenly felt unsteady, she sank down beside her mother and reached for her cup of chocolate.

"And Emilio's all right, you said the hospital are keeping him in - for observation?" Jorge queried.

"He's O.K. I think he wanted to come out but the hospital insisted he stay." Janni ventured. "I'd say he's quite a strong young man. Stella noticed that her mother was looking at the clock, it showed quarter past eleven.

"If you don't mind, Janni, David, it's past Stella's bedtime." For once Stella did not question the decision.

The couple got up from the couch. David bent down to the girl.

"Stella you'll have to tell me later how your project is coming along. Once the dust has settled perhaps Janni could bring you along to the museum again." Stella nodded wearily. At that moment the biology project into which she'd poured her energies and which offered such potential for all Spain's wildlife, especially the lynx, seemed not at all important. Jorge walked with their visitors to the hallway. Once sure they were out of Stella's hearing, he asked.

"David, do the police have any idea who carried out the attack?"

"I don't think so, at least they haven't said. They're insisting on questioning all the staff but everyone's so dedicated I can't believe they'd be involved."

"You said Jade's father saw a car?"

"Yes, a black car, it drove out of the car park with no lights. He couldn't tell for sure, but he thought there were three people inside. He only remembered the last two numbers of the licence. There is just one strange thing though. I mentioned the dart gun Emilio had with him, well it hasn't been found. The police think his attackers took it."

"It doesn't bear thinking about, could they shoot someone with a thing like that?" Janni asked tucking her arm through David's.

"I hope not, but it was only small dose, the type we give the animals. It's such a pity we lost two of them. Dr. Mansera's going to have to rethink Xando's security after this."

"Wouldn't it be possible to install some security alarms?" Jorge continued.

David shook his head.

"I really don't know," he answered. "But we've kept you long enough."

Jorge let them out of the apartment. Closing the door he leaned back against the wood and tried to make sense of the day's events. Dispirited and somewhat saddened, he shook his head and wandered back into the lounge.

NINE

At the same moment as Jorge Martin closed the apartment door, in another part of the city Sergeant Lobato was returning to his desk in the central police station. For the last two hours he had been out on a domestic disturbance case thankfully with no violence but the continued vociferous argument between husband and wife had exhausted him. He returned thankfully to the station to look at his messages. Bringing the steaming cup of coffee to his desk he sat down and perused the two slips of paper in his tray. He was surprised to discover that the message timed at 6.30 pm hadn't been dealt with on the previous shift, but it was perhaps fortuitous that both notes had been left for his attention. Once separated the connection between them might never have been made. He read both briefly, set them down and reached again for the coffee cup. The 6.30 call had been made by a Dr. Haloran, a teacher at the City High School. It mentioned the mid-week edition of the *Playa* and the letters they'd published. With the recent attack on Xando in mind, Dr. Haloran drew attention to the probable "false" address in Carlos Boulevard, given in one of the letters.

Sergeant Lobato glanced over the message, and had decided to place it in the 'crank' letters folder, when his eyes were drawn to the second message, timed at nine the same evening. The caller had insisted on anonymity. Late Wednesday night morning, perhaps about two a.m. he'd been driving back from a girlfriend's home when a black car slewed sideways, swerved front of him and ran into a parking lot, colliding noisily with a pile of rubbish. The car reversed savagely into the road only narrowly missing the caller's car a second time, and finally shot back into the empty lot to disappear behind a complex of commercial buildings. The incident occurred in Plaka Square to the east of Carlos Boulevard, the street given in the Playa as Juan Delgado's residence.

At seven next morning Sergeant Lobato placed the two messages in front of his senior officer.

"Might be worth looking into." He suggested. "Two calls about Carlos Boulevard." Detective de Horna glanced through the message sheet, shaking his head.

"You'd better look into the one about the car. It's the right time and colour, pity he didn't get the number. I don't know about this letter to the *Playa*, could simply be coincidence. I remember thinking it was a scenario for cranks. Be pretty stupid to put in an address you're connected with."

The detective laughed candidly.

"Some of the criminals we deal with don't have much imagination, and remember, the letter had to be written some days before the attack to get in the paper when it did."

"All right, I'll get the *Playa* to give us the letter - if they still have it, might be a clue there. I'm going back to this Xando place this morning to finish checking the personnel records. They're a close-knit bunch, difficult to get them to talk about their colleagues at all except to praise their work with those animals. Perhaps I'll pop into the hospital and see if this Mistral chap can remember anything more about the attack."

An initial survey by Sergeant Juan Lobato and Constable Luiz Johnson, of the commercial complex on Carlos Boulevard drew a blank. Each of the new properties bordering the boulevard was enclosed in its own compound by high metal fencing and comprised a grey-fluted metal prefabrication unit and parking lot. Most were guarded by the same security firm at the far end of town which they would have to investigate later.

By noon, the police officers had already visited seven of the units. A further two units at the rear bordered on a wide strip of scrubland where the few trees and shrubs struggled to survive, blackened stumps and burnt out oil cans littering the ground below them. They were older than the other seven, constructed of inferior material and the fence bore no identification or security logo. The gate to the first compound was locked with a rusty padlock and seemed unoccupied while the gateway to the second unit stood wide open. Along the front, bales of waste paper were stacked in untidy columns. A fork lift truck wandered among them loaded down with crates of scrap metal. It wasn't hard for the policemen to guess the nature of the business conducted within the compound. They exchanged comments.

"What do you think, worth investigating?"

"Doesn't look very promising, just a warehouse for junk. I doubt if they've any money for security guards, but while we're here, best ask if anyone noticed anything."

They had left their patrol car at the entrance to the vacant lot and walked towards to the open gateway. As they entered the property they heard a voice challenging them and an old man, wearing a grubby beige coat, came wandering out from the open warehouse doorway.

"You just stay put," he called.

"We're police officers Mr ....?"

"None of your business what my name is, just the caretaker that's all."

Both officers were in police uniform. It was impossible for the man not to know their profession. Both held up their police cards and the constable stepped across the threshold into the site.

"I said not to come any nearer. You're from those busybodies over there aren't you." He gestured to the complex of more modern buildings, - trying to move us off our land. Well we're not going. Understand!"

Sergeant Lobato stood by the gateway while his colleague walked towards the open doorway. The old man turned away and raised his hands as if gesturing to someone. The beige coat flapped in the wind showing several tears through its already worn hem. The constable had nearly reached the doorway and was taking out his notebook when his colleague shouted from behind.

"Look out Luiz, the door!" The man heard his colleague running towards him. "Look out!"

It was almost too late, a forklift truck drove rapidly out of the warehouse. It was piled high with stacks of paper, far more than was safe and the driver could have no way of seeing ahead. The policeman only had time to dodge sideways. He stumbled awkwardly to the ground as the truck blundered past just missing his feet. Dust swept over him in its wake.

"Told you not to come in. Dangerous it is here."

The old man offered ruefully. He turned away and would have disappeared into the warehouse but the sergeant caught him tightly by the arm. At the same instant he called back to his colleague. "You all right Luiz?"

"All right but for him," Johnson said getting slowly to his feet. He brushed the dust from his uniform and started rubbing at his right knee.

"Can't say I didn't warn you." The old man laughed, cocking his head. Then his attitude changed abruptly. "No harm done though, eh?"

"Do you have an office where we can talk away from any trucks?" Sergeant Lobato asked brusquely.

"Down the back, over there."

"You go first then." The sergeant said loosening his grasp on the old man's arm. "You O.K. to walk Luiz?"

His colleague nodded.

The 'office' proved to be a small area in a dark corner of the warehouse illuminated by one barred window overlooking the area of scrub. The office was partitioned off from stacks of newspaper piled almost to the ceiling of the twenty metre high building, by metre-high plasterboard nailed together. Alongside were three large skips overflowing with metal waste. The room was barely three metres square and housed an ancient rickety desk cluttered with sheets of papers. The only other furniture was a collapsible wooden chair. As soon as they entered the room the old man reached into a drawer for a packet, stuffed a cigarette between his lips and lit it with a petrol lighter.

"Not a very safe place to smoke old man, with all this paper," ventured Lobato.

"It is when you're driven to it." The man glared back at him and coughed.

Johnson stood at the narrow entrance to the office and wafted the smoke away with his notebook. It made little impression on the pall of smoke.

"Now will you tell us your name."

"Why do you want to know?"

"Well for one thing we want to be able to tell the owner who we spoke to."

"You're meeting him now, name's Jose Julio Fernandez, if you can believe it." Grumbled the figure behind the smoke.

"I thought you said you were the caretaker?"

"Owner, caretaker, buyer, seller - sometimes even the truck driver ..
but then I usually look where I'm going don't I?" He wheezed to cover the
sound of his sneer.

"All on my own I am, except for the drivers, and the boys that guard
the place at night. Can't be too careful with everyone trying to take the
business away from me, need someone to look after my interests."

"Well we'll need to speak to your drivers and anyone else on site in a
minute. You better give us details of these 'boys' too."

"They're only my nephews for Christ's sake. My sister's kids. She's had
a hard enough time of it bringing them up practically alone, I like to do my
bit to help out."

The old man shuffled awkwardly on the chair and lit another cigarette
from the dying butt of the old one.

"Nonetheless we'll need their addresses."

"I'll write it down in a minute but you'd better tell me pretty snappy
what you come for, I've got business to do."

"O.K., but first, just write the name of your employees and their
addresses too."

The man grabbed a strip of paper and began scribbling with the stub
of a pencil. He wrote three names on the sheet, scribbled an address at the
bottom and waved the sheet to the officer nearest him. Johnson looked up
from rubbing his bruised ankle and took the paper.

"You'll have to ask the drivers their addresses, I don't have them. Now
will you tell me?"

"We want to know if you saw anyone in the area near the commercial
units during the early hours of Thursday morning."

"Why would I be here at that time of night? I was at home. One of the
boys would have been here, you'll have to ask them."

"We will, don't doubt it." The officer fingered the piece of paper.
"And your wife will give you an alibi will she?"

"She will," the man grumbled, "and that sister of hers lives with us will
- she hates my guts so if she confirms it you can believe her."

"You haven't put the boys surname on here."

"Their father was - is - a bastard, I don't know whether she uses the
family name or his - it's Gonzales."

"How old are these boys, aren't they rather young to be left alone here
overnight."

"Now look they're not children, Paco is 21 and Jerome is about 19, sometimes Pietro comes with them for company, he's fourteen or fifteen."

"Two of them not really boys then. Do they drive themselves here?" The old man looked sideways at them and briefly inclined his head. The policeman exchanged glances. Officer Johnson thumbed through his notebook while the old man lit yet another cigarette. Ash had begun to accumulate on the desktop and across his knees. He began scribbling on a piece of paper ignoring the policemen.

"What colour of car do they drive,."

"I think it's black, yes black. Now look I've got work to...."

"Black you think. Now there is just one more thing, Mr Fernandez."

For a second the old man seemed to stiffen, his fingers froze over the paper then recovering himself he carried on scribbling.

"Mr. Fernandez, do you have a gun - a rifle perhaps?"

The hand with which he was writing relaxed slightly and the man put down the pencil.

"A rifle, yes I've got one, point 22, use it for hunting rabbits."

"So you still have it, you've got a licence I suppose?"

The man nodded twice slowly.

"And where do you keep it - at your home?"

The man shrugged.

"Wouldn't be much use there would it? The boys ..." The man narrowed his eyes and looked up at the sergeant, "... that is Paco and Jerome, use it here to shoot the rats, sometimes the place is infested with them, right scourge they are. They manage to kill a few rabbits out there too." He nodded towards a smeared windowpane, so coated with grim that it was barely possible to see through to the parched scrubland beyond.

"Probably take them home to their mother." He added with a gruff laugh.

"Perhaps if you kept the place a bit more hygienic, rats wouldn't be a problem," said the constable, nudging with his shoes at a mouldy crust of bread lying near the base of the desk . The old man sneered and remained silent.

"So you keep the rifle locked up here? Is it in this *office*, it doesn't look very secure."

"It isn't, that's what I've been telling you. There's other people the boys help, herding goats and the like....it's easier for them to keep it at home. I thought there was no harm in that."

"When was the last time you saw them with the rifle."

"Look I don't know. I trust them."

"Perhaps you're a little too trusting Mr. Fernandez. Did you ever check if either of them had a gun licence."

"Didn't think they needed it, the rifle's mine. It's just the sort of extra bureaucracy you Town Hall people invent to keep yourselves in work."

"But it's no longer in your care is it, your licence is only valid for you Mr Fernandez."

"Just a lot of fuss about nothing. The boys were still schoolboys, started using it during their school holidays. Look I'll get it back from them and take it home if that's what you'd prefer."

The old man grimaced and placed his cigarette down on the edge of his desk which showed the marks of previous burns. He looked up candidly and seemed to be assessing each of the policemen in turn.

"And afterwards, well if you need anything, parts for the car, well I have got contacts."

Sergeant Lobato swiftly interrupted.

"You're only making matters worse Mr Fernandez but I'll overlook that comment. We'll go see the boys ourselves about Wednesday night. I don't want you doing anything about the rifle, except to look out your licence and get a copy over to the central police station within 48 hours. D'you understand?"

The old man stood up suddenly, and tried to brush past the Sergeant. The office entrance was so narrow that for a moment he stood face to face with the man. His rheumy eyes peered up at the policeman's face, his breath so strong from cigarette fumes that the policeman turned aside to let him pass.

"I understand all right, a man tries to protect his property from vermin and he gets the police down on his neck. But when our fellow citizens try to put him out of business, move him on, then he gets no help from the Town Hall, none from you police." He spat a gob of saliva that fell on the constable's shoe, and walked away down the corridor between the towering bales of paper.

"You can see yourselves out." He called back. "You found your way in."

They heard the clicking of the cigarette lighter from within the paper mountain.

"He'll do himself out of business if he carries on like that," said the constable. "And I'd say it won't be any great loss."

"Except for that sister of his." The sergeant hissed. He gestured to his colleague encouraging him towards the perimeter fence. He clutched his notebook and remained silent as they walked back across the open lot. When they reached their patrol car he gestured across the bonnet.

"You know there's a lot of coincidences here. I just hope the old man doesn't realise yet."

"Coincidences - I don't get you?" The constable was still amusing himself picturing the old man burning down his own warehouse.

"Constable think! If this place really has any connection with that Xando attack then the old man and his nephews might be implicated. He said they had a black car didn't he - the same colour car as at Xando. And they've got his rifle, a point 22. The same type used in the shooting."

"The boys, his nephews? ...but surely they wouldn't attack the animal centre."

"Some people enjoy killing just for fun, first rats and rabbits, then.... besides I think I've heard the name Gonzales before. Something about school truancy and vandalism. But whether it's coincidence or not I'm contacting headquarters on the radio right now. Then it will be up to them. No don't drive off, they may want us to stay in case the old man leaves in a hurry. "

When Jorge heard the apartment's front door opening he hurried from the bathroom, where he was working, to greet his wife and daughter in the hallway.

"Come in, there's some news about Xando."

Anna sighed in dismay. That Saturday morning she had taken Stella shopping for school books to distract her from the Xando tragedy. The sea air had brought a little colour back into her face, now she watched her daughter's face whiten once again.

"Jorge can't this wait?" she begged.

But Stella looked up hesitantly at her father and replied in a whisper.

"What news Dad?"

"They think they've caught someone for the attack."

"Oh!"

"Let us at least sit down Jorge."

"Of course." He looked at his wife's face noting the warning signals she was trying to send him. Her eyes fluttered down towards her daughter.

"Come and sit down, then. Stella would you like a drink?"

"Cola, please."

Stella perched herself on the edge of a kitchen chair. Her colour had only partially returned when Jorge set the filled glass down in front of her.

She was almost too calm.

"What news Dad?" she pleaded again.

Jorge hesitated as Anna sat down beside her daughter. She patted her daughter's hand.

"Well you had better tell us."

Anticipating Stella's dismay, Jorge now shrugged rather unhappily. "There was a report on the radio just half an hour ago, the police have arrested two young men, brothers. "

He paused watching Stella's knuckles whitening around the glass.

"It seems their uncle employs these boys as caretakers in his property on Carlos Boulevard. Apparently they have his rifle on permanent loan and when the police visited their home they panicked. They and a younger brother to tried escape through the window, so the police arrested all three. A point 22 rifle turned up in a kitchen cupboard and .....the police also found something else."

Anna watched her daughter drain the last of her drink. Her hands were shaking as she silently set the glass down.

"They found a loaded dart gun, like one missing from Xando, under the youngest boy's bed. It seems he's also subject to a truancy court order, but he's only fourteen so they can't charge him. He's been taken into care."

"Pietro," Stella gasped suddenly. "It's Pietro!"

"Who's Pietro?" Both parents chorused.

"He broke the lynx.... the statuette."

"The little model, but I thought you said it had fallen from your bag."

"It fell out because Pietro snatched the bag from me. He was bullying us, Hanna and me."

"Why haven't have told us about this Stella?" Jorge queried.

Stella just shook her head and looked down at her lap.

"Jorge, let be," Anna cautioned. She took Stella's hands in her own and said quietly.

"Whatever he's done, this bullying, doesn't mean ......this Pietro, is the same boy, does it?"

Stella looked up hopefully, but said, "Pietro's been playing truant lately, his mother's being taken to court over him. And everyone knows about his older brothers too, they were always playing truant, perhaps worse."

"Well I think we'd better not make any judgements about him at the moment Stella. Regarding the bullying though, perhaps Jorge and I had better talk to the school. See if we can get something done."

"O.K. if you think it'll do any good. I'm sure it was Pietro who left a page from the *Playa* on my desk."

"On your school desk..... to be sure you read it?" Anna asked horrified.

"Yes, and after I read it, I looked up and he was standing in the corridor laughing. I haven't see him in school since."

"Well, I don't think we should dwell on this. It may turn out to be quite a different boy. I don't want you going to school on Monday with the wrong idea. Will you promise not to worry for the time being."

Stella nodded. Anna looked up at Jorge before continuing.

"Your father and I were discussing the summer, just a while ago. We wondered about taking a place near Gerardo and Lucia for part of July or August. It would get us out of the city for the worst of the summer heat. Do you think you would like that?"

Stella was taken aback. The events of the last week had distracted her. The museum and Xando now figured largely in her world and the contacts with David and Emilio had been as unexpected as they were welcome. She couldn't imagine life away from them. Nine months ago the prospect of returning to her grandfather's farm and the lynx family would have filled her with joy. Now her emotions were so mixed up she couldn't answer.

"What about Dad's work?"

Anna looked momentarily puzzled.

"Well, he's going to have three weeks off anyway and if we take somewhere for longer he could always spend the week here and come up at weekends."

"It won't be until school is over will it, I need to finish my project and ....?"

"No it won't be for at least six weeks, I just thought we all needed something to look forward to."

Stella thought of Emilio in his hospital bed and asked.

"I'd like to go back to Xando and, to see Emilio before... before the holidays," she finished, almost begging.

"Well Dr. Mansera has got some thinking to do about security. They may have to stop taking visitors Stella." Jorge saw the disappointment on his daughter's face. "But we'll see. David said he hoped to see your project soon, perhaps you can ask him."

TEN

A week passed before the children returned to the museum. The stressful time of examinations was approaching and school soon settled down to its normal routine; the Xando "incident" and even Pietro's enforced absence at a youth centre due, as Stella had suspected, to his involvement in the attack, were temporarily dismissed. Already, by early June, the summer heat had become oppressive, the city sweltered. By the end of each afternoon, the classrooms were unbearably hot and stuffy, teachers and schoolchildren alike grew irritable and were looking forward to the long summer break. Janni passed on the museum invitation at the end of a geography class, but Hanna sought Stella out immediately afterwards.

"I don't think I'll bother going to the museum" she confided. "I've used all the information they gave me and found some stuff on the web and Jamie wants to get back to his swimming club and enter their competitions. He's trying to get me to swim too but...."

"Won't he finish his project then?"

"Oh yes!" Hanna replied indignantly, "but he's almost finished it like me."

Stella was dismayed.

"But couldn't you come just one more time, if the trip's just for me Janni'll want to cancel it. Please won't you come?"

Hanna looked at her friend with a puzzled expression.

"I'd have thought you had nearly finished your project with the amount of work you've been doing. D'you have much more to do?"

"Not much really, only...."

"You know Janni wants the projects handed in before the end of the month."

"I know, it's just there are some things I wanted to ask David about. Won't you come, please Hanna, after everything that's happened."

"It's not just because you have a crush on him - it's something else isn't it Stella? "

Stella blushed, looked at her friend and only nodded.

"It's something to do with Xando isn't it, I heard a rumour that they're going to move away from the city, due to the attack."

Stella jerked her head up asking fearfully.

"Where did you hear that?"

"I can't remember, it might have been on the radio."

"Well I don't know anything about that, but will you come please Hanna?"

"All right, I guess I owe it to you after you stood up to Pietro for me." She saw a look of anguish cross Stella's face and hurried on.

"Of course I'll come," she concluded "I'll even persuade Jamie too."

"Oh would you, then Janni can't refuse...." She leaned over and hugged her friend.

Unusually, that Thursday evening Janni accompanied the three children into the museum and waited with them at the reception desk. Stella wondered whether she was waiting to see David, but the receptionist made it plain that security had been increased since their last visit. She simply took their names and made them wait in the busy foyer. As they waited, Hanna grew increasingly indignant.

"Well it isn't as if they don't know us," she insisted.

"Don't be so impatient, come and sit down over here," Janni chided indicating a leather-covered bench.

"Well I hope....." Hanna showed no sign of moving away from the reception desk. Stella interrupted, anxious to prevent more friction.

"Janni, are you coming in to see David?" she asked, moving past Janni and sitting down beside her. Jamie drew Hanna towards him, putting his finger to his lips. She pouted but remained quiet.

"Not immediately, I'll see him later," Janni replied. "You're getting on well with your project aren't you, I hope David's been helpful to you?"

"Oh yes, he has, and I've done a lot of work, but... I suppose this will be our last visit for the summer?"

"Well the whole point of these trips was to help with the projects and they'll be finished soon. But there's nothing to stop you coming with your parents, in the summer break if you want to."

"We're going away for the summer, I don't expect..."

But she was interrupted by David himself.

"Well here you are." He was standing beside the reception desk and beckoning to them both. Hanna and Jamie stood to one side deep in subdued conservation.

David walked over and pressed a kiss on Janni's cheek. A faint flush coloured her face.

"I didn't expect to see you until later Janni, are you coming in with Stella."

"No, we were just chatting. Stella was telling me that she's going away for the summer."

"Oh, where are you going... abroad?"

"No." Stella shook her head rather shyly. "We're only going to stay near my grandparents."

Stella saw a brief look pass between her teacher and David.

"But isn't that where...." Janni began, only to be interrupted by David who shook his head suddenly.

"It's up in the Tejedas isn't it Stella?"

As Stella nodded, David turned quickly back to Janni.

"We said six o'clock didn't we!"

Janni nodded but her face bore a puzzled look as he lead Stella away briskly. Before they reached Dr Mansera's room David opened a door to the right of the corridor and lead the way in.

"This is my own office now." He gestured around the room. It was only a few metres square but housed a huge desk on which sat a computer and several untidy stacks of paper. One tall window graced the only external wall and gave views between tall cypress trees onto a narrow lane at the back of the museum. The only other furniture in the room was a bulging bookcase and two chairs, one was piled high with computer paper. David moved around to his chair and began clearing a space to the side of the desk. Stella waited unsure where she was to sit. Somehow the biologist seemed rather distant.

"Here, sit here." David cleared the papers off one chair and beckoned Stella across. She moved hesitantly round the desk.

"We'll have to tidy this later. These are the results of some surveys we did last year, we've got a lot more work to do yet."

He edged the chair closer to his desk and Stella sat down rather timidly. She guessed from his hurried farewell with Janni that any time spent on her project would be curtailed.

"Now what have you got to show me Stella?"

She handed over her project folder and David began reading. He quickly thumbed through the first few pages and looked up.

"This is very good. Now, do you want a drink while we work, a lemonade again, I know you like it?" David had already risen from his chair when Stella shook her head.

"No I'm all right.

"Well, we'll crack on shall we? Janni's given me a list of criteria to look for but have you anything else you wanted to ask?"

Stella nodded.

"I wanted to know more about how they interact, not just the lynx..."

"All the carnivores? Well, that's not so easy, not much research has been done on that aspect. What have you been able to put in, can you show me."

Stella reached over to her typescript notes and indicated a page where she listed the carnivores in Spain and Andalucía.

"Yes, I see and you've put the estimated number of each species and the area they cover - well I don't think we can improve on that for the moment. I think you've probably done enough on that section, certainly for your school project. Was there anything else?"

Stella nodded, she gave him a sheet of paper on which she had listed various questions about the lifecycles of the Spanish carnivores: wolf, lynx, bear and genet. For the next fifteen minutes David poured over the project answering her questions, while she penned notes. At last David closed the folder and handed it back to her.

"You've done a good job, Janni will be pleased. You have to hand it in at the end of the month don't you. I'll mark it during the summer." Stella was surprised and said.

"I thought you'd mark it before the end of term."

"Well I am rather busy. Janni said there was no hurry to mark it. I'm sorry Stella I didn't think it had to be done before September. When are you going away?"

"Right after the end of term, the middle of July."

"And where is it you're going to stay?"

"It's to the south of our old village, Valdes."

David smiled and passed over the folder. Stella took this as a signal to leave. She stood up. Instead he waved her back into her chair.

"It was there you saw your lynx wasn't it?" He nodded as if he really didn't need an answer.

"Yes."

"There were three families at one time I think."

Stella looked up in surprise.

"Three but I only told you about....."

"I know, but we had already surveyed the area - we've been doing so for some years of course. It wasn't far away where the female cub, Marmit, was orphaned."

"Then you already knew about Pardito and his family?" Stella asked aghast, so upset she couldn't continue.

"Sure Stella we knew about some animals, from our surveying and radio tracking, but when you told me about them, and about the genet kill, I knew you'd seen more than all the researchers put together. Your information has been, and will be, very valuable."

Stella felt disillusioned, as if somehow David had mislead her, but she couldn't exactly say how. He sensed her unease.

"Stella I'm going to tell you something in confidence. Something that will help us."

Stella looked up from her lap, not feeling reassured.

"Us.. .?"

"Me, Liz, Doctor Mansera... and Xando."

"Xando?" Jade had told her that Emilio was back at work as if nothing had happened. But, as her father had warned, Xando had announced its closure to visitors for the immediate future.

"I heard a rumour ... that's it's going to move, will Emilio still be able to work.....,"

"Well Stella I'd like to know where that rumour started, it's not the only one we've heard."

"Then it's not true?"

"Not exactly."

"What do you mean?"

"Well that's what I was just about to tell you. You remember back in the spring I told you about our plans for a breeding programme for the lynx."

"I remember, Liz, Dr Delgado.... felt you shouldn't have mentioned it to me."

"Yes, that's Liz for you - all security." He nodded to himself.

"But you see our plans weren't finalised then, we were waiting for money and sponsors and also needed to assess the current lynx population, that's why your information was so important. You see it proved that lynx can survive quite effectively in the area."

"And that's important?"

"Very important, because that's where the project is going to be based."

"Near Valdes? Oh but what about......?" Stella sensed a lump in her throat as the old fears welled up. She couldn't speak.

"Your grandfather?"

Stella looked at him and shook her head.

"He'll never accept it... never."

"Stella, I'm sure he and all the farmers know that lynx and all the carnivores, are protected. Anyhow the programme will be based further into the hills, it won't be near any of the villages. The whole site will be fenced, just like the hunting reserves and there will be wardens patrolling all the time. What happened at Xando was a bad thing, but it brought us a lot of sympathy. And just as important we've more funding for educational work. That's where you can help - of course."

"Me?" Stella felt her stomach lurch.

"Well, you said you're going back to your old village. We are holding a travelling exhibition in the neighbouring villages, I thought you might like to help with the one at Valdes. Suppose I got your project back to you over the summer. If you leave Janni your address we could call in and bring the project. If your parents see now much work you've done they might want to help too."

"Dad would, I'm sure."

"There is one other thing Stella - this might be more difficult, but since you are going to be there for .... how long?"

"About 6 weeks, until the beginning of school in mid September."

"O.K." David remained silent for a full minute. He thumbed rather abstractedly through the computer records, then said.

"I said this might be more difficult. When we start work on the enclosure, sometime in August, we expect there will be some reaction locally. Since you'll be living there - do you think you could listen out for people's reactions and let me know if you hear anything ... anything that worries you at all."

Stella looked up from her project and felt her throat constrict. To David's surprise all she said was.

"Could I have a drink now please?"

"Sure." David hurried out of the room leaving Stella in a state of turmoil. He returned with can of cola and glass of water for himself.

"Sorry this is all we have."

David opened the can, the liquid hissed and bubbled onto the lid in a white foam and he quickly poured some into her glass. She took it, drinking down the fizzy liquid hurriedly until she felt composed enough to ask.

"Did you mean spy.... spy on people?" Over the top of her glass her eyes were dark with anxiety.

"No, not at all Stella, I wouldn't ask that. I just want to know people's opinions, whether they are happy with the project, whether there's any dissent. What people say in general." He paused and sipped thoughtfully from his glass. "But no Stella I'm not asking you to *spy* on anyone at all. Perhaps I shouldn't have asked you this at all, I just thought since you're so local and..."

"It's all right David," Stella said. "I don't mind doing just listening, ...and I'll know won't I, if there's anything I should tell you?" David looked down at the girl's pale face. She seemed suddenly very mature. Stella put her glass down and asked.

"The female at Xando - Marmit - she's going to be part of the programme?"

David nodded.

"And the little cub - it's a male isn't it?"

"Yes, he's still very young, but we'll soon be introducing him to Marmit. It's best for the young cub to be with others of its kind."

"Will Emilio... will he be involved?"

David nodded. "Yes, he's going to be in charge of the new enclosure."

"You'll only have two young animals though, will that be enough - to breed?"

"I can see your studies have been worthwhile Stella. No two isn't enough. We'll have to bring in some other animals, perhaps from the wild."

"From the wild, but won't the ones nearby be related?"

"Probably but it's a risk we might have to take at the start. There aren't many other zoos or reserves with surplus animals. We've been surveying a group of animals over near the coast - beside the big Palmiri reserve, do you know it?"

Stella nodded, she remembered driving along the coast road with her father the previous summer. The reserve boundary ran along the road for many kilometres.

"No lynx were reported in the area for five years and we wouldn't have known there were any there until we heard of a couple of accidents."

"Accidents?" Stella asked, concern showing in her small face.

"Yes, I'm afraid a young female was reported killed on the new Granada road back in the winter, and a lorry driver I know who helps me on my surveys, had a collision with an adult lynx a couple months' ago."

"Was it killed too?" He sensed the concern in Stella's voice.

"We don't think so, no. Lamas, that's the driver, realised it was a lynx. We went back together and surveyed most of the Visua valley and found signs of at least two lynx."

"And are you radio tracking them too."

"No yet, Stella. We think they may have just been dispersing."

"You mean they might have moved on - not be there any more?"

"That's right, but recently I've heard some disturbing news about the rabbits in the area - you know they are the lynx's main food?"

Stella nodded.

"Well there have been recent reports that the population is suffering badly from disease this summer: myxomatosis, and haemorrhagic disease. When we did our initial surveys there seemed plenty of rabbits about - now, I don't know."

"Will you do any more surveys?"

"If there's time, perhaps. I've got to concentrate on the new reserve first and...." but he was interrupted by a knock on the door which opened before he could respond. Janni stood in the doorway smiling.

ELEVEN

When the family arrived in the village of Valdes three days previously, the rented cottage with its dark tiny rooms came as a shock to them all. The building stood in a small plot of land shrouded by groves of olive trees whose leaves shaded all but the eastern side of the house. The trees were past their prime and only a few wizened grey fruits hung from the gnarled branches, they were diseased Stella's father insisted and should be grubbed up. Her parents were to have taken a flat in a new block near the village centre, but they'd had been let down at the last minute.

The tiny cottage had only been the only rented accommodation left in the village for the summer and Jorge had rented it for the full six weeks. A young couple now living in El Rosal had recently inherited the cottage from an elderly uncle. They intended to refurbish it as a holiday home but had not even started on the project. In the meantime, Jorge agreed to take it at a reduced rent. The old man's tired worn-out furniture was to stay in the house for the duration. Stella and Andras had both been disappointed, complaining bitterly to their parents. All the rooms were small and smelly, the decor drab and boring, with only one shower for all four of them. The kitchen outhouse contained the only toilet. When they both chorused their dissent their parents had given them the choice of returning to the city for the summer. Both refused.

Over the last few days Anna had tried to make up for the cottage's deficiencies by brightening up rooms with fresh bright bedding and curtains, while air fresheners and pomanders wafted away the stale smells that clung to the house. She and Stella scrubbed and scoured the kitchen surfaces until they shone, while Jorge and Andras found some old tools in an shed at the rear of the long garden and lopped off many of the low olive branches that crowded against the walls. After three days, when the work was mostly finished the family relaxed with a barbecue in the garden with a fire fed by dense fragrant olive wood. The rich smoke deliciously scented the churritos and chopped apples and melon were wrapped in foil and tossed into the ashes to bake. As they ate, laughing and talking beneath the olives, the cicadas' strident evening song filled the air.

Next day they were at last be free to visit Gerardo and Lucia for the first time since their return. It was to be a disturbing visit for them all. Lucia hadn't seen the children for six months but she greeted the family with her usual reserve. If she had felt neglected over the year she gave no sign, even querying their gifts of special foods: melon, pineapples and cakes from the patisserie, as they carried them in from the car.

"Anna why do you let them buy these things, don't you think we have enough to feed you?" Lucia asked scornfully.

Gerardo had appeared round the side of the cottage. He was dressed exactly as Stella had last seen him. An old working jacket, the colour of charcoal, hung loosely about his shoulders and a plaid shirt, sweat stained and ill-fitting, was tucked awkwardly into brown moleskin trousers. His boots were worn and so clung to his feet that she wondered if he ever took them off. As he swaggered towards them Stella sensed from the slight dulling of his eyes, that he had aged, perhaps not outwardly, but inside and occasionally when he thought no-one was looking his shoulders drooped dejectedly.

"Leave be woman, they're just trying to show how grand they are now, living in the city." He scowled then caught sight of Stella standing half hidden behind her father. His eyes softened momentarily, and a smile crossed his face, to be quickly replaced by a frown.

"Best let them come in." He nodded to the children who quickly ran into the cottage. Stella had forgotten how dark it was inside the building. Even in July the thick walls and tiny windows let so little light into the room that her eyes took some time to adjust. In the darkness, the mustiness and dank charcoal smells assaulted her senses. Andras rushed over to the ancient pump and began pumping water into a cup. The water bubbled out of the tap, clear and sparkling.

"When I've been to college I'll get this old thing replaced by an electrical pump," he announced.

Gerardo blundered forwards pushing his grandson away from the pump handle.

"You'll do no such thing. There's nothing wrong with this pump, it'll last me out."

"But Grandpa, I'll be able to do a lot for this place, once I've been to college."

"Well when you've been to college, that'll be soon enough Andras," Gerardo grunted

"Will the two of you get out of my kitchen," Lucia interrupted. Stella noticed a brief smile crossing Lucia's wrinkled face. Gerardo and Andras moved sheepishly into the centre of the living room. Jorge had settled a box on the wooden table but upon hearing Lucia's muffled protest he quickly removed it to the floor alongside the settee.

"How are the goats?" He asked casually.

"Same as when you came last time!" Gerardo began packing his pipe with fresh tobacco from one of the boxes. "Same as the time before that, and the time before that."

"O.K. so nothing changes. But what about the pastures, there's an awful lot of building in the valley below the town, doesn't that affect them."

"If I want to take my goats down the valley for water, then I take them. Don't let no houses stop me." Gerardo exclaimed, his weathered face lit up by a burning match.

"But doesn't it take longer, and more houses are being built all the time, how will you cope?"

Gerardo drew heavily on his pipe. The thin spine of the match was blackened as the flame drew down into the pipe's crusted bowl. When the flame reached his fingers he extinguish it with a quick shake of his hand. A thin veil of smoke rose towards the ceiling and curled down the dark stone walls. When Gerardo coughed, the sound came from deep in his chest.

"Still plenty of space, no cause for you to worry," he grunted at Jorge. As far as he was concerned the matter was closed.

Stella had settled herself on the sofa next to her father. Talk of goat-herding reminded her of the previous summer. She suddenly remembered the feeling of freedom it had given her. In the city she had forgotten the freshness of the air and the stillness when the breeze dropped and birds called from the oaks high up on the ridge. All of a sudden she wanted to be outside, to be close to the pines and the dense fragrant scrubs which clothed the hillside and perhaps to her lynx, Pardito.

"Can I.... can I go out with you tomorrow, with the goats?" She asked.

"What, I thought my little goatherd had deserted me altogether." Gerardo pointed to her with the mouthpiece of his pipe.

"She'll need her old clothes to come goat-herding, not those flimsy things," Lucia gestured to the pink top and shorts she was wearing. Gerardo grunted a subdued laugh.

"But they're back in the city." Wailed Stella, "I can't get them now."

"Well you better take my old trousers Miss Goatherd." Andras offered laughing at his own joke.

"If you must go Stella, I think I left a jacket here last time. I helped Gerardo chop some wood, but it was raining so hard the thing got soaked. Do you remember Lucia, an old corduroy thing, now where would it be...?"

"In the shed beside the goats I shouldn't wonder."

"I'll go and look for it." Stella was half way to the rear door when Anna called her back.

"Just a minute young lady, there's dinner to prepare and I seem to recall that you were going to make something special for dessert. The coat can wait."

"Oh yes, the churros," Stella remembered shamefaced.

She turned back to the table and reached into one of the boxes searching for eggs, flour and sweet molasses sugar.

"I'll need the fat very hot Mum."

"Well we'll stoke the range and you can do them while we prepare everything else. Now Lucia what do you want us to do."

The next two hours were spent in preparing and eating lunch. Despite their poverty Lucia laid on a broad spread of cold meats, bread and fruit which Anna guessed had been begged from Lucia's neighbours. For all her obvious coldness, the meal was evidence that Lucia had missed the family over the past year. It made Anna and Jorge feel guilty. When it was time to leave Stella had forgotten about the corduroy coat. They were already outside the cottage approaching the car when Anna reminded her.

"What about that coat Stella? Best get it now so you can wear it in the morning."

"I'll find it after you've gone." Gerardo offered.

"It'll need a bit of airing before she wears it Dad," Anna argued

"Yes Stella." Jorge added before Gerardo could argue. "Why don't you just pop round to the shed now, you'll probably find it on one of the pegs against the goat pen."

"Wait for me then." Stella yelled disappearing behind the cottage.

"No we're going to let you walk." Quipped Andras, quickly getting into the car and slamming the door loudly so his sister would hear.

Anna embraced both her parents noticing the look of dismay on Lucia's face.

"Remember, we're only in the village. We'll see you often."

"During the summer," Gerardo barked.

"Why yes the whole summer - six weeks, into September."

Lucia looked at her daughter and shook her head.

"Six weeks." Was all she said.

Anna noticed unshed tears brimming on her mother's eyelids.

"Oh Mama." Anna cried turning back from the car. "Why don't you come and live with us, you know we want you to..,"

Lucia stiffened and looked across to her husband. "He wouldn't come."

Gerardo snorted. "In the city, call that living? Never!"

His hand dived into his pocket and drew out his pipe. Jorge sat at the steering wheel as Anna entered the car. There were tears on her face. Several minutes passed since Stella disappeared. Jorge finally looked at his watch. Although already 9 o'clock, it was still light. He got out again.

"Stella?" He called. "Where's that girl?"

"Stella," Andras mimicked loudly through the rear window.

"I suppose I'd better go and find her."

Andras got out of the car beside his father.

"You stay here with your mother Andras. I don't want you disappearing as well."

Andras grinned in agreement.

"O.K!"

He would be quite happy for Stella to remain with his grandparents, it would give him more space in the cottage.

Stella had very quickly found the coat. The shed had no windows and was almost in darkness except for the doorway, but there was enough light to see the coat hanging limply from a peg on the inner wall beside the goat pen, just as Jorge had said. As she reached up to pull it down from the wall the coat peg snapped in half. The coat slipped from her grasp and plummeted down into the darkness beside a clutter of equipment balanced against the wall. At first she could only see the prongs of two rusty rakes and some cogs from a broken tractor but the coat had fallen down the back of the tractor where it was completely dark.

At first she tried reaching across the machine, stretching her hand out, but the coat eluded her grasp. In desperation she went back to the doorway and managed to force the door ajar to give more light. She looked back into the shed and waited for her eyes to adjust to the semi-darkness. It was then that she saw it: the sharp prongs and the evil curve of the trap staring at her from the shadows. The metal of the outer rim gleamed as if recently burnished but the central plate was marred by a dark liquid stain. Small scraps of some pale fibrous material clung to the outer teeth.

As Jorge turned the corner of the cottage Stella came flying towards him. She raced up the rock-strewn slope as if chased but as she drew near him she stumbled and crashed down almost at his feet. He reached down to pick her up and noticed she was shivering.

"Where does it hurt Stella?"

Stella shook her head and clung to him so tightly that he couldn't see her face. He thought he could hear stifled sobbing. Gently he raised her up and brushed the fine hair away from her face.

"Can you walk, you went down with such a crash, honey?"

Stella wouldn't look up at him, she simply nodded and kept her head bent.

"Yes I'm all right." She leant down and began rubbing her knees. The skin was raw and roughened.

Jorge bent down with her.

"The skin's all broken. Shall I carry you?"

"No I'm all right," she insisted.

"Better get back to the car, your mother can take a look."

Stella insisted on walking, but she was shaking so badly as they reached the front of the cottage that Jorge had to support her. Andras was the first to see them.

"Didn't you find the coat then," Andras taunted as they approached the car. "Do you want me to get it?"

"No Andras," Jorge cautioned. "Just stay there....,"

Andras slid back into the car and hung out of the window.

"What's wrong with little Sis then?" He laughed.

"She had a fall, she's a bit shaken."

Anna quickly got out and ran round to her daughter. Stella wiped her face clear of tears.

"Where does it hurt dear."

"My leg, I fell on my leg but it's better now, really."

"Let me see." Anna leant down and examined Stella's legs. Without Jorge's support the girl seemed close to fainting. She laid her hand on her mother's shoulder.

"I'm all right, really."

"Well if you're sure, I've got some ointment back at the cottage. "

Anna turned to her parents who were waiting patiently in the cottage yard.

"I think we'll get straight back there and clean that cut. I'm sorry Mum, I'll see you in a day or so."

Lucia smiled weakly, her eyes running over her granddaughter's slight form.

"She's in shock, likely." It seemed a strange pronouncement.

Anna nodded thoughtfully.

"Andras get in the front will you, I want to travel in the back with Stella."

"In the back Andras, in the front Andras," the boy taunted.

"All right that's enough, son," Jorge glared at him as he opened the door. Andras remembered Jorge's accusation weeks before when his father had called him callous. Stella had been the cause of his censure on that occasion too.

In their kitchen Anna cleaned her daughter's leg. All the time Stella kept her head turned away, almost ignoring her mother.

"Do you want some tea darling, something to eat?."

The idea of food repelled her.

"I just want to go to bed."

Anna shook her head, "Just some toast and chocolate?"

"I don't want any food Mum. Please I just want to go to bed."

Her mother was still kneeling down. She looked up at her daughter and shook her head.

"If you're sure."

Stella had gone straight to her new bedroom. Her legs ached but she hardly felt them. The deeper inner pain would take longer to heal. Later when her mother brought in a tray of buttered bread and hot chocolate, Stella turned her head away pretending to sleep. The tray still lay untouched on the floor beside the bed where Anna had placed it.

"Grandfather, grandfather don't...!." She was struggling to hold onto his arm as he raised the loaded gun. Twice she had managed to pull it down. Now her strength was failing.

The old man shouted, "Leave me be," and shook her off. He was scowling as he raised the gun. She leapt at him once more. This time he pushed her aside so angrily that she spun round, caught her foot against a rock and tumbled to her knees on the rocky soil. Her breath was hot in her throat, and her chest ached as she tried to cry out. When she attempted to get up, her leg buckled beneath her. She looked up at her grandfather. He was raising the gun again.

"Don't..". she gasped, but already he seemed unaware of her presence. She clawed her way towards him over the rough ground. Spines caught in her clothes and rasped at her hands, bright red blood trickled from her fingertips. As she drew level, she caught hold of his trousers and pulled herself slowly up to her knees. Streaks of blood darkened the material. Her grandfather didn't move, he held the gun steadfastly out in front of him. Stella could only gaze along the line of the gun. A hundred metres away a thick patch of shrub gave way to an open glade.

An animal was pacing slowly across it, its body moving sinuously. At first it seemed undisturbed by the commotion behind it. Then the lynx turned its head and peered from its mask of dark fur directly across at her grandfather. The dark ear tufts twitched anxiously and its eyes struck gold and piercing in the sunlight. Stella cried out again but strangely neither her grandfather nor the lynx moved; both stood transfixed, their eyes drawn to each other through some inner struggle. Then suddenly Gerardo raised his arm. Something flashed in the lynx's eyes. It spun round and raced across the remaining metres of bare soil, but as it began to run Stella cried out in desperation. "No. Not that way."

"Not that way," she screamed again, managing to draw herself up. Despite the pain in her legs she began running. Behind her she heard several clicks, the sound of the rifle being primed. Still she ran, faster and faster, trying to head off the lynx, trying to turn him away from the ghastly trap, its hungry metal jaws half-hidden under the juniper. She was flaying her arms in warning as a whistling sound passed her and the first shot tore up a strip of soil only half a metre behind the lynx's hurtling frame. The animal veered towards her, she saw its eyes, they were blazing with fear. There was another shot and the animal hesitated right in front of her, Stella staggered to a halt and collapsed helplessly in front of the lynx. The ugly trap was only centimetres away, its jaws open and primed. She heard herself cry out again... No, don't ....please don't, then suddenly there was only darkness.

Stella's pillow was wet from her tears. She awoke in the little box room unable to recall where she was. She sat up quickly but the tears continued to pour down her cheeks. Her chest was tight and painful as if she had really fallen. Gasping for breath she scrambled out of bed and fumbled through the darkness towards the little window set high in the wall. It faced east and the sky showed as a thin pale blue line near the horizon. She fumbled awkwardly with the catch and finally had the window open. A welcoming breeze, cool and refreshing caught at her wet face. Slowly as her breathing eased she turned back towards the room. Beside the narrow bed was a heavy wooden chest in which she had neatly folded her summer clothes. Now on its roughened wood were strewn the pink top and flowery shorts she'd worn the day before on the visit to Holm Cottage. Despairing she slipped down beside the chest, rashly crumpling the fine material of what she'd thought of as her very favourite top. Clinging to it with wet hands she revived the terrible nightmare, sobbing: "Oh Pardito, don't let it happen!".

The goats bleated constantly, jostling each other as they struggled along the stony hillside. The bells around the leaders' necks rang out clearly across the hillside and dust pearled into the air from beneath their feet. The dense smell of their bodies and dung mingled with the fresher scents of pine resin and sage. Gerardo held to the track ahead, his head bowed into the slope of the hill, his pipe sometimes clasped to the corner of his mouth, sometimes thrust into his pocket. Occasionally he looked up at the milling herd and cast a stone at a lone straying kid. There was no dog to do the task. Dogs were expensive to feed. Sometimes you got one which was difficult to train, often it became a threat to the herd - then you had to shoot it anyway. The last one had died five years before. He hadn't replaced it.

Gerardo was leading the herd out as Stella arrived. He scrutinised Stella's rough and ready outfit - a loose shirt of her own, a pair of Andras' trousers which he had almost outgrown, and an old jacket of Jorge's. Gerardo nodded to Anna, gestured with his stick for Stella to follow then turned up the narrow track into the shadow of the holm oaks. Stella trailed behind. Earlier Anna had questioned the wisdom of Stella walking so far after her fall. Stella refused to listen. Still concerned Anna now watched her daughter until she, Gerardo and the goats disappeared around a bend in the track. Neither her daughter nor her father turned to wave back.

They'd walked for almost an hour without speaking. Hugging the ancient tracks across the ridge, wrapped in the sounds and scents of the jostling herd. There was a reluctance for either of them to speak, yet the atmosphere hung heavily about them. Trapped in her own thoughts, Stella hardly noticed when the track opened up and the goats spread out to wander on the open hillside. Gerardo sensed a strangeness in her. Previously his granddaughter had accompanied him up the hillside chattering constantly. Now her silence troubled him. She had been away for almost a year, living a life in a city that would always be alien to him. The girl had grown more mature, not just in years but in temperament, more thoughtful too. The easy relationship which had grown between them over the early years of her childhood had gone, replaced almost with diffidence. And yet here she was accompanying him and the goats to their summer pasture. Why?

Gerardo drew level with the top of the ridge where the goats were feeding dubiously on a patch of scrub already dry from the summer drought. Two large sandstone blocks stood at the top of the ridge. Gerardo placed his stick against one and leant back on the other. He teased tobacco from an old leather pouch, pushed it well down into the bowl of his pipe then lit a match and drew the flame down into the tobacco. With his gnarled fingers he carefully crushed out the embers of the match and let it fall beside the boulder. He looked down the track through a thin veil of almost blue smoke and watched his granddaughter walking slowly towards him. Her head was bowed. She trudged heavily, each step an effort. When she drew level with the ridge she looked across the long lines of hills and intervening valleys and briefly smiled. Then she noticed Gerardo resting between the boulders. Scenting the rich tobacco smoke her smile faded. She squinted ahead to where the next valley dropped away revealing the Tejeda hills to the north. Holm oaks framed an area of lush pale green vegetation where a stream still flowed. Stella felt herself stiffen. Surely that was where David said the reserve would be. She hadn't realised it would be quite so close.

She stopped two paces away from the boulders and forced herself to look at her grandfather. He clutched at his pipe and gestured towards his sack which lay on the ground. She looked down. It was the same sack he took everywhere on the hill. The roughly-cured leather was scuffed and worn, the once colourful braid of the strap now dark and evilly stained. On occasions the sack contained snares, sometime a rabbit corpse or a mangled pheasant. Today she knew it probably only held a water bottle, and some wedges of bread and cheese. She shook her head and sighed.

"Well?" Gerardo asked, taking the pipe from his mouth. "You want to go back, is that it?"

"No, I don't but....."

"Too much the city girl now eh, outgrown your goat-herding ways?" Gerardo said, purposely misunderstanding her.

"No that's not true ... only...,"

She turned and involuntarily looked towards the more open landscape plunging down towards the coastal plain. The city, her schoolmates, even David and Xando seemed very far away.

"Only.....?" Gerardo demanded tapping impatiently on the boulder with his stick.

"I did a biology project before the end of term."

She looked towards her grandfather and silently willed him to understand.

"A project, what was it on then?"

"The tutor's going to mark it and bring it here in a couple of weeks. There's going to be an exhibition in the village hall and David's going to....,"

"David? Who's this David, another pupil?"

Gerardo frowned and shook the burnt tobacco from the pipe. It fell at his feet where the tiny embers quickly died. Stella remembered her father's initial strained attitude when she'd used her tutors' first names. She looked at the ground.

"No he's a scientist at the museum - Dr. David Foster, he's English."

"An English scientist, I thought you said he was your tutor. Why would he want to mark this project of yours, it's for the school isn't it?" Gerardo's tone was disparaging. He clutched his stick then pushed himself away from the boulder and set to walking along the line of the ridge where the majority of the goats were clustering.

"Grandfather," Stella called out and ran until she was pacing alongside him.

"I love it here - the hills, everything." She gently took his arm and urged him to stop.

"You love it do you....?" Gerardo looked down at the girl. He hadn't realised how much she had grown, her face already level with his shoulder. She looked up at him with eyes that were clear brown, like the pale streams which ran in spring down from the hills. He nodded and looked from her towards the ridge and the scattered goats. The rich tones of their mottled coats merged with the landscape making them hard to distinguish: black and white hides against the dark pines, pale beige rumps fading into the ochreous sandstone, crusty brown horns like dead branches held against the distant rock. Only the tolling bells fastened loosely around the goats' necks gave them away as they moved hungrily from shrub to shrub. The land was dry and hard, savaged by seasonal extremes, the thin soil lifeless, offering little for the goats or the people who herded them. It was knowing how to tend it, how to herd the goats to the better pastures as the years moved past, that was important. Gerardo didn't "love" the land but it was this knowledge that tied him to it - and it to him. Stella stood beside him gazing out across the same hillside, but seeing quite a different, landscape.

They walked for a further few minutes in silence, sensing the divide between them, unable to cross it. Eventually Gerardo gestured with his stick towards a ruined hut in the distance. Stella had taken little notice of the route he'd chosen. She started as she saw the hut, the jagged wreck of the wall, the boulder-strewn surrounds. There was no doubt. It was the place where she'd watched Pardito's mother kill the genet last September. She hung back as Gerardo loped towards the hut. He settled himself on one of the boulders and pulled the water bottle out of the sack, then laid a red cloth out on the ground placing on it thick wedges of bread and cheese. Stella hadn't joined him so he gestured towards her.

She walked slowly forward and sat down on the wall, the stones were hot from the morning sun. They almost burnt her bare skin. Without thinking she picked up the bread and a hunk of cheese that Gerardo had cut from the wedge with his knife. The lynx: Pardito, his mother, the other two cubs, seemed suddenly very close. She swallowed a mouthful of food and reached for the water bottle. The original stopper had broken long since and Gerardo had replaced it with a cork from a wine bottle. The cork was ill fitting and he'd wound a strip of cloth about it to stop the bottle from leaking. It was a normal part of her grandfather's life but she wondered briefly what her classmates would think of this totally unhygienic arrangement. She drank quickly then laid the bottle aside. Studying her grandfather's face she said boldly.

"When I was up here last time I saw a family of lynx. "

"You saw lynx?" Gerardo spluttered over his hunk of bread nearly choking. "A whole family...," he coughed angrily. " When was this?"

"Last September, before we went away," she said, calmly replacing the cheese down on the cloth.

"And you didn't tell me...."

Gerardo stared into the brown eyes of his granddaughter. She stared back defiantly.

"You still kill them."

"Yes I kill them, girl. What of it? They're vermin, I can't believe you didn't tell.....," Gerardo hesitated and spat on the ground near his feet.

"They're not vermin, they're protected. I did my project about them, David says....,"

Gerardo's anger erupted quickly.

"Your project. What do you know, what does this... this David know about living up here. Has he ever tried?"

"No, but he's done a lot of research."

"Research," Gerardo spat again.

"You shouldn't do that."

"Shouldn't kill them?" Gerardo asked confused. "My folk, your folk, have lived up here for hundreds of years. Herding's what we know, what we do. If we let these vermin, these lynx, survive we won't survive ourselves."

"But there's hardly any of them left, that's why they are protected - not just here, not just in Spain, but in the whole world."

"Then let the whole world look after them." Gerardo took a long drink from the water bottle. Stella watched his Adam's apple moving up and down under the loose weather-beaten skin of his neck. She felt soured by their argument.

"The rabbits are dying out too."

"Too much predation by your lynx."

"No, that's not true, it's not by the lynx." She stood up quickly and felt light-headed. Briefly the hillside went black, then came into focus again. "It's not the lynx, they rely on the rabbit for food.... the rabbits are diseased, when they die out the lynx dies out too. People hunt the rabbits in the summer, then in the winter there aren't enough for the lynx. That's why they sometimes grow hungry and ......and perhaps take a occasional goat. If people weren't so greedy.....," Stella gasped almost out of breath.

"Greedy, what do you know?" Gerardo struggled awkwardly to his feet. He leant on his stick for support and gasped out savagely. "What do you really know Stella? Haven't I watched your grandmother wear herself out, seen her grow old before her time. Hasn't she worked on the land through the heat of summer, clawing at the soil just to make a few crops grow. Is it greed to hunt a few rabbits to make her life easier....just a little bit easier," Gerardo spat out the last word.

Stella was stunned by his argument, she turned away and clawed at the wall, the stones hot, burning her hand. Somehow it didn't matter.

"You could come and live with us."

"And what would I do girl? Sit in a chair in your city apartment and wait to die."

The idea horrified Stella as Gerardo meant it to.

"We could move back here. You could still have some goats."

"I was born to this life Stella, I'll die before I give it up."

Gerardo turned away from her. Bending down, he wrapped the uneaten food in the cloth, stoppered the water bottle and rammed both into his sack.

"I saw the trap - in the shed. You can't use it again - I won't let you."

Gerardo shrugged.

"How will you stop me girl?"

Gerardo picked up his stick. Without another word he walked across to the nearest group of animals. The lead goats, their bells jangling harshly, were congregated around a sage shrub, the plants grazed almost to the ground. In a metre wide circle around each shrub the goat's hoofprints stirred up the dry soil and nothing grew there. There was no food for rabbits nor any other herbivore now that the goats had had their fill. Gerardo walked on. He would use the information to guide them to different pastures as the year wore on and next spring the plants were sure to grow again. Stella remained by the hut.

"I *will* make you stop you," she cried out to her grandfather's back, "when David comes………,"

David Foster arrived two weeks later. The August heat had driven the family indoors for a siesta in the early afternoon. Jorge was first to emerge. At three o'clock, alerted by the sound of a car he eased himself from the bed where Anna lay sleeping and reached the tiny hallway when a knock came on the dried wood of the front door. Sounds of movement came from Stella's room to the left. Jorge was near the end of the hall when her door opened softly. She peered out. Her light summer dress was crumpled, she too had been sleeping and her eyes had a dreamy look .

"Who is it?" She whispered through dry lips.

Jorge laughed quietly. Putting his finger to his lips, he said

"I'm not a mind reader. Let's see shall we, young lady?"

The door faced west and the sunlight played brightly on the pathway. Two figures stood close together near the door. With their faces in silhouette Jorge did not recognise them. He held the door open and stepped out onto the gravel track for a better look. He hadn't taken two steps before Stella was beside him, pulling at his arm.

"It's David...Oh, and Janni too."

Jorge shaded his eyes with his hand.

"Of course, Stella said you might come."

"I hope it's convenient," Janni asked. She looked up at David, putting her hand around his left arm. He clutched a bulging briefcase in his right hand.

"I didn't call because, ... well we didn't finalise arrangements until yesterday."

Jorge felt Stella pulling at his arm.

"Ask them in Dad," she whispered.

"Of course, come in out of the heat both of you. I'll get you something to drink."

"That's very kind, it's pretty hot ....but...." Janni hesitated, looking at David.

"I hope you don't mind." He said, "we've brought some friends you might like to see." He turned and gestured with the briefcase down the length of the path. Half hidden in the olive grove, stood an old range-rover, its battered paintwork overlain by a pale film of sand. As Jorge shaded his eyes to look down the path, he heard Stella gasp. She dragged her hand from his arm and ran towards the vehicle. The rear door was thrown open and two figures emerged into the shade of the olives. The first was a tall man, slim to the point of gauntness, the second a girl of no more than fifteen.

"Emilio, Jade," Stella cried, rushing up to the young man. Beaming with pleasure Emilio embraced her.

"Stellita," he cried out to Stella's amazement. "How is my little Stella?"

Stella blushed with embarrassment, quickly turning aside she greeted the girl.

"Jade .... I didn't know you were coming."

"It was a last minute thing, Emilio's was coming and so...."

Without waiting for her friend to finish Stella grasped her hands and twirled her round on the shifting gravel of the path.

"Enough, enough Stella, the stones are scattering under me."

Stella let go of Jade's hands and felt suddenly self-conscious.

"I'm just so happy to see you." She laughed. Looking briefly up at Emilio she said.

"Jade I've missed you so, I just didn't realise quite how much until now."

Jade had noticed her quick glance at Emilio.

"I'm glad you missed one of us," she countered in amusement. Emilio's usually calm face coloured slightly.

"Come in, come in all of you."

Stella heard her mother calling from the house. She grabbed Jade's hand then turning to Emilio calmly took his arm and lead them towards the house. Anna had woken from a dream to hear voices in the doorway. She'd risen quickly and looked flustered at receiving unexpected guests.

"Jade, lovely to see you again." She bent down and gave the girl a quick hug

"And this is Emilio?" Anna asked. Jade nodded and the man gave Anna a soft smile that seemed to light up his whole face.

"We've only spoken on the phone, are you quite well now.... after ...,"

Emilio saved her from mentioning the attack on Xando. He nodded.

"Quite well, as you can see."

"And you don't need to worry about his weight, Mrs. Martin." Jade added. "He eats constantly but he never puts on any fat, he's nothing like the rest of our family."

"Perhaps you just work too hard Emilio?" Anna teased looking enquiringly at the young man.

"No, that is not true Mrs Martin. I just enjoy my work that is all."

As Jorge entered the cottage he decided its tiny lounge would be too small for the visitors.

"Lets go through to the garden."

He lead them down the hallway and through into the kitchen area. Anna called out behind him, she knew the lunch dishes had not been cleared away.

"Where are you taking our visitors Jorge, the kitchen it'll be.....,"

"Out into the garden, and I'm sure they won't mind a little mess."

"The garden will be better I suppose."

"Oh Mrs Martin, we should be the ones to apologise for arriving unannounced," Jade ventured. "I know my mother goes spare when she has unexpected guests - except Stella of course - she's no bother at all." Stella blushed.

"Just go straight on through the door to the garden. Stella, will you help your father move the garden furniture out."

"Oh Mrs Martin I must do that."

Emilio pushed ahead but at the rear doorway he saw David and Jorge carrying garden chairs into the shade of the olives.

"Once the sun's off this section of the garden it's really pleasant." Jorge commented. He and David set out the chairs along the rear wall of the cottage in the deepest shade. Alongside a small trellis a terracotta urn, over a metre tall, contained a wizened jasmine flushed with white flowers. Jorge ushered Janni towards a chair nearest the container.

"You can sit here Janni." He offered. "If you like jasmine."

"Oh, I'd love to Jorge, it's such a sweet scent." She leant towards the clustered branches of the bush and breathed in the heady fragrance. "It's beautiful."

"That's what Anna always says. I find it a bit heavy myself. Now

David, we'll need another table."

"Oh please, Mr Martin, let us do that." Emilio strode from the kitchen doorway.

"Jorge I don't think there is another table," Anna called.

"But I saw wooden one folded up inside the shed."

Anna shook her head.

"It's rotten, I looked at it last time I was down there."

Jorge shook his head in disbelief.

"Are you sure, shouldn't I check?"

"I'm sure Jorge! And anyhow, it won't be in a fit state to use.... Now Jade, Janni, won't you sit down. David, Emilio, here by this little table. That's right." She watched her guests settle themselves gratefully into the shade.

"Jorge will look after you while Stella and I prepare some drinks."

"Oh Mum, I wanted to talk to David," Stella complained.

"I'm sure David will be happy to talk to you once he has a drink Stella. Isn't that right David."

"Sure. We're in no hurry to get back to the city, that new road's so easy."

"That's right," Jorge agreed. "I was really surprised when I first used it a few months ago. The journey time's more than halved. Now, I suppose there'll be even more development heading this way."

A frown crossed David's face.

"All too true."

Stella sighed and followed her mother into the house. In the kitchen Anna gathered together an assortment of soft drinks while Stella hurriedly filled a fruit bowl. She loitered near the door eager to listen to the buzz of conversation in the garden. Emilio hurried to the doorway as she emerged with the filled bowl.

"Please, let me take that." He placed the bowl on the table and turned back to take a laden drinks tray from Anna.

"David was just telling me about a project he's begun." Jorge called across as she handed out the glasses.

"I hope you like this." She gave the first glass to Janni. "It's a fruit cocktail, very refreshing."

Janni put the glass to her lips and tasted the orange liquid.

"Delicious."

Anna handed out the remaining glasses then sat down thankfully beside her husband.

"Oh, is it something to do with Xando?" Anna glanced at Stella.

David nodded.

"Yes, it is." He took a sip of his drink. "But Emilio's going to run the project." David hesitated.

Emilio was standing silently against the cottage doorway but he declined the offer to speak.

"Yes, it's to do with Xando of course. But this is a new enterprise for us. We're up here to survey land we've purchased. It's going to be a wildlife reserve."

"Up here?" Jorge quizzed. "Did you know about this Stella?"

Stella gave a slight nod, then looked down into her drink. David smiled conspiratorially.

"I may have told Stella a little about what we hoped to do. You see the land is in the Tejeda foothills, barely thirty kilometres from here. In fact we've just come from looking over the site."

"But won't there be some opposition? The farmers are pretty conservative around here. What sort of animals will you keep."

David put his empty glass down on the ground and leant forward.

"It's a captive breeding programme - for the lynx. And you're right Jorge. There may be some opposition, and to forestall attacks like the one on Xando we're taking exhibitions to local villages. We want people to understand our work."

"I certainly hope it's successful," Jorge mused. "Where're the exhibitions going to be?"

"We have a exhibition trailer. It'll be taken to each village in turn. Starting next week we'll bring the trailer to Valdes, to the school yard. With your permission Jorge, I'd like to ask Stella to help."

"If I can," Stella said shyly remembering their earlier conversation.

"What do you have in mind?" Jorge asked.

"It's to do with this actually," David said, bending down to his briefcase. He lifted out a folder which Stella recognised as her own.

"My biology project," she exclaimed.

"Yes, it's your project Stella." Offered Janni. "David and I marked it together and I think it's one of the best year-nine projects I've ever seen." She got up and walked around the back of David's chair where she leant over and leafed through the pages of the project.

"The introduction and text are exceptional for someone so young."

Stella felt the praise wasn't justified.

"But I had so much help - from David and Liz," she exclaimed

"I guess that's true Stella." Janni smiled. "But Jorge, the most exciting sections are when Stella puts in her own ideas."

Janni took the folder and quickly scanned through to the back.

"Look, here's what Stella wrote: 'The Iberian lynx has been part of the Andalucian landscape for many centuries, sharing it in harmony with mankind. Now that harmony and the lynx's own existence are threatened. But anyone who has seen this beautiful animal stalking its prey, or the tiny sandy-brown cubs of *Lince purdinus* playing beside their mother, cannot but mourn the loss of this creature from our lives.'"

Stella lowered her head in a mixture of pride and embarrassment. Jorge took the folder and thumbed through the pages. He motioned his daughter to his side. Putting his arm around her waist, he asked, "Did you really write that Stella?"

Stella looked up into her father's eyes and saw the pride they conveyed. She nodded.

"Janni and I were so impressed with the project, we gave it 95%, and we wondered if you and Stella would allow it to be displayed in the exhibition."

"Of course you can, can't they Dad?"

Jorge nodded. "If that's what you want. I don't see any problem. What about Janni, do you want the project back."

"No, it's Stella's to do with as she pleases."

"I was wondering," David continued, "if Stella could help in the trailer, just while it's in Valdes. You'd be welcome to come with her of course. My staff will be in attendance, it would just be a case of displaying Stella's work and answering any questions. If people know a school project had been done by a local girl they might be more interested. What do you say Stella?"

"I'd like to come very much, especially if you think it would help."

"Will the exhibition be open all day David?" Anna asked.

"No, just two hours in the morning, say 10 to 12 and then again at 4 pm for another two hours. It's just too hot around noon."

"I think I'd better come with Stella, perhaps we could go down for one or two sessions."

"Oh Mum, why can't we do every session?" Stella pleaded.

"Because we do have a few other commitments Stella, but we'll see. Jorge will want to come one day, won't you dear?"

Her father nodded.

"Of course."

"There's one more thing Anna, before we go. Although we went to the reserve today Emilio wants to go back there tomorrow to check on some details. We were wondering if Stella, and perhaps yourselves, would like to come with us."

"Oh you must go Stella," Jade burst out. "It's a wonderful site, so close under the foothills with a stream too, I don't think I've seen a more beautiful landscape."

"Oh, I'd like to see it very much."

"Then you shall Stella, and I think I'd like to see this place. How about you Anna, will you come too?" Jorge turned to his wife.

"I would have, but I've arranged to go back to Holm Cottage tomorrow."

"O.K., it'll be just Stella and myself, David."

"That's settled then."

Later, as the range rover drove away, Stella stood sadly in the roadway watching it disappear. Her parents remained in the olive grove. Behind them Andras came walking up the path. Squinting into the sunshine he asked casually, "Have I missed something?"

TWELVE

The range rover turned off the narrow paved road onto a gravel track. Stones spun under the tyres and dust swirled up into the pines which cloaked the valley sides. After less than twenty minutes the vehicle emerged from the shade into a wide stretch of grassland. Above, the tall Tejedas mountains stretched away east and west, the bare grey limestone forming a long row of rounded hills. Below, the foothills were cloaked in a open forest of evergreen oaks and pines interspersed with low shrubby garrigue. Lower still and running alongside the perimeter road to the south, ran a belt of juniper, the darker green contrasting sharply with a strip of fresh green marking the course of a stream which wound its way through a dense swamp emerging into a broad grassy prairie before dipping into a shallow gorge to flow towards the coast. David pulled the vehicle to a halt in the shade of some tall pines.

"Well, we're here," he announced getting out of the car.

Stella, who had taken the front seat beside him, opened the passenger door, assessed the half metre drop to the ground, and quickly jumped down onto the dusty soil. She raced around the front of the vehicle where David stood. Pointing down the hillside to the green scar within the browning meadow grasses, she asked breathlessly.

"Is that the stream, it looks so green in all this dry vegetation."

"Yes, it runs out of the limestone just a little way above the oaks. We had a geology survey done and they found a clay band running all along the valley, it keeps the water from disappearing into the sandstone. We'll also build a small reservoir to retain the water through the summer. It's down there just out of sight, I'll show you later."

Stella turned round as Emilio and Jorge drew level with them.

"It looks a pretty isolated spot David, yet we're not far off the road. How far will the reserve stretch?"

"Well we've purchased the land from above the oaks, along to that distant plantation and right down to the road. We're going to have to fence off the road and put an entrance gate just inside the boundary. The reserve fence proper will begin just beyond where we're standing. "

"Will you be fencing the whole estate?"

"Only about a third. We're going to restrict hunting on the rest of the estate. The landowner neglected the place for so long that most of the local farmers have been used to hunting over it. It'll take some time to get them used to the idea."

"Can we see where the fence will go David?" Stella pleaded. "Will it be a really big reserve?"

"Probably as large as some hunting enclosures. If we go down the path a little I'll be able to show you the area we propose to fence. But Emilio and I need to check on the actual layout with the plans. The contractor was up here last week and has set out the markers but Emilio doubts they'd been laid out properly." Emilio nodded.

"I've got the plans here." He reached into the range rover. "Here's the GPS handsets and the latest maps."

"GPS? Is that satellite positioning Emilio?" asked Jorge looking with interest at the black handset.

"Yes, have you ever used it?"

"Well no, but I'd like to see how it works."

Emilio set both map carriers on the ground and turned his attention to the handsets. He turned a switch on each one and scanned the dials.

"David and I will each take one. I think we decided that I'd take the northern sector and he'll go down across the valley to the farthest corner and then work back parallel with the stream. Is that right David."

"Yes that's O.K."

Emilio spread one of the maps out for Stella and Jorge to see.

"See Stella, this is where we are and the fence will go in along this line.

He drew his hand in an arc across the terrain." Stella puzzled over the detailed map.

Emilio began explaining the GPS system to her father.

"I'll take one of the maps, checklist and a handset." David said as Emilio handed the equipment to him.

"It's looks like Emilio has an apprentice Stella." David said laughing at Jorge's concentrated look. "Shall we leave them to it and carry on down the track before it starts getting too hot." Jorge looked up from the handset and smiled sheepishly.

"What do you want to do Stella, come with us, or go with David?"

"I'd rather go with David. If I come with you and Emilio all I'll hear is GPS talk."

"OK, off you go then."

David laughed.

"If you come with me you'll have to work Stella, I'll want you to record the GPS numbers that I read out and I also want you to count the rabbits you see as we walk."

"Count rabbits," Stella said sharply then, realising the joke, laughed.

David lead the way from the shelter of the pines out onto the dry track and into the fierce morning heat. A faint breeze riffled almost soundlessly through the distant trees making their branches sway in time with the rustling of the grass stems. Behind them the baked white mountain slopes stood out in stark contrast. The peace and seclusion of the setting overcame Stella. David heard her sigh. She walked thoughtfully beside him casting her gaze at the sweep of rich vegetation that formed the valley bottom and marvelling at the emerald coloured sedges along the length of the stream. In the far distance she spotted a rabbit grazing leisurely. It seemed unaware of their presence until a pebble shot out from beneath David's shoe. Even then the rabbit stood up on his hind quarters for a few seconds before bounding into the cover of a cluster of low rosemary scrub.

"They seem very tame," Stella observed.

"There's not much hunting at this time of year Stella, later in the autumn you'll be lucky to see any."

"Will there be enough for the lynx in the reserve?"

"Perhaps, but remember we are going to release some rabbits as well, there's good evidence that the rabbits will do well in the damp grassland here."

"Where will you get the rabbits, will you need a lot?"

"Rather a lot yes, they're being bred for us over in the Sierra Morena hills, but we'll have to release them over a longish period so the numbers can build up. Some won't survive very long, some will fall prey to the raptors. Hanna's favourite birds remember."

"Oh, yes she'd be happy here. I bet some of her eagles are watching us right now."

"Well perhaps not eagles, maybe some buzzards. There'll also be plenty of foxes who'll take advantage of an easy meal."

"Would they get through the fence then?"

"Hopefully not. Now look here's the first marker."

He gestured with the handset to a white painted peg hammered into the earth at the side of the track. He checked the readings on the GPS handset and Stella wrote them down.

"Well that one's O.K. anyhow. Let's get on down towards the stream."

"David, you were going to show me how far the reserve will stretch."

"Ah, yes. I'll show you here on the map first. Do you see where the stream comes out of the woodlands into that dark band of grass."

Stella glanced up at the hillside then scrutinised the map.

"If you take a line from the stream to a point just above the trees, then that's the northern boundary. Follow the trees along to the third peak to the west, then drop down to the top of that broken limestone crag."

"The one with the jagged top? It looks like the ones at Torcal."

"That's right. It's the same type of limestone so it weathers in the same way. But I don't think there are any ibex round here for you to see."

"Why is that, aren't they here too?"

"I guess it's because Torcal's a protected area and this estate has been hunted over for a long time."

A sudden frown clouded Stella's face which David didn't notice.

"The reserve runs down to the valley from that crag, but the estate runs on along below those two further peaks and the boundary is marked on the far side by that pine plantation, it's outside the estate."

Stella studied the range of hills then with her finger traced the line of the reserve on the map.

"You said you're going to fence only a third of it. Will you put notices around the rest to restrict hunting. What if people ignore them?"

"We just have to try and stop them, but it's not going to be easy. That's where the exhibitions come in I hope. Come on let's find the next marker." He picked up the GPS set while Stella looked at the map. David took a step away from her. Stella did not move, she held her finger over the map and measured out the distance to her grandparents' village. It had taken only forty minutes to reach the reserve from the village, but on the map the two looked so very close.

"Come on," David chided. "It's getting hot already, the shelter of those trees looks welcoming."

Stella didn't move.

"But what if you *can't* stop them hunting, what will you do?" She asked.

David looked back at her noticing the section of the map she was pointing to.

"Your village?"

"It's only just over there, isn't it."

David nodded.

"It's more than twenty-five kilometres from here over some pretty rough land."

"I walked up with grandfather the other day. I guessed where the reserve was from .... from that ruined hut I told you about."

"Where the genet was killed?"

"Yes, the genet. But I haven't seen any sign of lynx since I've been back, they should have been here....," she agonised.

"They're probably still in the neighbourhood! But some of the young animals would have dispersed by now."

"Even Pardito?"

"If he's a male as you thought, then he might have travelled a long way - right out of the region."

"What about the other cubs though?" David noticed that Stella's face bore a deep frown, the colour seemed to have washed from her skin.

"I can't say. Just because you haven't seen any sign of them doesn't mean...."

"It might mean that.......that they've been trapped, illegally mightn't it?" Her faced suddenly flushed red.

David stepped back towards her. The map was shaking in her hands. He took it from her and laid it down on the ground with the GPS.

"Stella, have you any reason to think they have been trapped?"

"No...... yes, Oh, David I don't know." She seemed to be imploring him to understand something she could not, would not, put into words.

"Your grandfather?" David asked simply.

Stella kept her eyes fixed on his face and nodded.

"But you don't know .. not for certain."

"No I don't but....."

"But...?"

Stella remained silent, her eyes blazing defiantly.

"If .. if someone was found with a trap - an illegal gintrap, would they ....would they be arrested?"

"Well only a wildlife warden is allowed to search their place. But if a trap was found then it would be confiscated."

"Only confiscated." Stella repeated. "The owner wouldn't be arrested?"

"I don't think so. No. And if it is private property, the warden would need good reason, some evidence or information, to make the search in the first place."

"Oh," Stella mused. "But if they did the search, and they found evidence suggesting that the trap had been used recently, what then?"

"I guess it depends what sort of evidence. There would have be to some...," he hesitated before continuing. " Stella, you haven't seen....?"

"No!" Stella shook her head violently. She bent down to pick up the map case and GPS. "We'd better get on, hadn't we!"

David was puzzled by her sudden change of mood. Clearly Stella wasn't going to tell him any more. He watched her striding down the track, her head raised and constantly turning, her eyes busy over the hills and forest scrub as if her life depended on knowing every inch of the landscape. When she reached the first swathe of green vegetation in the centre of the valley she stopped and turned. Her faced was flushed and bore a determined expression.

He ran the last few steps towards her.

"Stella, If you want my help with anything, you know you only have to ask."

The girl only shook her head, she would not be drawn. Clearly she had made a decision and meant to act on it without further help from him. She gestured with the map and peered into the GPS set.

"Are these the figures you want. Top line reads...," she read out a set of numbers.

"Stella, won't you tell me," he tried again.

She raised her eyes briefly from the set, stared into his own and shook her head. She read out the figures again. Frustrated by the girl's reluctance to reply David could only note down the figures. The two of them continued in the same way, locating three more markers, Stella calling out the figures, David noting them down. Beyond this neither of them spoke. After thirty minutes they reached the greenery bordering the stream. Even in the summer heat, the ground was distinctly damp. Instinctively Stella knelt down, tucking the GPS set into her lap. Her face was hot, her skin tingling fiercely. She let the cool stream play over her hands, then raised them to her face. David walked towards her, water oozing from beneath his trainers.

He expected her to turn around but she continued to gaze along the stream. Beside her water gushed out from a pool behind a bank of sedges, the flow tumbling into the main stream with loud gurgling sounds that seemed wholly unnatural in that parched landscape. The girl's previously hunched shoulders relaxed. Sunlight played on the rippling stream and reflected on her pale face.

"Stella!" He knelt down beside her. The girl was very still, she hardly seemed to be breathing. She spoke without turning towards him.

"Where do you think he is?" She asked enigmatically.

"Who?"

"Pardito."

David turned away and looked towards the dense oak forest. "I don't know Stella....I really don't know."

THIRTEEN

Late on Friday afternoon, at the same time as the exhibition trailer was pulling into the school yard, Stella turned into the track leading to her grandparent's home. She had walked alone up the four kilometres from the village along the dusty road. By the time she entered the tree-lined drive she was grateful for the shade of the tall trees. But the oak leaves hung dry and dusty at the end of the long hot summer, their brown edges contrasting with the stiff green needles of the Aleppo pines. Even the heady fragrance of the herbs had lessened.

Stella's course took her along the side of the track where leggy branches of rosemary and gorse masked the boundary between gravel road and heath. In a few minutes she would be in sight of the cottage. The faint rangy smell of goats wafted towards her in the breeze. She knew if the goats were corralled the scent would be overpowering and hoped her grandfather had taken them out on the hillside as usual. No fresh curls of smoke came from the cottage chimney. Lucia had gone with Anna to El Rosal for supplies and should still be there. The air was very still with no detectable signs of activity. Even so, Stella decided not to approach the farm directly, she headed away from the cottage towards the lower end of the farm where a ragged stone wall lay half hidden under a thick fringe of bramble and gorse.

She carried with her an old hessian sack bearing the logo of a corn company that had long since ceased trading. She'd found it folded up on a shelf in a dark corner of the garden hut. Although stale, the material was strong and without mildew. When she reached a place in the wall where several stones had fallen into the track, Stella took out a small axe which her father used for splitting kindling for the barbecue and hacked through the frieze of bramble making a small opening in the vegetation. Through the gap she scanned the lower field and could just make out the goat shed some hundred metres away. The pen above was empty. She picked up the sack, carefully putting the axe inside and scrambled through the opening.

As Stella edged round the corner of the field, the rear of the goat shed was in clear view, masking any view from the cottage. She continued up the slope eventually coming level with the top wall. She would have to enter the pen around the front facing the cottage. Clutching tightly to the sack Stella ran the last few metres towards the broken door. A family of rock pipits flew up noisily up from where they were feeding on some dry seedheads and tumbled across to the shed roof. The birds' calls echoed within the oaks, then there was silence again. Stella squeezed through the doorway, her heart beating rapidly. After the bright meadow the interior of the shed was very dark. She closed her eyes briefly, steeling herself for the sight which would greet her. The clutter of tractor parts lay against the wooden partition just as before, the rusted metal coated in a thick layer of dust and grain husks. Lodged against the rear stone wall where she'd seen the trap previously, stood a small harrow wheel and a broken fork handle.

There was no sign of the dreadful mechanism. Stella panicked, dropping the sack in disbelief. The trap had to be in the shed. She scrambled over the rubble of tractor parts, pulling the harrow wheel and wooden handle from the wall. Beneath lay only a dusty pile of logs. She searched around anxiously but the windowless shed contained only piles of rusted farm equipment. She edged through the shafts into a small pen beyond the partition which served as a nursing pen for young kids and their mothers. The kids were usually born in the late spring, so the pen hadn't been used for many months. Piles of coarse hay, grey with age lay beneath her feet, coating her white trainers in a fine dry straw dust. Stella looked around the stall then kicked impotently at it filling the air with dust. She coughed violently, caught her foot on some obstruction and fell awkwardly against the wooden partition. Still coughing she clasped her hand over her nose and looked at the ground where an angular shape protruded from beneath the hay. Realisation dawned. Still coughing she sank down on the stall floor and pulled the hay towards her. Thick mildewy dust rose into the air, making her skin itch. Feverishly she cleared all the hay from the metal frame of the gintrap, then leant back and gazed sullenly at the feared half circle of spikes. The warm stall had grown suddenly cold. Stella shuddered. Although clasping her arms to her chest, the sound of goat bells jingling in the distance intruded brutally on her trance-like state. The goats were coming back.

She leapt up scattering clouds of hay and dust into the air and looked around for the sack. It was nowhere to be seen. She must have dropped it on the far side of the partition. Quickly squeezing past the wooden slats she grasped a corner of the sack, without noticing the axe tumble out. The jingling bells were getting closer. Gerardo would be at the top of the pen. There was no time to carry the heavy trap away. Her grandfather would come straight down to fetch the milking pails. In panic she climbed back into the pen. She tried to pull the trap upright but it was heavy and too unwieldy for her to stand it upright. Instead she had to drag it desperately over to the wooden partition and used all her strength to push it under the horizontal beam. As she balanced it on the beam one of the metal teeth stripped a slither of skin from the top of her finger, then the trap clattered into the dusty hole. Stella thrust her aching finger into her mouth and sighed. A shadow fell across the shed doorway.

"Lucia, is that you?"

Stella quickly leant down and kicked the sack into the shadows behind her. Her father's axe rolled into a corner, forgotten.

"No grandfather, it's Stella."

Stella stepped out into the bright sunlight.

"I didn't know you were coming."

"I've just arrived, grandfather. I thought I'd get the pails ready."

Gerardo looked down at his granddaughter. His face bore a puzzled look. Stella guiltily returned his look. The goats were milling in the pen behind him, their faces jostling over the rough-cut bars of the fence. The bells of the leaders blended with the noisy bleating of the younger animals anxious to suckle. If left too long the nannies' udders would be empty. Gerardo turned away thoughtfully.

"Come on then, I'll separate the kids. Be quick now."

Stella turned back into the shed and hurried to fetch the milking pails.

It took them nearly an hour to catch and milk all thirty nanny goats.

While Gerardo was releasing the last goat from the milking bay Stella heard the sound of a car driving up the farm track. She poured the last pail of milk into a metal churn and helped Gerardo carry it through the gate in the lower pen. Without waiting to be asked she took the pails to the side of the cottage and rinsed them out in a trough. Gerardo lifted the churn onto his back and gestured to Stella to accompany him. Unable to think of an excuse she followed him around the corner of the cottage and into the lean-to.

"Stella," she heard her mother exclaim. "What are you doing here?"

Stella said nothing. She dropped the rinsed pails on the kitchen floor for Lucia to cleanse later.

"I thought you were in the village with your friend Carla." Lucia stood in the main room of the cottage unbuttoning her coat. Although it was about 40 degrees outside the old woman persisted in wearing a coat whenever she left the farm. Anna, wearing a light summer blouse and skirt, bustled past her carrying a box of groceries.

"You should have told me where you were."

"Carla had to go out. I only found out when I got there." Stella tried hard to make the lie sound convincing.

"Oh I see. Well try to remember to tell me in future. Now help me get some of Lucia's parcels in from the car."

Stella obediently wandered out to the car. She wondered if she would have time to slip round to the shed but her mother called out from the cottage doorway.

"Lucia wants to give us some tea. Have you had anything?"

"Not since lunch no, but I don't feel very hungry. I thought I might walk back home."

"Don't be ridiculous Stella, there's no need to walk in this heat when I can drive you. Now do you want to stay to eat. Lucia seems to think you're underweight though I'm not sure I agree."

Stella blanched involuntarily and looked quizzically at her mother.

"But I'm perfectly all right."

"Well Lucia thinks otherwise and we want you fit for this exhibition don't we? I saw the trailer in the village as we drove through."

"Oh, the exhibition, I ...... I'd almost forgotten."

"Well you're going to have to explain it all to Lucia. I mentioned it while we were out."

"Do you think she wants to see it?"

"Perhaps, you'd better convince her hadn't you."

"Grandfather won't come."

By the time they re-entered the cottage Lucia had laid out the table with slices of tinned meat, bread and fruit.

"Lucia you shouldn't have opened these, " Anna remonstrated with her. "They're for your store cupboard."

"The girl needs feeding," Lucia insisted, setting a huge glass of the foaming milk, warm from the churn, in front of her granddaughter.

"Sit down Stella, there's plenty for a growing girl to eat."

Stella wanted to say that she wasn't hungry but a quick frown from her mother stopped her. Obediently she sat down on one of the wooden chairs and reached for a slice of meat to roll between the wedges of bread. Lucia nodded to herself and sat down on the opposite chair. Stella noticed that she made no attempt to eat.

"Anything for me to eat then?" Gerardo asked from the kitchen where he was pouring the warm milk into stone bottles. Later Lucia would churn some of the milk to produce a soft rustic cheese. The watery whey would be mixed into meal to feed their chickens. Nothing would be wasted. Lucia drew a plate towards her, laid a piece of meat on a hunk of bread and twisted around to place it on top of the pump-housing beside Gerardo. He was pouring the last of the milk into the stone bottles and grunted approval.

"We'll eat properly later." Lucia explained. "Now young Stella, what's your mother been telling me about your school project and an exhibition?"

Stella had just taken a mouthful of food, she continued to chew on the meat and bread, grateful for the delay it offered. Gerardo stood beside the pump alternately munching on his food and bending down to swill out the churns as if determined to ignore their conversation.

"I told grandfather about the project."

Gerardo didn't look up. There was no knowing whether he'd heard.

"Well he didn't tell me about it, but that's nothing new, so can you?"

"It's about the wildlife, here in Andalucía."

"Ah!" Lucia nodded and looked across at Gerardo. He was bent over the wheezing pump, directing some of the cold water into a large pewter flask. When he had filled it he let the pump handle settle. Silence returned to the room.

"Much of the wildlife is protected."

"Protected?" Lucia mused over the word phrasing it into three long syllables.

"Yes, protected so they won't die out..."

"But if a creature is dying out then isn't it God's will?"

"Not if we're the ones causing it, David says it's *our* fault!" Stella saw the blank look on Lucia's face. "David's a biologist at the museum, he's running the exhibitions and helped me with the project." She rattled on.

"And how does this ….this David know all this?"

"He's researching Spain's wildlife."

"And when you told your grandfather about this project what did he have to say?"

Stella was eating a chunk of bread and the question made it lodge in her throat. She swallowed hard and stared back at Lucia. Gerardo had finished eating, and was very still. Stella sensed her grandmother was manipulating the conversation, though she couldn't tell to what end. Anna was seated on the wooden settle near the fireplace, sorting through some bills. Ignoring the direct question, Stella summoned up the courage to say.

"The lynx particularly, is threatened with extinction." Gerardo was now staring at her intently. Her mouth had become very dry, she reached forwards to grasp the glass of milk. The warm fluid hardly seemed to touch her lips.

"Why should that be?" Lucia demanded folding another piece of meat into a slice of bread and pushing it towards Stella. The girl sensed her grandfather's eyes boring into her and lost courage.

"It's all in my project, you'll see if you go to the exhibition."

"She'll not go," her grandfather insisted.

"Why not?" Anna objected. "It's very good, Stella got top marks. You should you go yourself Dad."

Gerardo shook his head, dismissing the subject.

"I'll come Stella," Lucia announced stiffening her back ready to repel Gerardo's protestations. But her husband stood unmoving beside the pump.

"Waste of time," he said angrily, throwing open the door of the lean-to, it slammed behind him.

"I'll come to see your exhibition Stella." Lucia beckoned her around the table and took her by the hand. She nodded towards the door. "But you'll never change your grandfather, no matter how much you try."

It was an ominous forecast, one Stella was to remember long afterwards.

In the week the exhibition trailer was in the village school, time passed too slowly for Stella. She attended at least one period each day and every day came home daily more dispirited by the general disinterest and low number of visitors. During the weekend a few pupils from her junior school days came with their parents but she realised she had grown apart from them since the move to the city. Most of the children were only mildly interested in her project. Some looked through it briefly, giggling, only to place it back in the case David had prepared for it. Only one of the parents, the mother of a boy called Julio, who lived in the next village was really interested. She and her husband worked a smallholding growing corn and salad crops. It was a hard life and the whole family was involved. Stella guessed Julio too would soon have to leave school to work there, but as the boy was leaving he turned to Stella saying, wistfully, "I envy you.

Only a few of the village elders passed near the school and none showed any interest in entering the trailer. Silvio too, was dispirited by the poor turnout and on Tuesday morning he placed more posters around the village. By coincidence Lucia's grandmother chose that afternoon to visit the exhibition. Anna fetched her in the car. To Silvio it might seem that she was responding to the extra publicity. As Anna drove into the school yard Silvio went out to greet them. Stella had grown used to Silvio's quiet charm. He was a tall man, with a thin face and tawny coloured hair cut long around his ears. He was barely thirty years old but had the bearing of a much older man. His conversations with visitors to the exhibition were always courteous and, to Stella's eyes at least, extremely persuasive about the needs of wildlife. As Silvio opened the car door, Stella noticed her grandmother's usually stern expression soften under the influence of his charm. She watched them approach. Silvio took Lucia's arm.

"And you are grandmother to our Stella, I am proud to meet you." He winked at Stella but this approach was far too forward for Lucia. She stared at Silvio then removed her hand from his arm.

"I can get up these steps on my own young man." Lucia placed her foot on the bottom rung of the quartet of steps. She was unused to stairs and despite her pride would need help mounting them. Stella tripped down to the bottom step and took the old woman's arm.

"Careful, the wood's pretty slippery grandmother. Let me help you."

Lucia stood still for a moment and looked up at the posters on the outside of the trailer, then she let Stella lead her into the exhibition area. The old woman quickly sensed she was out of place. Her drab woollen clothes lent a poor contrast to the brightly lit room with colourful images of Andalucian countryside. For Stella it reminded her, very favourably, of the cheerful lecture hall at Xando. There were the same magnificent images of the region's wildlife: ibex and deer, wolves and lynx, even Hanna's eagle. She was sure the exhibition would make a similar impression on her grandmother. But Lucia sensed in the bright photographs things that Stella could neither see nor feel. In sixty years of marriage what the spectacular Andalucian landscape meant to her were days of toiling at parched soil in searing heat, longed-for crops wilting under the annual drought, the habitual depression as autumn drew into winter with a half-empty store cupboard, goats gone dry and often no milk for her small child. Anna came up the steps behind the old woman. She saw the bleak look on Lucia's face and wondered whether it had been wise for Lucia to come.

"Isn't it wonderful. I'll show you my project. We haven't had too many visitors, but now you're here perhaps some more ... more older people will come. See there's even a seat for you."

Stella gestured towards a chair and took her precious folder from its case. Lucia sat down unaided. Without looking up at her Stella thrust her folder onto her grandmother's lap and began turning the pages.

"Look this is all the information they gave me at the museum, David and Liz - that's Dr Liz Delgado, they were both so helpful. And here's what Emilio told me about the young lynx and about breeding them."

Without waiting for a response she left the folder in her grandmother's hands and began gathering up free leaflets on wildlife and conservation. She turned to place them on top of the folder only then looking up at her grandmother. She was immediately disappointed. The old woman's face was grey, her body shrunken. Stella was used to seeing her grandmother in charge of her own world. Away from the tiny cottage which she dominated by a severe force of character she seemed crushed. Lucia simply turned over the leaflets barely glancing at them, many of them slipped to the floor unheeded. She waved one leaflet with an orange and green stripe at Stella.

"What's this?" Lucia insisted.

Stella looked at the leaflet and read the logo upside down. "It says 'Sustainable Farming'."

"Well Stella what's that supposed to mean?"

Stella heard the challenge in the old woman's voice.

"It's farming while looking after the countryside and.... and the wildlife." The old woman stared hard at Stella.

"How do they suggest your grandfather and I do this.... this sustainable farming then?" Lucia asked bitterly.

Stella was quelled, she looked down at her feet and mumbled, "I don't know."

"But why don't you know Stella, doesn't it tell us - in your project."

"Well. There are grants you can get - to encourage wildlife, to help you farm sustainably, perhaps grandfather could....,"

"Gerardo. I told you he won't change, he can't .. not unless....," she paused and shook her head. "Anna it's time we went to the merchants. I want to get some oil."

Lucia thrust the folder and remaining leaflets into Stella's hands and stood up brusquely. In a few more moments Anna was driving her away. Stella stood on the top step of the trailer watching the disappearing car. Silvio noticed the tears running down her cheeks.

"Your grandmother is a very strong woman Stella. She's also very proud of you I can tell."

Stella shook her head and turned away. She quickly wiped the tears from her face and walked down the trailer steps onto the dusty tarmac.

"I think I'll just go for a walk, if you don't mind."

"Of course." Silvio stood in the exhibition entrance and watched the girl walk away. He wondered how many other women there were like Lucia, wives of elderly peasant farmers, stubbornly clinging to the only life they knew while the world around them changed forever.

At six o'clock on Friday evening the exhibition closed. Stella had decided to stay late and was helping Silvio pack the leaflets into the trailer cupboards for the move. She heard a car drive up and shortly afterwards heard David's voice.

"Hi Silvio, how did it go?"

Silvio got up from the floor and called through the doorway.

"Good to see you David, not too bad I think."

Shoes thudded up the steps and David appeared in the doorway. He glanced at Stella.

"Stella I didn't think you'd still be here."

"I'm just helping Silvio pack up. Dad was with us earlier but I decided to stay for a while."

"If you want to go now Stella, I can finish this, there's not much left to do," Silvio offered.

"O.K." Stella moved to the top of the steps and took one more look round. She had thought the exhibition would be fun, instead she'd been badly disillusioned.

"Hold on a minute Stella, I've been too busy this week to phone but there's something I want to tell you." Stella took her foot from the topmost step and turned back to face David. "But first, I wondered whether you'd be happy to leave your project in the exhibition or if you wanted it back?"

Stella looked back at the case holding her folder. In her mind she saw her grandmother's hand slowly turning over the pages. She sighed and shook her head.

"No that's fine, it can stay."

David thought the girl looked depressed.

"Just a minute," he called as she turned away. "Look Silvio will you be here for a while, there are some things I want to tell Stella?"

"Sure, it'll take me half an hour to pack up. I want to get a quick meal in the hotel before I move the trailer off anyhow. You can find me there if you like."

David nodded. He followed Stella down the trailer steps

"Bye Stella. Thanks for all your help." Silvio called out behind them. "Don't forget what I said - about your grandmother."

"What did Silvio mean Stella?"

"Nothing, she.... she came on Tuesday. She didn't seem very impressed."

"But you heard what Silvio said."

"Yes, but ...you said you had some news," she asked trying to turn the conversation.

"I have, but some of it's not very good. Look do you want me to walk you home or....,"

"Is it bad news then... about Xando?" She had glanced up quickly at him, concern evident in her pinched lips.

"Not about Xando no."

They were approaching a group of plane trees near the centre of the village where a seat had been constructed from the fallen trunk. The village houses were set back from the dusty roadside and the seat was sheltered by a rash of shoots growing around the bowl of the fallen tree.

"I'd rather you told me here, not hear any bad news at home."

She sank down on the edge of the seat. David shook his head, he had noted her mood. He walked to and fro in front of her before speaking.

"Do you remember me telling you about surveying for lynx in the lower Visua valley, near the Palmiri hunting reserve?"

"I think so, you said it was a new group you didn't know anything about."

"Yes, we think there were at least two adult lynx, possibly more."

David sat down at the far end of the bench from the girl and thoughtfully twirled some of the green shoots in his hands. Stella turned to him noting the muted tone of his voice.

"You said your news wasn't all good."

"No it's not. Stella I think you've learnt enough this year not to be surprised or too upset by what I have to tell you."

Stella nodded but didn't speak. She watched David's hands twisting the plane leaves. They had begun to shred between his fingers. Small green fragments fell near his shoes. Stella waited patiently for him to continue.

"This summer, the students spent several weeks living in the area and discovered that a female with two quite young cubs was using the area. The students use powerful binoculars but they only saw the cubs in the distance a couple of times. Then the rabbit population in the area crashed badly as I told you. One of the cubs disappeared back in June, now they've found the body of a second cub. It appears to have died quite recently, probably from malnutrition."

"That's really sad. Was it disease that killed the rabbits?"

"As far as we can tell, yes. The area's quite isolated, what with the hunting reserve to the east and all that development on the coast. Probably the rabbit population had no built-in resistance to disease."

"Is the mother lynx all right?"

"Yes, they think she's still O.K. It's a hard thing to say but without cubs to feed she'll at least be able to travel further to hunt and there are still healthy rabbit populations in the valleys beyond the hunting reserve."

"Do you think that's where her mate is too?"

"I don't know Stella. We hadn't known of any lynx in that area, not for many years. But there was something else." He paused and Stella looked expectantly at him.

"Is it about Pardito?" she asked breathlessly. She held herself very stiff, tensing against the expected trauma.

"Not directly. I was reading the student's notes the other day and ,.......of course it may only be coincidence, but they list identification points for each animal they observe. It appears the female lynx has a slight v-shaped nick in her *left* ear."

"Pardito's mother," Stella exclaimed, "could it be her, would she have travelled that far?"

"We may never know Stella."

"But is she still in the area - can I go down there?"

"I'm afraid the students have finished their survey already and the female wasn't seen for several days before they pulled out. But there is some better news - probably coincidence again."

"What is it?"

"Emilio has been up at the reserve site for the last five days. Initially he was just checking on the contractors and organising the work huts. But he got rather fed up with that, not his sort of work he says, and he's taken to surveying the high valleys north of the reserve, the land above the trees, do you remember I showed you where the boundary ran."

Stella nodded

"We wanted to purchase the land right up to the mountain top but unfortunately it's still in private ownership."

"Why unfortunately?"

"Because that's the area where Emilio has seen the lynx."

"This week, Emilio's seen lynx just this week."

"Well, he says it's only signs, sleeping areas, rabbit hair, seems the rabbit population there has escaped disease this year. I've a suspicion Emilio may have seen at least one animal but he's not saying."

"Why ever not?"

"Because, after the attack and publicity about Xando earlier in the year, Dr. Mansera wants all confirmed sightings made directly to him. He wants us to catch and radio track as many lynx as we can this coming season. Once we know how wide an area they travel it'll be evidence for getting protected status for the whole area, he's already started the process. That'll mean abolition of all hunting except under special licence."

"All hunting - rabbits and the carnivores?"

"Yes rabbits too, but the protected status will bring money to pay compensation to all the hunters, and the farmers."

"Like Gerar ....my grandfather?"

"Just like your grandfather Stella."

"But how will it work?"

"It's a bit complicated but I suppose if he can estimate the number of rabbits he's caught in previous years he should get some reimbursement to equal the loss."

"Even if it was that simple he'd never do it, he's too proud."

"There'll be advisers to help Stella, he'll come round."

"And if he doesn't?"

David looked across at the girl. He didn't speak but Stella could hear the words in her head just as if he had spoken them. *"If he doesn't, if he carries on hunting, he will pay the penalty!"*

FOURTEEN

"I'd better go now."

Stella left David seated on the village seat and walked thoughtfully back to their rented cottage. Summer was already slipping by, her father was returning to work on Monday and in less than two weeks they would all return to the city. From the roadside she looked at the crumbling plaster and dry woodwork of the rented cottage. Ironically her parents had sought out the village as a refuge from the trauma of the city, but too much had happened for Stella ever to think of it as home. She couldn't say now where she most wanted to be. The old block of houses where they had lived had been pulled down for development. She had walked past it just that the afternoon, looking for signs of where she'd grown up. Stark metal girders rose four storeys above her head, and the tiny garden where Ramon had once planted flowers for Anna was full of builder's rubble. It seemed incredible that she could be looking forward to returning to their small city apartment. Her project, the museum visits, were finished, Xando closed to visitors. And Emilio - he would be involved in the reserve and she would not be there to enjoy or share the work with him. Somehow the loss of his friendship saddened her more than anything else. Hanna believed she had a crush on David. That was never true, she'd only wanted to learn about his work with animals. With Emilio it was different. She yearned for his companionship far more than she did her other friends.

She pushed open the front door. Her mother was talking to Andras in the lounge - arguing with him over some adolescent misdemeanour. Stella slipped past the doorway and went into the kitchen. Through the window she saw her father working on repairs to one of the garden seats.

"Can I help?" She called out rather more happily than she felt.

"Oh Stella, you're here at last. Your mother's waiting to get the barbecue started, does she know you're back?"

"I'll tell her in a minute. What are you doing?"

"I was putting a new strut in this seat, I've had to saw out a strut on the arm from one of the broken chairs in the shed, I wanted to shape it just like the others but I can't find my small axe anywhere. I'm sure I left it on one of the shelves in the shed." Stella remembered her devastating visit to Holm Cottage fully a week ago. She'd never gone back. The hessian sack and the axe would be just where she had dropped them on the floor of the goat shed.

"Perhaps it's fallen down behind something, I'll go and look shall I?"

Stella prevaricated.

"Maybe, but tell your mother you're here first of all, I'm famished."

"I will, right away, but I ....I wanted to ask you something Dad."

"What is it Stella?"

Jorge settled the mended chair back on the ground, seated himself in it and beckoned to his daughter. Stella moved to the side of the chair.

"Nice job." She said smoothing her hand along the bare wood of the new arm.

Jorge sensed her reluctance to speak.

"Well come on, out with it."

"I know it's the last weekend before you go back to the apartment but I wanted to ask a favour."

"But I'll be coming back next weekend."

"I know but could we go out walking tomorrow - just you and me, up on the hills."

"Just you and me. You don't want Andras around is that it?"

"I just want to go walking, Andras wouldn't want to come anyway."

"But if he goes out that leaves your mother on her own."

Stella bent her head.

"Is it so important?"

"Yes."

"Then I'll just have to find something for your mother to do? Perhaps a little trip with my credit card."

Stella laughed.

"Better save that for the new school books in September."

"Have you decided what you want to do - what options you'll be taking?"

"I think so but .... can we talk tomorrow..... ."

They watched Anna drive back down the gravel track, dust rising behind the car's rear wheels quickly hiding the car from sight. Jorge took Stella by the hand and set a brisk pace up the path leading from the track onto the shrub covered hillside. The leaves of the holm oaks rustled slightly in the faint morning breeze. Soon they reached the top of the ridge forming the watershed between her grandfather's property and the next valley. Jorge stopped and looked down into the dry valley bottom. Water had not flowed there for seven months. He released Stella's hand and scanned the range of hills towards the coast shading his eyes. The morning sun was already strong. On his back he carried a small rucksack containing lunch for the two of them and sweat had already begun to trickle down beneath it staining his pale blue T-shirt. The pack was light but he was breathing heavily. He looked down at Stella.

"Looks like I'm out of condition," he laughed

"You'll have to get more exercise then. Like walking."

Stella teased and walked away from him following the track towards the top of the hill.

"Hey, not so fast!" Jorge ran the few steps to catch her up and looked towards mosaic of pine and oak woodlands in the north-east saying, "Is that where the reserve is?" He asked pointing towards the greenery. "I can't make out the details, but it looks in the right direction."

Stella had already identified the place. She kept her eyes focused on the green shimmer of vegetation just below the woodlands.

"I think so, that's the stream."

"Still running in this heat." Jorge was impressed

"David said they were going to make some small dams to retain the water throughout the summer, with sluices to control the level."

"I didn't realise that. Look I can't make out any details, do you think they have started the fencing. We should have brought the binoculars."

Jorge settled himself down on an outcrop of rock poking up through the heavily grazed vegetation.

"I haven't got them."

"Did you leave them back at the apartment?"

"No. I brought them back here only.... I must have lost them."

"Lost them. How did that happen?"

The memories of that day, now almost a year ago, were still very strong. A slight tremor passed over her body.

"Here sit down." Jorge patted the rock beside him and swept dry rabbit pellets from its surface.

"Did you use them at all?"

"I did try to use them Dad, really, but..."

"But they weren't much good," he nodded. "Well, I'll have to think about buying a better pair."

"Would you do that...only I was going to ask."

"Is it about school?"

"Not really no. I wondered, could we keep the cottage on for a few more weeks?"

Jorge stared down at the girl. He shifted the rucksack off his back and pulled at the wet T-shirt.

"I thought it must be something like this. Don't you want to go back to school in the city, you were doing so well?"

Stella raised her head and looked directly at her father. Her light brown eyes studied his face with an steady maturity.

"It's not about school Dad." Stella paused breathlessly, "I've already decided I want to go to university to study biology, but ..... I couldn't bear it when we left here at first, but it's different now. I do like school enormously Dad, I just want to come back weekends."

Stella looked away from her father. He followed her gaze towards the Tejeda range and then down to the foothills where the new reserve lay .

"To come back weekends," Jorge mulled over the idea. "For how long?

"I thought until Lucia's birthday - she's going to be eighty isn't she, at the end of the September."

"But it's not just because of your grandmother is it?"

Stella shook her head and looked down at her feet which rested on an abandoned anthill.

"I ...I thought if I could just be here .... when they complete the reserve. If I could just convince grandfather that lynx conservation was a good thing. I thought Lucia might encourage him to come to the exhibition. But he wouldn't come and hardly anyone else came."

"But Lucia came didn't she, your mother took her down."

"She did, she even looked at my project but ...."

"Yes, your mother told me something about it. Lucia and Gerardo have had hard lives."

"I know. But nobody in the village seems to care about the wildlife. I think they despise David, even fear him for what he's doing. When I walked back last night I saw a couple of men pull an exhibition poster off the wall. They ripped it up."

"Did you recognise either of them, were they from the village?"

"One was, Mr. Sanchez. Grandfather goes hunting with him sometimes."

"And the other man?"

"I'm not sure ... He's probably a farmer, I think I may have seen him at El Rosal market."

"And did you tell David about this?"

"No, I'd already left him. I'm going to tell him of course - but Dad I think there's going to be trouble when people find out about the Hunting Ban."

"The ban on the open part of the reserve. I think people will get used to the idea."

"No, not just the reserve. David told me Dr. Mansera is putting in for Protected Status for the whole region, it's going to be like a national park, with no hunting at all."

"That can't be right Stella, so many people rely on the hunting."

"David says they'll be compensated for any losses and the government would get money from Europe."

"Well I suppose that would make a difference."

"But you can't expect grandfather Gerardo to ask for compensation. He thinks he has a right to hunt. Lucia says he'll never change... never, and Dad he's still got a gintrap. I'm so frightened that...."

Jorge pulled his daughter gently towards him. She nestled her head on his left shoulder and stared back at the mountains. She felt drained.

"You've seen this trap?"

"Yes, it's in the goat shed."

"Does Gerardo know you've seen it?"

"I don't know. Last time I went there it was hidden under some hay. I was going wrap it in a sack and take it away but grandfather came back so I tried to hide it behind some old tractor parts."

Jorge was silent for a long time, then he said.

"Stella do you feel like walking a little more?"

"Yes, why?"

"It's early yet. I think we should work up an appetite before lunch. Afterwards I want to go down to Holm Cottage."

Stella gasped.

"Come on." Jorge slipped the rucksack on his shoulders. He seemed very thoughtful. Stella remained silent, she settled into an easy pace beside him.

"Stella, when does David expect to have lynx in the reserve?"

"I don't know, I think sometime in October."

"Then we need to book the cottage until the end of October."

"But that's another month." Stella looked up at her father quite amazed. He said nothing more and they walked on in silence.

Just after four o'clock they came down the track and pushed through the gateway at Holm Cottage. A thin spiral of blue smoke issued from the chimneystack. Voices raised in heated conversation could be heard behind the cottage. Jorge gestured Stella to stay behind while he walked slowly around to the side of the cottage. Stella followed him hesitantly. She thought she could detect her grandfather's voice angrily answering a second man. Jorge reached the corner of the cottage and was walking across to the goat shed when Stella clearly heard the man say.

"Well what can we do about it... why even your own granddaughter ....,"

There the man caught sight of Jorge and stopped speaking. Stella edged forwards until she stood directly behind Jorge, keeping in his shadow.

"What's the problem Gerardo?" she heard her father say.

"Nothing." The gruff reply did not inspire confidence.

"Mr Sanchez isn't it?" Jorge quizzed. The man was standing close to the goat pen, he had one arm stretched across a horizontal bar as if he had just turned round. Stella looked past her father. Gerardo was standing in the middle of the pen, one of the lead goats nuzzled up to him, its bell ringing clearly in the silence that had fallen between the three men.

"Sanchez, yes." The man mumbled at Jorge. He turned back towards Gerardo.

Jorge was not to be deterred. "I thought I heard you say something about Stella?"

The man turned around again and spat on the ground. Gerardo pushed the goat away. Ignoring Jorge he began walking down to the goat shed. Sanchez shook his head and slouched away from the fence heading for the top of the hill. Gerardo's back was turned towards Jorge.

"Stella." Jorge became aware of Stella's presence behind him. "Go inside to your grandmother."

"But don't you want me to show you...."

"Stella, you heard me."

Stella stepped back to the side of the cottage, she had no intention of leaving the scene.

"Gerardo!"

Jorge called but the old man had already disappeared. Undeterred he pushed past the broken shed door. Stella ran across and peered in. Jorge stood the gloomy darkness waiting for his eyes to adjust to the shade. Beyond the pen he could see the wood store which he had spent most of last winter filling. It was almost empty and would need attention soon. A hessian sack, grey with dust, lay on the wooden partition. He placed his hands on the wood for support and edged past piles of rusting equipment to the front of the pen. Listening outside the shed Stella heard him ask breathlessly.

"Now where did she say it was?"

Gerardo's voice echoed from the end of the shed. "What you looking for?" His voice was low and gruff.

"I think you know." She heard her father say. She sensed him moving equipment about and heard a sudden curse as metal thumped onto the ground. Stella edged nearer the door. The sunlight was so bright she couldn't make out anything inside. She pushed her way inside. Her father was bent over near the partition, rust from the tractor wheel staining his hands.

"You're bleeding Dad." Stella said rushing forwards.

"No Stella, it's just rust."

"What you're looking for's down there."

Stella looked into the gloom. Gerardo pointed at the wooden partition. He wasn't looking at her father, his eyes were fixed determinedly on her. She watched as her father bent down into the dusty darkness. The trap was covered in dust and cobwebs.

"Ah," Jorge exclaimed "Stella pass me that sack."

She fingered the rough hessian. Gerardo had found it on the shed floor. She sensed he was playing a game with them. She handed her father the sack and watched as he poked the trap down into it. She was thankful to see it disappear, but once it was out of sight she realised that it was old and rusted, not shiny and black like the one she remembered. Gerardo must have switched it for the one he normally used. Stella found it impossible to speak, she couldn't accuse him of falsehood right in front of her father. Jorge dusted down his trousers then ushered Stella through the door. Silently he lead the way back alongside the cottage wall. He obviously intended to return to the village straight away but as they passed the cottage door Lucia called out.

"Jorge, I thought I heard your voice, what are you doing here?"

"Just talking to Gerardo, Lucia. Stella and I've been walking."

Lucia tutted and looked over the pair of them. Jorge carried the hessian sack awkwardly under his left arm, the rucksack was swung over his right shoulder. His blue T-shirt was smeared red.

"Whatever have you been ......?" she began as Gerardo stepped into view. She looked from her husband back to Jorge.

"Well you must come in."

"No it's all right Lucia."

"But I insist, I can't let Anna see you like that."

They entered the house reluctantly. Gerardo followed them. As the door closed Jorge slid the hessian sack under the dining table. Gerardo pushed past him. Taking his pipe from the mantelpiece he sat down ruefully in his usual chair and gestured with it to the floor, saying with a sneer.

"Won't make no difference."

"Come to the pump and wash yourself Jorge." Lucia urged. Jorge nodded. Stella settled down on the chair opposite her grandfather. There seemed little to say so she remained silent. Jorge washed his hands then opened the door of the lean-to where he stripped off his T-shirt shaking it free of rust. He wondered what Anna would make of the rust marks. When he re-entered the cottage he found Gerardo and Stella staring silently at each other. Gerardo's pipe was empty. But as Jorge re-entered the room he leant down towards the grate where a packet of tobacco lay. Instead of picking it up he fumbled between the logs and brought out something small and shiny.

"Knew someone had been here." He said, throwing Jorge's axe on the table where it spun round several times, the metal glimmering against the dark wood. Jorge looked surprised.

"What's that doing here?"

"Came stealing she did - like a thief." Gerardo clucked to himself.

"Whatever Stella's done," Jorge began angrily...." she did it to help you. That.. that obscenity in there." He gestured to the sack, "is illegal. You know that Gerardo."

"Now stop this, can't you." Lucia stood beside the pump, the knuckles of her hand showed white and bony against the black metal. Rare tears brimmed on her eyelids

"You're right Lucia, we *should* stop this nonsense." Gerardo barked. He gave her a sour look and began to fill his pipe.

"I'll make a drink."

"I'll have coffee thanks Lucia. Want some lemonade Stella?"

Stella nodded.

"And Gerardo?" Jorge turned towards his father-in-law, who only grunted.

"He'll have coffee," his wife declared.

Stella was given her lemonade immediately, then Lucia scurried to the stove and poured out coffee from the metal percolator which stood permanently on the heat. She gave Gerardo and Jorge their drinks then retreated to the kitchen. Gerardo leant forward and heaped three spoonfuls of sugar into his earthenware mug.

"You went to the exhibition Lucia."

The old woman nodded noncommittally.

"....and saw Stella's project?"

Lucia looked awkwardly at her husband. His eyes were glazed over as if he had withdrawn from their company.

"Yes, I saw it. Her tutors say it's very good."

"It is Lucia, they are very proud of her. And what did you think...... of the exhibition, about the reserve."

Again that guilty look at Gerardo.

"She doesn't need to think anything about it, Boy. It's nothing to do with her."

Gerardo tucked a loose sliver of tobacco into the bowl of his pipe and rapped it on the table.

"But it's going to affect her as much as you, you can get some compensation."

He saw the way Lucia's eyes lit up briefly, but she didn't speak. Jorge tried another tack.

"If you came and lived with us you wouldn't have to..."

The old woman blinked, but Jorge wasn't permitted to continue.

"Compensation, huh." Gerardo studiously ignored the invitation, as he had many times before. He struck a match against the stone fireplace with such force that the wood splintered and fell into the grate carrying the fiery flame. Angrily he struck another match. Stella watched the flame flicker brightly about the pipe bowl, dense acrid smoke circled over the table.

"Don't you get most of your cash from hunting?"

"That little reserve isn't going to stop it."

"But it isn't a little reserve - the fence only encloses a quarter of the land. Didn't you see the plan in the trailer Lucia?"

Lucia took hold of her mug and looked away. She wasn't going to answer.

"Interfering that's all they're doing - it won't last." Her husband barked.

"What won't last Gerardo." Jorge demanded.

Gerardo banged his pipe on the arm of his chair.

"All this carnivore conservation, it needs nipping in the bud - vermin that's what they are, always have been, always will be."

"That's not what the government believes, they're putting funds into the reserve - doing more research all the time."

"Then why don't their researchers come here and speak to me."

"Gerardo that's just what they are doing, it's what the exhibition's for. There are people ready to help and ....,"

Gerardo had had enough, he stood up awkwardly, pushed past Jorge's chair and disappeared into the lean-to. The outer door slammed behind him. Stella watched the pipe which he had dropped, roll off the chair and onto the stone flags. The bowl made a tiny pinging sound when it hit the floor as if the wood had split. She looked at the wounded expression on her father's face and decided not to pick up it up.

FIFTEEN

As they turned off the new main road just three kilometres from the cottage, the phone rang.

"It'll be David." Stella yelled, lunging forwards from the back seat. "Oh let me have it."

"Stella don't be so rude," her father called angrily from the driver's seat.

"But it's bound to be David, you gave him the number."

Anna took the mobile phone from her handbag. The warbling sound grew louder, and Stella's gestures more urgent. Lifting the phone to her ear, she said, "Yes, but you don't know if it *is* him Stella."

Anna spoke into the handset.

"Hello David, yes, thanks. Stella's here, we're on our way back up to the cottage at Valdes, we've kept it on for a few extra weeks."

There was a long pause in which Stella squirmed impatiently in her seat. Jorge took a long twisting bend on the road and Stella fell against Andras.

"For heaven's sake, watch what you're doing," he yelled, piqued as usual by his sister's behaviour.

"Well, yes if that's what he says, then I'm sure Jorge could drive up, hold on a minute."

She cupped the handset and twisted around.

"For the last time will you two behave." Andras smirked and slumped back in his seat.

"Don't know why we had to come back anyhow," he complained.

Stella pulled herself upright, her nails were biting into her father's seat

"Well we're here and that's an end to it. Now Stella, David has some news from Emilio at the reserve. He's asking if you'd like to go up there -

this evening. Jorge, you could go straight from the cottage. I'll have dinner ready when you get back."

"All right by me."

"Thanks Dad, let me speak to David." Stella yelled.

Anna handed over the handset.

"David, it's Stella."

Stella listened to the scientist for many minutes, then, rather thoughtfully, handed the set back to her mother.

"O.K. David, Jorge thinks they should be there in half an hour. Does Emilio have a phone number - Oh hold on, we're still in the car, I've no paper........ yes, if you could tell him to expect them. Thanks again, Bye."

"Has something happened at the reserve?" Jorge queried as he drove the car between the first of the village houses.

"Stella your father's asking you a question." Anna looked towards the rear seat where Stella was gazing out of the window apparently oblivious to her surroundings.

"Stella!"

Stella blinked.

"Yes?"

"Your father wants to know what David said."

"He said.... he said they've caught a lynx - a *male* lynx." She paused, her lips so dry she had to moisten them.

"Well go on .. Dreamyhead." Andras nudged her side.

"They've caught a lynx?" Jorge repeated, taking the car tightly around a corner in the village centre. On the far side the new apartment block was almost complete, at four storeys tall it towered over the old cottages.

"Is it for the breeding programme?"

"They don't know yet."

"They have to check it's not closely related to that female in Xando, isn't that right Stella?" Her mother looked back at Stella.

She nodded. "If it is they'll have to let it go. Emilio's waiting for blood tests, they'll know tonight....... or tomorrow morning." Stella said quietly.

"You're so looking forward to seeing your first really wild lynx are you?" Andras mocked, amused at the solemn expression on his sister's face.

"I don't know ... I don't know."

Stella returned to gazing through the car window, acutely aware of a tightness in her stomach that hadn't been there before the phone call.

Ten minutes later Jorge drove with Stella back through the village. After some minutes he realised she hadn't spoken since they'd left the cottage together. He turned to look at his daughter.

"I must say, you don't seemed very excited, little one."

Stella smiled back but said nothing.

"I would have thought you'd be happy to ..."

"It might....it might be Pardito." She said almost in a whisper.

"Pardito?" Jorge queried.

"He's a lynx, a cub I saw here, with his family last year. He's why I wanted to do the project so badly."

She paused unwilling to tell him everything, particularly about the lies she'd needed to tell. Jorge slowed the car and pulled off the road onto a strip of rough grass. He looked down to examine his daughter, noticing her pallor for the first time. Her hands were tightening on the hem of her T-shirt.

"You never told us Stella. I wish you'd...."

"But how could I? Everyone said they were vermin. I've been so scared in case grandfather found out and used the trap." Jorge nodded to himself thoughtfully then, after a few seconds, asked.

"How often did you see this cub, was it just once, on the farm?"

"No I saw them several times. Pardito was just a small cub at first. There were two others. I looked out for them all through last summer."

"And you never said," Jorge sounded amazed but with sudden insight asked. "David, does he know?"

"Yes." Stella replied quietly looking down at her feet.

"And Emilio?"

"I don't really know, I think perhaps David...." She began to feel ashamed.

"You really are full of surprises young lady. Well you'll be pleased now if it is him?"

"No I won't, he'll ......he'll be in a cage." She sobbed.

"But Stella, you've seen animals in cages before, there's Marmit, and the cub."

"But Pardito, he's a wild lynx."

"It might not be your Pardito, but Stella........ you knew didn't you, right from the beginning that some animals would have to be captured."

"I know, only...."

"Only Pardito's special, is that it? You've seen him as a cub, growing up in the wild."

"Yes, but I don't want to see him in a cage Dad, not even in that big enclosure."

"But this may be the only way to save the lynx."

"Yes, I know. " By now tears were brimming on her eyelids.

"It's a year since you saw him, how will you know if it's Pardito?"

"I suppose it might not be him." Stella said solemnly.

"Well do you want to go on? We can always go back to the cottage."

"No, I want ..... I want to go on."

"O.K. then."

But as Jorge switched on the car engine he felt his daughter's hand on his arm.

"Dad, you don't have to tell Mum, or Andras do you?"

Jorge shook his head and drove on.

They nearly missed the turning, Jorge drove straight past the tall metal gates without even looking about him, then Stella started in her seat.

"Dad, you've missed the track."

Her father jammed on the breaks.

"Are you sure, those gates....?"

"They're new Dad, don't you remember David telling us about them."

"Well if you say so."

The road behind was clear. Jorge reversed until the car was level with the trackway. A high wire fence now ran along the roadway apparently enclosing the reserve. The large gate stood wide open, but a thick chain wound round the gatepost made it look intimidating. They drove quickly along the track and Jorge heard his daughter gasp as they drove towards the clearing where they had parked before. This had been a wide area set against pine woods with the valley sloping away to the southwest.

Once a peaceful place beneath the enduring limestone hills, it was now all bustle and movement. Giant fence posts and chain-linked fencing surrounded the upper half of the valley. Over a kilometre away people worked with a large machine that wound out fencing. Both fence and men looked tiny at that distance and the machines were far enough away that only a few metallic sounds reached the car. Part of the nearby hillside had been gouged out to make a flat compound layered with fine gravel, on which stood three green-painted portacabins. Two cabins stood at right angles facing towards the hillside and opposite them a car and a dark range-rover had been parked. The third cabin was smaller and positioned at the far end of the parking lot. It housed a washroom and chemical toilet.

"This is it then - looks rather different doesn't it?"

Jorge nudged the car forwards until it was beside the range-rover. He got out and Stella followed him rather timidly.

"It all looks so strange - I didn't think...."

"Hello, Stella, Jorge."

A young man emerged from one of the portacabins and was striding towards them across the gravel. He was tall, wearing only an pair of faded jeans cut off well above the knees and an old white T-shirt. His skin was tanned the colour of hazelnuts and his dark hair had pale streaks where the sun had blanched it. Jorge put up his hand in greeting.

"Emilio, good to see you."

"I got David's message. Stella, it's good to see you." Emilio beamed at the girl and held out his hand to her. Stella held back timidly. This extrovert Emilio was a new phenomenon for her, she was a little shy of him.

"Stella," he asked quietly, when she wouldn't take his hand.

"Come on Stella." Jorge encouraged.

Emilio noticed her reserve, he smiled at her sympathetically.

"It's O.K. Jorge, Stella thinks I've turned into a workman." He pulled at his loose shirt. "But it gets so hot in these cabins."

"I don't, Emilio, I don't," proclaimed Stella.

The men laughed. She found herself relaxing.

"Come into the cabin and you'll find out. And I want you to meet a colleague, as you can see we've quite a big setup here."

"It must cost a bit to build that fence Emilio."

"Oh, it has Jorge and you should see the equipment we've been donated. Here in this cabin."

They preceded Emilio up a couple of steps into the first cabin. The noise of a generator filled the room, and although it was now seven in the evening the excessive heat was instantly apparent. The room was furnished with three computers consoles.

"This is where all the work's done, we'll monitor all the animals and keep records on the computers."

One man was sitting behind a computer in the corner of the room, he had his back to them and was working on a piece of equipment. A large chartboard containing maps and sketches was positioned on the interior wall. A doorway to the right led into a corridor with two more rooms..

"Do you sleep here then." Stella asked, then felt a blush warming her face.

"Two of us are here all the time, but Liz only comes up during the week. And the three students camp in tents just behind here, but they've gone to town for the evening."

"Liz?" Stella asked.

"Yes Dr. Liz Delgado from the museum, I thought you'd met her. She's left for the weekend."

"Yes, I know her, she ... she helped with my project."

"I heard about that, David tells me it was so good he put it into the exhibition."

"Yes, we're rather proud of her Emilio. Do you think the exhibition had been successful."

Emilio's expression clouded slightly.

"It is hard to say. The trailer's gone down to El Rosal, I think David is expecting some trouble there."

"Why?" Stella asked loudly. The man at the desk looked up.

"There's been some opposition to the project, from El Rosal hunting lobby naturally. It's all rather political."

Emilio turned to look across at his colleague.

"But first let me introduce you. Lamas is now our full time technician. He has a daughter rather younger than you Stella. "

The man looked up briefly, nodded without smiling, then concentrated again on his work.

"There's just Lamas and myself here at the moment. Dr. Mansera comes up occasionally. We don't have a vet on site, but there're always one on call at Xando, it doesn't take long to drive from the coast.

"Doesn't David work here?" Stella asked.

"Well, he's in charge of the whole project but Liz is organising the trapping and radio-tracking with the students. I think David spends most of his time contacting other zoos checking on animals for breeding."

"That must keep him pretty busy."

"Yes, Jorge, along with his other work, but he keeps in touch by phone as you know."

"But where's the lynx, we saw the fence, it isn't half completed yet."

"That's just the main pen, it won't be finished for another couple of weeks. The camouflaged quarantine pen is behind these vans in a much quieter area, I don't suppose you even guessed it was there."

"What do you mean quarantine pen, is the lynx ill?" Jorge sat down on the nearest stool. Stella looked at Emilio in horror.

"No it's a very healthy animal. When the whole enclosure is complete we will have to be careful not to bring disease in. So we have separate pens, where any new animals are observed before mixing with others. It's completely camouflaged and we'll control entry into the main pen without being seen, I'll show you shortly."

"Lamas?" Stella mused looking at the man seated behind the desk..

He looked up as Emilio was speaking, now he smiled directly at her. He seemed quite friendly so she asked.

"David mentioned a driver named Lamas. He helps with the surveying."

"That's me. " Lamas answered. "Now I'm working full time for David. But to be honest ..." he looked across at Emilio and laughed, "I think I work harder and longer here than when I was driving."

"Take no notice Stella, he loves it here."

But Stella was remembering a conversation she'd had with David back in the summer.

"David told me you had an accident, down near the Palmiri hunting reserve."

Lamas scrutinised the girl's face and nodded.

"That was me, yes."

"And there was a lynx... in an accident."

"Now I wonder why you should mention that - you see I have been arguing with Emilio here. I think this lynx is the same one. It has a faint scar running down his left thigh. I can't remember much about the accident, but I know the lorry tyre caught that lynx on the left thigh."

"But Stella, as I've told Lamas, it's probably not the same animal. It's most unlikely this animal made the forty kilometre trek and back even if it was looking for a territory."

But hadn't David said Pardito's mother had been seen in the same area? She mused watching Lamas shaking his head. It couldn't be coincidence could it?

"Well, anyhow the blood test will show whether he is related to little Marmit, and whether he's from a local group." Emilio concluded.

Lamas shook his head and Stella found herself warming to the man.

"David found her as a cub didn't he." She asked.

Lamas glanced at her.

"He told you the story?"

"About how her mother was killed, yes."

"It was a very sad thing." Lamas' voice wavered as he spoke.

"Were you there?"

"Yes....." Lamas nodded slowly.

"It was a terrible thing Stella," Emilio interrupted. "But we must find her a mate as soon as we can. Now shall we go to the pen." Emilio motioned Jorge and Stella out of the cabin.

"Here you might find these useful." He handed Jorge a small pair of binoculars. "Lamas, bring the camera will you?"

Emilio lead the way across the compound and into the belt of trees. Jorge took his daughter's hand. It was quite dark within the oaks. Holding a finger to his lips Emilio motioned them silently forwards.

"I can't see any pen, can you?" Jorge whispered to his daughter.

"Neither can I - wait, what's that."

Ahead lay a grove of pines with a dense stand of oak scrub beneath. Within it they could just make out a fence swathed in thick green webbing. Emilio waited. He peered into the gloom behind them.

"Lamas?" he mouthed silently.

Stella nodded and pointed back. Lamas was ambling along behind them. In his hands was a small digital camera. When he drew level with her Lamas winked. Emilio unhitched a small section of webbing. Stella found with delight that she could look directly into the pen through the wire. Inside the dense woodland was broken by a small glade and on the ground was a scatter of broken pine branches from a tree whose tall trunk soared high above the pen. They stood in silence for what seemed an age. Stella held her breath for minutes at a time then she felt her father's hand on her shoulder, Jorge was pointing back to Lamas. His camera was focused directly into the pen. Under the ancient pine a lynx was standing at the centre of the fallen branches.

Jorge handed Stella the binoculars. After a quick glance, she lowered them carefully. She hardly needed them. The lynx was so close, looking directly towards her, his golden eyes searching the fence. She heard a tiny squeak. The lynx's dark ear tufts twitched. He was fooled, as they all were, by Lamas' mouse impression. It sank behind the broken wood and began to stalk around the mound of earth, its ears twisted forwards accentuating the dark ruff. The magnificent broad face bore a determined look. Suddenly the animal became aware of their presence. It lifted its head searching for scent and a second later flashed from sight, bounding away into the undergrowth.

"It was him." She whispered to herself. "Pardito."

"Your lynx," asked Emilio knowingly. "The one you studied?" Stella nodded.

"How can you be sure?" Jorge asked.

"How can you be sure?"

Emilio questioned from the steps of the portacabin.   Stella stood defiantly before him, her arms crossed tightly over her chest. Jorge and Lamas were talking quietly inside the cabin. The evening sunlight cast through the nearby pines and sent fingers of shadow across the now illuminated windows.

"I'm sure. I don't know how - but I know it was Pardito."

"Well, we'll never be able to prove it, even when the blood tests arrive."

Just then a phone rang in the office. They heard Lamas talking, then he brought out the handset to Emilio.

"Hello, yes Liz, it's Emilio, do you have some news."

Emilio's listened, then he shook his head slowly.

"O.K. Do you want to be here when we release him."

Stella heard a woman's voice talking loudly but she couldn't make out the words.

"No, of course not, so when will the vet be here? O.K., I'll wait for her call."

He paused, said goodbye then flipped the phone closed.

"Well you were lucky to see the lynx tonight Stella."

"You're letting him go?" Jorge was standing at the top of the steps.

"Yes Jorge, you see ...." He paused and looked back at the girl. "The DNA proves he's very closely related to Marmit after all, we certainly can't risk mating them."

"Can we stay till you release him?"

"That'll be early morning Stella. The vet won't arrive until just before dawn to anaesthetise him. Then we have to take him back to the capture site. It's quite a long way."

He gestured towards the pine plantation on the hillside beyond the oak forest.

"You'll still be fast asleep in your bed when we set him free."

He laughed quietly to himself. Stella's face bore a strange look, rather of elation than disappointment. Her lips moved but he couldn't be sure what she said. It might have been just one word "Free!"

SIXTEEN

Stella was still in bed long after the lynx, or Pardito as she insisted, was released into the pine forests at the open western end of the reserve. She awoke suddenly to the sound of the front door slamming, followed by the noise of a car driving away. She had slept fitfully, waking often to muddled dreams about the lynx and her grandfather. She tossed back the bedclothes and dressed thoughtfully, wondering where the lynx would be, what he was doing. She tried to remember what Emilio had told her about the anaesthetic and how long it took to wear off when the lynx, or Pardito as she insisted, would be most vulnerable. When she entered the kitchen her mother was reading a magazine. The kitchen clock showed nine-thirty.

"Ah, you're up at last sleepyhead. What do you want for breakfast?"

"Just some juice plus toast and honey, please."

She looked out of the window to see her father talking on the phone. He had his back to her and was standing very still. Once he rubbed his hand through his hair, it was dark brown with a strong wave that she envied. He seemed rather pensive.

"I thought someone had gone out in the car?"

"That was a friend of Andras, you remember Theo."

"And I suppose he's still asleep, he's never up before..."

"Quite the opposite, Theo's taken him out in the car. He's staying with relatives in the village and they told him Andras was here. So it seems we did the right thing bringing Andras here after all," she said with a wry smile.

"Oh, yes I suppose Theo's old enough to drive. Do you know where they've gone?"

"No, but Theo's at the technical college so they'll have a lot to talk about."

Stella smiled as she finished her toast. She was fingering spilled honey on her plate when a shadow fell across the kitchen doorway.

"Stella that looks pretty unhygienic to me." Jorge chided.

Anna glanced at him. He looked upset. He tipped the mobile phone onto the table and sat down opposite his wife. Stella got up and began washing her dishes. Her back was turned to Jorge.

"That was a rather worrying call."

"Who was it?" Anna asked.

"David, he ...."

Stella spun round from the sink, her wet hands spun water over the floor and down her clean shorts.

"Stella be careful."

Stella ignored the request, and placed wet hands on her father's arms demanding: "Is it about Par. .." Stella began, then remembering that Anna would not know him by name, continued. "About the lynx, is he all right?"

" Stella it's not about the lynx, only... look you've made my arm wet, get a towel and sit down will you."

"Don't keep us in suspense Jorge."

"All in good time Anna. David said there were some people demonstrating against the lynx project at the exhibition in El Rosal yesterday. Emilio suggested as much last evening. Seems the media's up to its old tricks, playing one side off against the other."

"Xando," Anna said softly.

"Not Xando no."

"What's happened then?" Stella begged.

"David had a phone call this morning from El Rosal Town Hall, the exhibition trailer was parked in their car park, nice and central. Too central probably. This morning when the caretaker was checking on the building he noticed the trailer had been smeared with graffiti and it was sitting lopsided on its axle. When he peered inside he saw that the whole thing had been torn apart, posters ripped and leaflets tipped into a pile and a small fire started which luckily didn't take hold. David's there now trying to sort things out with the police - only he wanted us to know before we heard it from anyone else - you see Stella's project is missing. Either burnt or taken, they can't be sure."

"That's awful for you." Anna patted her daughter's hand.

"For me...," Stella parried. " I've only lost the project. What must David be feeling?"

The maturity evident in her daughter's reaction surprised Anna. Jorge nodded.

"David thought it must be senseless vandalism at first, the caretaker didn't mentioned the slogans splashed on the trailer walls. He saw them when he arrived. 'No ban on hunting' or 'No to Lynx reserve', most of them said."

"Does he think it's a serious threat?"

Jorge shook his head.

"He's talking about armed guards for the reserve, but I don't think he's convinced there's a real threat. He's taking advice from the police."

"He won't let Emilio get hurt again will he?" Stella's voice rose to fever pitch.

"Of course he won't."

"But it'll be Xando all over again," she insisted.

"Be sensible Stella, that was just misguided youngsters," Anna insisted.

"Misguided youngsters with a rifle," Jorge reminded her. "Anyhow there's nothing we can do about it, David will know how to act I'm sure."

"There is one thing we can do Anna..., " here Jorge paused and looked down at his daughter.

"He wants us to let him know if we hear or see anything odd. Valdes is the nearest village to the reserve."

"But surely David doesn't suspect the farmers round here. Why they're poor peasants like my father, eking out a living, they couldn't, wouldn't organise anything.....,"

"I don't know what David thinks Anna, he just wants us to report anything vaguely suspicious to him - or even to the police - that's all."

"I suppose so." Anna said firmly. She patted her daughter's wet hands but Stella remained very still.

"Stella, shall we get some material for that dress you wanted for the party." Anna said thinking to take the girl's mind off the subject. "We can go across to Coralli's shop to see if she has any nice material." Stella didn't reply immediately.

"Stella, what do you think?" Her mother demanded.

"Yes let's." Stella said rather noncommittally. "But I thought you wanted to see Lucia and get things organised for her party next Saturday."

"That's O.K., I'll slip over later this afternoon."

It was well past four when Anna drove her car up to Holm Cottage. A protracted visit to the shop where Stella took ages to choose material, meant they had arrived at the rented cottage just in time to join Jorge for a late lunch. Andras was nowhere to be seen.

Later as Stella rushed from the car she declared, "I want to help Gerardo with the milking. There won't be many more weekends and.....," she began explaining. But the shock of another attack and the loss of the project had unsteadied her. She just had to get away and think things through.

"No of course not, but I thought.... well never mind. Lucia will be happy to see you I'm sure."

Stella guessed Jorge had told her mother nothing about the dreaded gintrap, and equally she had never told Jorge about the shiny trap she had originally seen in her grandfather's shed. It was all such a terrible mess and the problem seemed to be getting more dire each day.

Anna opened the car boot to collect some parcels.

"I'll just go up the track, I think I can hear them coming...," she yelled. "Don't wait, I'll walk back home."

"But Stella, could you help me with ......," but Stella was already racing up the track.

"Stella!" Anna yelled. She was growing increasingly exasperated with her daughter's unpredictable behaviour.

Stella didn't even hear her call. She rounded the first bend in the track where the rosemary and juniper bushes cloaked the bank side and slowed to a trot. By the time she reached the ridge where the oak understory opened out to scrub she was out of breath. She sank down on the side of the track and breathed deeply. Opposite was another small side track, it was overgrown with oak saplings but a few of the branches were broken allowing her to see an unusual red metallic gleam through the foliage.

She heard voices coming down the main track and decided to hide beside the old blue and red car parked there. It had a large shiny grill but its battered mudguard and old number plate were evidence of age. She was still staring at the car, wondering if it was 'suspicious' when she heard her name called out. It was too late to hide, she had to turn and face the speaker. A young man had just pushed his way through the bushes, he was tall with a very thin frame with almost gawky legs and arms that swung by his side as if moving of their own volition. Under a thatch of unruly brown hair his face had a ruddy complexion and bore a coy smile that was vaguely familiar. Another figure limped to his side, Andras. The two of them gawked at her for several seconds without speaking.

"My little sister," Andras said, "always appearing where you least expect her."

"I ... I was looking at the car."

"Yes wonderful isn't it," said the boy grinning with pride.

Andras was also grinning. Her embarrassment was amusing him.

"You look as if you don't remember Theo."

Stella had a mental picture of a gangling youth, several years younger than the lad in front of her, but with the same loose almost athletic frame.

"Theo.... of course, I haven't seen you for ......,"

"Two, three years." Theo offered.

Stella's mouth remained open.

"I've grown about ten centimetres since then."

"Oh I did recognise you - only not right away."

"Come on Sis, you....."

But Stella was not to be deflected.

"What are you doing here, I thought these old... cars were for racing, you can't race here."

"Well you could," Andras taunted.

"But we're not going racing are we Andras. Go on, tell her what we've been doing." The boy placed an old rucksack beside Andras' feet and nudged him playfully.

"He's just a little shy," Theo said hugely enjoying the joke. "Come on lad, it's no secret is it? All right if you're not....," he urged.

"No, I'll do it." Andras bent over to undo the straps of the rucksack, then pulled out a clipboard with several sheets of paper. Unhappy with the speed he was moving Theo dived into the sack and brought out a strong bulging cotton bag and a map covered with bright colours which Stella didn't recognise. The bag rattled as he moved it.

"Bring the stuff over here," said Theo. He moved across to the car, unfolding the map across the bonnet and called proudly to Stella.

"There, do you know what this is?"

Andras smirked at her consternation, and said disparagingly.

"It's a geology map of course."

"What do you want that for Andras?" Stella quizzed, expecting to be repulsed but Andras decided to be serious for once.

"Theo's going to help me with a feasibility study. I have to do one as an entrance examination for college."

"A feas..... "

"Feasibility. Bit of a mouthful isn't it." Theo said sympathetically sidling up to her. She edged towards the rear of the car. Sunlight piercing through the leaves fell directly into her eyes, for a moment she couldn't see anything. Theo pursued her again, obviously attracted to her. He was a gawky youth. Although not unattractive, Stella was in no mood to enjoy or respond to his advances. He sensed her rejection and turned his attention away saying almost with chagrin.

"And what about these?" He shook the cotton bag till it rattled.

"Look out, you'll drop them." Andras yelled, lunging for the bag.

"No chance." Theo placed the bag gently down on the map and began retrieving its contents. A pile of small and some not so small plastic bags appeared out of the sack. Each had lettering written in bright blue ink.

"Here Stella, this one's sandstone." Stella let him place the bag in her hand. The rock fragment glowed yellow in the sunlight.

"But it looks just like this." She said indicating the earth beneath her feet.

"Ah, but look at this one, and this, and this." Theo cradled the bags in his hand and thrust them at Stella. She resisted the urge to push them away.

"But they are all the same," she said in disgust

"You're wrong there." He took the bags back and gently twisted each one round.

"This is coarse ironstone, and this is much finer, but this - the best of all, it's very fine and has tiny fossils embedded in it."

"Why does Andras want all these?"

"Because I've got to test them for porosity, whether they hold water or not."

"And you need this for your feas...feasible study."

"Feasibility study. Yes. You see I want to help grandfather Gerardo. His land's so parched, if only we could build a small reservoir for his crops, then once I finish college I'll come back here to live."

"But you'll be away for years studying, anyhow Gerardo won't let you change anything, you know that."

"Oh he'll change, I'll bring him round."

Stella looked down at her feet. "He'll never change," she repeated Lucia's words under her breath.

"What was that?" Theo was standing close to her. Andras hadn't heard, he was gathering up the rock samples and putting them back in his bag.

"Nothing, nothing at all. I have to go now."

Andras was fumbling with the straps of the rucksack. She tried to push past him.

"Don't you want a lift ... in this magnificent racing car?" Theo asked. He seemed genuinely disappointed when Stella shook her head.

Without explaining further, she ran past the car into the valley following the dry streambed until she was too tired to run any further. She climbed to the top of the ridge and trudged on aimlessly. She had forgotten all about the goats. She thought back to her conversation with the boys. Nothing seemed to make sense any more. Lucia had a hard life but wouldn't move when her parents offered them a place in their own home, Gerardo would never change, but here was Andras envying their arduous life. Did he really think he could make a difference just by building a reservoir when there was never any rain. All the good soil had washed away long ago and anyhow where was the money to come from for all the work?

She sighed and walked on, reaching the ridgetop in another ten minutes and realised that she had walked as far as the ruined hut. She could hear goat bells jingling from the distant end of the ridge. Her grandfather must be nearby, but she was so hot and breathless that she decided to wait for him in the shade of the hut. She sat down feeling the warm stone against her back. Flies buzzed over some nearby goat dung and the jingling of the bells grew closer. But the heat haze was so strong Stella couldn't keep her eyes open.

Something was nibbling as her skirt, its warm breath moist on her legs. She opened her eyes and looked directly into the straight I-shaped pupil of a goat's eye. The bell hanging from its leather neck strap clattered into her consciousness. She tried to get up but other goats nudged forwards forming a phalanx around her. More were trotting past watching her speculatively. She reached out and tried to grab the strap of the lead goat but it nudged forwards and nibbled expectantly on her fingers. She felt the hard rasp of its tongue and pulled her hand away. More goats were streaming past the rear of the hut, out of sight. A coarse shout from her grandfather called the herd away. She sat back on a grassy mound as they passed, deciding she would catch up with him later. She was contemplating her conversation with Andras and Theo when a voice, not her grandfather's, jolted her out of her reverie.

"But you're the nearest, why can't you...?" She knew the voice, it was Mr Sanchez.

"I can't do it, don't you see."

"But we can't go in from the front, they've built a ruddy great fence and entrance gates they lock up each night. Your track is the only way through."

Stella had heard enough, she cowered down behind the wall and made herself small. Several of the goats had moved away but the lead goat with the loudest bell continued to pester her. It bleated continually but she dared not shush it away for fear of discovery.

"Then they can do it without me, there's enough of them pays their dues after all."

"I'd have thought you'd want to be a part of this, I thought you'd be in the forefront." The man's voice was raised. He was in deadly earnest.

"I would, only it's the date, I told you before, Saturday was no good."

"Well it can't be changed now."

"I told you, I'll give you all the help I can, leave the gate unchained, you can even have the rifle."

"Well I don't understand you, it's not just the date is it - that granddaughter of yours, she's twisted you up in knots with all her conservation nonsense and fancy exhibition."

"No such thing, I won't have that said, do you hear. We'll get this thing stopped somehow."

"And what if we're not successful this time."

"Then I'll be with you the next time, and the next until we are."

"That'll have to do then. I'll be in touch by Friday."

Stella heard heavy footsteps on the track, then the sharp noise of someone - her grandfather she guessed - blowing his nose. The goats moved away, the jingling of their bells fading as they moved down the hill. She pulled herself up on shaking legs, until she could just peer over the top of the wall. Some goats had stopped to nibble at an oak sapling but the main flock had already gone over the ridge. She caught sight of her grandfather's coat disappearing into the nearest oak scrub.

Saturday, the man had said Saturday. They could have been planning anything from trespass to an assault on the reserve. There was such horrible malice in Mr. Sanchez's voice, and he *had* mentioned metal gates like the new ones at the reserve, and her grandfather was going to leave his own gate open. It was the only track that lead across to the new reserve. But Gerardo had declined to take part in whatever was planned, she wouldn't feel like a traitor if she told David about the conversation. She started walking back down the open hillside worrying over what she'd heard. Then it hit her. Next Saturday was the day of Lucia's 80th birthday - the day Gerardo 'couldn't make'. He hadn't wanted to commit himself because of the party. It all fitted. She must phone David and warn him as soon as she reached home. When she approached Holm Cottage her mother's car was no longer there. Relieved, she ran on past the cottage and down through the village.

Andras had taken charge of the lounge, together with the mobile phone. Stella nodded to her mother as she pushed open the kitchen door. Anna frowned.

"We didn't expect you so soon, milking over?"

"I... I didn't catch up with them in time."

"I gather you met Andras and Theo though - right after you left me in the lurch."

"I'm sorry Mum, I wasn't thinking straight."

"Sometimes it would be nice to know what you *are* thinking my girl."

Stella steeled herself, expecting further questions but Anna's attention was drawn by the beeping of a kitchen timer. She slipped into her bedroom, leaving the door open to listen to Andras. He seemed to talk forever. As soon as he had finished one call she jumped off her bed and raced into the lounge. Andras was already dialling another number. She slumped down on the sofa and glared at him. But Andras only played to her mood and dragged out the call. Cooking smells had grown stronger. Andras got up and dropped the handset into Stella's lap. She dialled David's number only be to disappointed by an ansaphone. She left a desperate message asking him to call. Moments later her mother called them in to eat. She carried the phone into the kitchen and sat down with it beside her.

"Now Stella, you know we don't use the phone during mealtimes," her mother cajoled.

"I'm waiting for an urgent call," she insisted.

"And how urgent is that Stella?" Her father walked in from the garden.

"Urgent enough." Stella looked down at her lap.

"But not so urgent that it can't wait, eh!" Jorge switched off the mobile and placed it on the shelf behind her. She caught sight of Andras and guessed he would grab the phone just as soon as the meal was over. Predictably enough he made two more long calls and by ten-thirty Stella had bowed to the inevitable. She sat watching the flickering images on the television screen with glazed eyes until her mother prompted her to bed.

"Can I just check there haven't been any messages on the phone."

"I think Andras has just finished a call, he's in the kitchen making himself a drink. Jorge can you bring the mobile in and see if we've missed any calls while our son has been spending your money."

"He'll have to earn some of his own money soon. I think it's time we got him another set."

"Not more expenses." Anna groaned

"Dad.. please?"

Jorge punched buttons on the phone and looked down at the tiny screen.

"No calls. Time for bed."

On Sunday morning Stella tried David's number several times without success. The phone rang just once, she leapt to pick it up but it was Theo again for her brother. Andras laughed. Taking the handset out into the garden he taunted her, "My we're jittery today aren't we".

Stella turned to see her mother watching her quizzically.

SEVENTEEN

"Janni, Janni!" The teacher heard her name yelled out along the school corridor. Stella raced down the smooth woodblock floor almost colliding with her. It was Monday morning, Janni's day for the senior classes.

"Hello Stella. What is it? It's not your class today."

"No, I've been trying to call David, I've left messages but there's no reply."

"There wouldn't be, he's at a conference - in Madrid."

Stella reeled giddily.

"Madrid, but he didn't say anything about a conference."

"He wasn't due to go. Dr. Mansera was but he was taken ill on Saturday."

"But when does it finish, how can I get hold of him."

"I don't think you can Stella. Is it something urgent?"

"Yes, yes, it's very urgent, so urgent that...."

"That what Stella?"

"I ... I can't say." The girl lowered her head in despair.

"Can I help?"

"I don't think so."

"Well he'll probably call me by the middle of the week. He's due back either Thursday or Friday, do you want me to tell him you called?"

"Not till Friday?...I don't know ... eh, it might be too late."

"Too late for what?"

Stella shook her head, turned and drifted thoughtfully down the corridor.

"I'll tell him to call you then shall I?" Janni called after, but there was no response from the girl.

Janni was left shaking her head.

Stella walked towards her classroom still puzzling how to contact David. She was not aware of anyone else in the corridor.

"Stella!" She spun around. It was Jade's voice, the one person who might help. The older girl stood in the doorway some ten metres beyond Stella's own classroom. Hanna, walking ahead, was watching expectantly as Stella drew level. The school bell rang. The first lesson was mathematics and the teacher was a stickler for timekeeping. Hanna beckoned.

"Aren't you coming in...?

"In a minute."

Jade had nodded to her as the bell rang so she moved into her own room. Stella ran past Hanna ignoring the open classroom door.

"Oh thank goodness Jade, just the person I wanted to see."

"Stella, it'll have to wait 'til after class."

"It can't wait, I have to contact Emilio, David's at a conference and....," she said breathlessly.

"Stella Martin!" The voice of the mathematics teacher boomed down the corridor. "Two seconds or...."

"I have to see you," she mouthed anxiously to Jade.

"After class." The door closed in front of her.

Stella's attention constantly wavered throughout the maths lesson and at the sound of the bell for the lunch she grabbed her books and rushed from the room. She needn't have worried, Jade was waiting for her outside the door.

"Can we go somewhere ......private?"

She hadn't hear Hanna walk up behind her. The girl was already at her side.

"Somewhere private?" Hanna repeated, "Well if that's the case, don't let me detain you. But you dropped this in your hurry."

Hanna held out Stella's pencil case, a jealous half-smile twisting her features.

"Oh, I didn't mean to......"

Stella blurted out, but Hanna was already walking down the corridor with another girl completely ignoring her. Stella grimaced.

"She'll come round Stella."

"I have to get hold of Emilio," Stella said desperately, unable to think of anything else.

"Well I think he's working up at the reserve, didn't you go and see it?"

"Yes, yes of course we went, but it's important I speak to Emilio."

"Is it about some....some animal?"

"No.... yes, look I just need to speak to him. Janni's just told me that David had suddenly to go to a conference so I have to contact Emilio. Do you have the reserve number?"

"Well I don't," Jade said looking puzzled. "If it's really important couldn't you phone that researcher at the museum - Dr. Delgado wasn't it?"

"I ... I couldn't talk to Liz."

"Why not?"

"I don't think she ever liked me, she always seemed to resent giving up any time for my project and..."

"Well you could tell her you wanted to talk to Emilio in David's absence surely."

"She'd only ask why."

"I suppose so."

"Look," said Jade. "I know it's against the rules but I've got my mobile here. Have you got the museum number with you?"

"I think it's on Liz's notes." She pulled a computer sheet from her bag trying not to let Jade see the tear where Pietro had shredded the page. By now they were walking along outside the school cafeteria. Jade walked past three boys from her own class. Jade knew one of them, a boy named Guy, had a crush on her. He sidled up to Jade and with false bravado asked.

"Can you give *me* your number sweetheart." The other two boys laughed and chorused. "Yes, give him your number, and us too."

Jade gave Guy one of her sweetest smiles. He blushed as his two friends guffawed behind him.

"Come on Stella, let's get away from this sideshow."

She took Stella's arm and walked her quickly away. The boy's laughter followed them down the hallway only lessening as they pushed open a first floor door and stepped out onto a metal staircase.

"It's a fire escape, should we be out here?"

"No we shouldn't, but we'll get a good signal here and hopefully……." Jade looked back through the reinforced glass panel of the doorway "no-one else will disturb us. Now if this call's so private, do you want me to stay with you?"

"Yes... oh yes. I just want to ask Liz for the number." Jade nodded, indicating the computer sheets which were filled with text.

"O.K. But you won't want to write over those notes." She handed a small notebook over to her friend and turned to watch the activities in the courtyard below. The yard opened onto the school's delivery bay and a small truck had just drawn up near the storeroom. The driver was a young man. He paused as he unloaded a large parcel, caught sight of Jade and smiled up at her. Stella quickly keyed in the number then heard a ringing tone.

"Hello is that the museum... 'um, could I speak to Dr Liz Delgado, yes .. yes it is business." She squeezed Jade's arm in embarrassment. Jade turned to watch her.

"Hello, Liz, I mean Doctor Delgado, it's Stella Martin, you remember my biology project. Is David….?"

"The project, yes of course. David's away and…"

Stella sensed Liz's steely reserve.

"It's not about that," Stella barked, her panic breaking through.

"Well what is it then?" Liz sounded only slightly more conciliatory. A tight knot formed in Stella's stomach.

"I wanted to speak to Emilio and he's...,"

"At the reserve yes."

"We'll I don't have his number and I wanted to speak to him

urgently."

"I don't think I can give you the reserve number, it's privileged to Xando personnel - especially after the trailer fiasco. Why do you want to talk to him anyway?"

Stella ignored the question.

"Could you give him a message please, ask him to call me at home."

"All right, next time I speak to them I'll ask him. Give me the number."

Stella couldn't remember the number. She had to fumble in her bag and in doing so managed to drop Jade's notepad. It fell through the slats of the staircase onto the ground, landing in a small puddle beside a flowerbed. Jade grimaced and began walking down the stairs. After a few seconds Stella found the phone number and read it out to Liz.

"Well I'll do what I can, but I can't promise to speak to him today, he *is* very busy you know."

"Oh, but it is very, very important, I have to speak to him."

Jade was walking back up the staircase. She held the limp notepad out, droplets of muddy water falling from her fingers. The young driver was calling after her and she smiled back at him briefly before noticing Stella's worried frown.

"I'll see what I can do!" Liz barked. The line went dead.

Stella eyed the notebook. She was nearly hysterical with tension but the sight of the soggy pages made her want to laugh. She met Jade's eyes and watched a smile crease her friend's lips. The two girls doubled up with laughter. Stella hugged Jade's shoulders unable to tell whether the tears pouring down her face were from laughter or tension.

By Wednesday evening when Stella arrived home from school she was growing frantic wondering what to do next. Saturday was fast approaching and she hadn't heard from Emilio or David. Luckily, just as she opened the apartment door the phone rang. Emilio's voice asking for her. She looked furtively into the kitchen listening for any signs of occupancy and sighed.

"Emilio, is it really you?"

"Liz said you wanted to speak to me, something important....?"

"Yes, it is, at least I thought so... can you hold on a minute."

"O.K. but be quick, the signal breaks up here sometimes."

Stella raced down the corridor checking the lounge and her parents room, they were empty. The door to Andras room was tight shut but she didn't dare try it in case he was inside. She crept back to the hallway and pulled the door closed.

"Emilio are you still there." The phone crackled but Emilio's voice came over strongly.

"I'm here Stella. You know you should have seen that lynx racing away up the hill into the woods, it was......," he paused hearing Stella's sigh. "You'd better tell me why you called Liz."

"David's away and he told us to mention anything....anything.....," Stella's voice exploded into the earpiece.

She began to feel a little foolish. Even in her own memory, the significance of her grandfather's conversation with farmer Sanchez had faded.

"Anything.....?" Emilio encouraged.

"Anything suspicious."

"Because of what happened to the trailer?"

"Yes." The line crackled badly, she was afraid the connection would fail.

"Yes, after the trailer.... I.....I heard a conversation, at the weekend."

"A conversation, between who?" Emilio's voice was cool, patient.

"I can't say - don't ask me, only I think .... at least I thought they were planning an attack on the reserve. That was four days ago, but now I'm not sure of anything."

"Can you give me more detail Stella, think now." Emilio was being patient with her. "If it's someone you know, you don't have to tell me their names, but I'll need to have a little more information to tell the police and....,"

"The police, I thought David..... but I suppose you have to tell them." She was suddenly very scared.

"David might not be back until late tomorrow, perhaps not even till Friday."

"That's why its so important. Whatever it is, will happen on Saturday I'm sure of it because....,"

Stella gasped, the door to the kitchen was swinging slowly open. She held her breath but nothing stirred. It must be the wind. She turned back to face the front door.

"Saturday you say, when on Saturday?"

"I don't know, night-time I suppose. I thought, well David did say to report.."

"Yes," said Emilio thoughtfully. "I expect he told you we now have some extra protection." He emphasised the last word, knowing she would understand. David had mentioned armed guards, the reserve would not be unprotected, like Xando.

"Yes."

"Stella, I'll get in touch with David somehow. Now you must put this out of your mind. Leave it all to us."

"All right, I'll try."

"One more thing." Emilio paused ominously. "Are you staying in the city this weekend?"

"No we're going back to the village, there's a party on Saturday for ..... a party."

"Well Stella, promise me you'll keep away from the reserve. Try to keep your family away too. All your family, do you understand?" By all, Stella knew he really meant her grandfather. She nodded sagely into the phone.

"O.K."

She put the phone down and turned away. The kitchen door was opening. Andras stood in the doorway. His face bore a look of disgust.

"Keep away from the reserve, ...Keep away from the reserve", the words pounded in Stella's head as the car travelled irrevocably across the coastal plain and up the new mountain road. Friday evening had arrived The family were on their way to the cottage ready to celebrate Lucia's 80th birthday next day. Jorge had suddenly decided to bring some work with him and had thrust his briefcase onto the floor beside Stella's leg just as they left. Each time the car rounded a corner the briefcase knocked against her ankles. Desperate to know if Emilio and David were taking the threat to the reserve seriously she was so keyed up she wanted to cry out with rage. Had they evacuated the reserve, maybe just left the guards in charge? Perhaps nothing would happen. It would be a relief, but then she would feel like a meddling fool.

The cottage was just as they had left it the previous weekend, the windows lifeless, the olive trees a little more bowed under the sun's heat. It had been extremely hot that day, particularly for late September. As they drove through an empty village even the new apartment block, usually busy with all manner of workmen, was devoid of life.

"I think I'll just check the phone for any messages." Jorge walked through the house to the kitchen and unlocked the outside door. "I was hoping Harry would contact me about this stuff before we left." The briefcase thumped heavily down on the garden table.

"Did you have to bring work home, this weekend of all weekends?" Anna complained.

"Got to be done love. It'll only take a few hours, I promise."

"Well make sure you keep to that."

Jorge dialled his phone and started listening to his messages. Harry had rung back. Jorge dialled his number and began writing notes. After almost fifteen minutes he finished the call. By then Stella was lying down in her room. She had unpacked her few weekend clothes taking especial care to hang up the new dress her mother had made for her. She would wear it for the party. It was of a silk-like material, pale blue with tiny white flowers dancing across the surface, the neck decorated with fine white ribbon. She was even thinking that Jade might be jealous when she heard her father say.

"Anna, there's a message to call Consuela."

Stella's ears pricked up.

"Well, why don't you call then?"

"Oh, Anna you know she'll keep me talking for hours. It's hot out here, I was going to get a quick shower and then work on these notes."

Stella instantly shook off her unease.

"Shall I take it?" She ran down the corridor into the kitchen.

"If you like Sweetie." Her father tousled her hair and headed thankfully for the bathroom. She noticed that his hairline was wet and streaks of sweat marred his smart office shirt.

"Coward," Anna laughed after him

Stella took the handset and ran out into the garden. She sat on her favourite chair and punched in her grandmother's number. The voice answering the phone was faint. Ramon's wife never trusted the phone, she always held it a couple of centimetres from her ear. Since she was also more than a little deaf, this did not allow for good telephonic communication.

"Granny," Stella shouted into the phone.

Anna laughed quietly.

"Is that you Stella?"

"Of course it is, we're looking forward to seeing you tomorrow, what time will you get here?"

"Get where dear?" Consuela's voice was slightly louder. "Oh yes, well that's what I called about, is your father there?"

"He's in the shower granny, will mother do?" She could already hear water rushing down the outlet pipe.

Anna appeared by her side and took the handset.

"Hello Consuela, are you all right for tomorrow?"

Anna listened for a moment.

"Can you get a little closer to the phone dear, I don't think I heard properly."

She wiped a wet hand on a washing up towel.

"Yes, yes..... but are you sure he'll be better by Sunday."

"Is granddad Ramon not coming," Stella cried out.

"Yes, yes, give him our love. I'll phone again tomorrow. 'Bye dear."

Anna placed the phone on the table and turned towards Stella.

"Oh dear Lucia's going to be disappointed. Ramon's gone down with a stomach bug."

"Isn't he coming tomorrow?" Stella cried.

"No we're going to have to move the party to Sunday." Jorge came into the garden wearing a bathrobe.

"Ah that's better." He laughed down at the phone, then at Stella. "Finished the call already?"

"Your father's got a stomach bug. I'm going to have to run up to Lucia to tell her we're putting the party off until Sunday. I'll call Juana when we get back, I hope they can all make Sunday."

"I wish you'd get them to accept a mobile phone. Will Ramon be well enough by Sunday?"

"According to Consuela, yes. Now you know it's no hardship to run up there in the car, besides neither of them would use a phone. "

"I know your father wouldn't, but it would be reassurance for Lucia wouldn't it?"

"Only if she learnt how to use it! I'll go now, do you want to come Stella?"

The girl froze.

"No....eh, why don't you wait until the morning, granddad Ramon might be better by then."

Stella said, desperately searching for a reason not to cancel the party. Saturday was the day Sanchez had mentioned, the day of the possible attack. If Gerardo realised the party was cancelled he might feel compelled to join in.

"Unlikely little one," her father said.

"Well if you don't want to come...."

"No, no, I'll come."

Gerardo sat woodenly by the fireplace.

"I hope you're not too disappointed Lucia."

"Nothing disappoints her." The old man quipped, tapping the table as if waiting for a reaction.

"I'll phone Consuela tomorrow, but we don't need to decide until Sunday morning whether to go ahead."

"What about Juana, can she make Sunday?" Lucia asked. Jorge's sister lived in El Rosal, nor far from her parents. Lucia always seemed vaguely jealous of the relationship.

"I haven't spoken to her yet."

"If we don't speak to them we may have to have two parties, one on Saturday and one on Sunday."

Stella glanced guiltily at her grandfather. "So we'll see you tomorrow, just in case you're very disappointed." Stella realised that she sounded like a petulant child, disappointed at the postponement of a longed-for treat. She didn't care, she would do anything now to keep her grandfather at Holm Cottage tomorrow. Lucia gave one of her rare husky laughs.

Saturday dragged on incessantly for Stella. Jorge spent long hours working on his papers in the lounge discouraging interruption. Andras slept until twelve, had suddenly risen, grabbed some cakes his mother had just baked and gone out to see friends. Stella hadn't brought any school books with her and was bored. After helping her mother in the kitchen all morning she had retreated to her bedroom throughout the noontime heat. At first she tossed and turned but couldn't sleep. The new pale blue dress her mother had made for the party mocked her from its hanger. After an hour she made a decision. She got up and searched through her case and then through the whole room for the old pair of trousers Andras had given her. They weren't anywhere. Exhausted by the heat she slumped down on the bed again and this time went to sleep. She awoke an hour later to the sound of Andras bumping noisily through the door of his room.

"Where have you been?" She called out.

"Out with my friends. What about you - do you have any friends left?" Andras pushed open her door and stood in the doorway laughing.

Stella glared back at him then leapt off the bed.

"I'm going up to see Lucia."

She brushed past her brother and headed towards the front door.

"Did you say Lucia?" Jorge called from the lounge.

Stella already had the front door open.

"Yes, I said I would. She made out she wasn't disappointed about the party, but I knew she was. I told her I'd see her today."

"Hold on a minute." Jorge appeared in the doorway.

"Anna, have you spoken to Mum yet today?"

"Not yet," Anna called from the bedroom.

"Look Stella, if you wait a minute, we'll give her a call and you can tell Lucia how Ramon is."

"O.K." Stella groaned and closed the door but refused to push past Andras a second time. She waited while Anna dialled the number

"The line's busy."

"You'll have to wait a little longer Stella," her father said. "Besides I've done enough work today, I think I'll come with you, I could do with a walk."

"Oh great, Dad."

"If you're going for a walk then you'd better have a drink before you set out, it'll still pretty hot out there."

Anna gathered up juice and lemonade and lead the way out into the garden. Jorge followed her and immediately noticed the increase in humidity. Even the olive leaves hung limply and the garden was fearfully hot. Jorge looked up at the long lines of cloud streaming in from the coast, thunderheads were forming over the tops of the Tejeda mountains.

"Rather looks like the weather's breaking."

"I wish it would do it soon. I thought August was hot enough. Shall I get us some food, Jorge you look washed out. I told you not to work so hard," Anna coerced.

"Now don't nag, I'm fine but a little cold omelette would be great, what do you say Stella, before the walk?"

"O.K. I'll get some from the fridge."

"You know I think I'll come up to grandfather's with you." Andras emerged from the kitchen and grabbed a glass of lemonade. He drank it down in one long swallow. Stella stopped short in the doorway.

"What do you want to come for?" She asked suspiciously.

"To see granddad, that's all."

"Why, you never like walking, you'll only slow us down."

"What's got into you Stella, don't be so cruel," Jorge countered.

"Well he only wants to interfere, he always does."

"Stella, none of us will go if you don't behave. But if it comes to it we could all go in the car."

"But I wanted to walk and Andras only wants to talk to grandfather about his stupid feasible study."

"Feasibility. I've started the college project for next year already Dad."

"Well I'm impressed, by one of you at least."

Stella grimaced. She'd practised several times to say the word properly but it had come out wrong again and made her feel ashamed in front of her father. Just then the phone rang.

EIGHTEEN

The evening was humid and sultry with the gathering clouds offering dubious promise of freshness. The family started out much later than Stella had intended after another protracted phone conversation with Jorge's mother. It was already after six and in September darkness fell about eight. With dark clouds looming Jorge was sure to insist they spent only a few minutes at the cottage. The first hint of thunder rumbled from the head of the valley. Andras carried a small rucksack over his shoulder. Stella wondered if it contained his plans for her grandfather's property. She desperately hoped Gerardo would be there to see them. Her brother walked fast at first, setting the pace but as she predicted after two kilometres he slowed markedly. Jorge offered to carry the boy's rucksack but received an adamant refusal. Andras continued to struggle up the long slow hill. Stella was racing ahead as they rounded the cottage wall. With one last burst of energy Andras speeded up and the two of them raced towards the cottage. Andras found himself at the wooden door ahead of his sister and knew she had allowed him to win. He vented his resentment by puling so hard that the cottage door sprung back missing Stella's face by a few centimetres.

"Now you two... ," shouted Jorge angrily "behave!

Andras took no notice but Stella who was facing away from her father poked her tongue out slyly at her brother.

"Happy 80th Birthday, Grandmother," Stella called, hardly able to imagine what it was like being so old. Grumbling sounds from the lean-to indicated that Lucia was doing nothing out of the ordinary on her 'special day'. She appeared in the kitchen doorway carrying a bucket of firewood in one hand and a half sack of pea pods in the other. Stella tried to take the load from her but was shaken off with a grunt. Lucia dropped the bucket beside the stove and shuffled into the living room. Still holding the sack of peas she nodded to Andras and kissed the top of Stella's head. Jorge strode across the room and gave his mother-in-law a hug. She accepted it wearily then lifted the pea sack on to the table and sat down. Stella noticed that the old bucket in which she collected vegetable waste for compost, was already beside the table.

"Lucia, Happy Birthday. Anna sent you a little present in anticipation of the party tomorrow. We've just spoken to Consuelo, she insists Ramon will be fine by Sunday, Juana & Luis are coming too." Lucia looked at the small colourful parcel on the table, then pulled the pea sack towards her and placed some of the pods in her lap.

"Time enough, tomorrow."

"Where's Gerardo, out the back? I was going to chop some logs, supply's pretty low again." He patted Lucia on the shoulder and moved towards the lean-to.

"And I want to show him my plans," Andras added.

"What plans are these?" Jorge asked half turning towards the boy.

"The ... the feasibility study, of course." Stella mocked, pleased to pronounce the word correctly at last.

Andras had already pulled his notes from the rucksack and was now spreading sketch maps out on the table. He picked up his grandfather's pipe meaning to use it as a paperweight then noticed a sharp break in the bowl. He shook his head and put it down carefully on the logs by the fire.

"Well you'll be disappointed then," said Lucia at last.

"Why's that, is he ill too?" Jorge asked looking through the semi-darkness towards the closed bedroom door.

"Not as you'd describe ill."

"He's gone down to the village has he?" Jorge asked, "we didn't pass him on the way. Still I can get on with the logs, do you want to help Andras?"

"He's *not* gone to the village, I'd be happier if he had." Lucia looked towards the corner of the room where Gerardo's gun habitually stood. As Stella followed her gaze a sudden spasm seized her chest. Her blood ran cold. For a moment she couldn't breath.

"Dad," she gasped. Andras was leaning over the table. He looked up at his sister and asked idly.

"What's the matter Sis?"

Jorge looked back into the room. In the darkness of the lounge the pale orb of Stella's face stared back at him, her eyes were wide open and appeared quite black. She was hugging her stomach as if in severe pain.

"Whatever's the matter Stella, do you feel ill?"

"No I don't.......I don't ......" The room spun around her for a moment. Lucia's hand tightened on her arm, she felt herself pushed down onto one of the hard wooden chairs. Her grandmother's coarsened fingers pressed into Stella's skin. Slowly she regained her senses, roughly pushing off her grandmother's arm she shot upright.

"We've.... we've got to stop him. What time did he go?"

"Stella whatever are you talking about, stop him what.......?"

"He's only gone to do a bit of shooting," Lucia offered. She glanced sharply at Stella, then returned to shelling the peas.

"He's gone to join Mr. Sanchez hasn't he?" Stella shuddered. She was holding onto the edge of the table for support.

Lucia shook her head without looking up.

"Isn't it a little late in the day to go hunting?" Jorge demanded of her.

"He said he was going to get a few rabbits, there'll be more about, with the storm coming."

"But Mr. Sanchez hasn't gone hunting, he's....a group of them are going to attack the reserve. I overheard them last Saturday!" Stella shrieked

"Yes and I heard you phone your animal friend. What did he say - that the police will be waiting for them."

Andras voice was steady but Stella could tell from his blackened pupils that he was enraged.

"I don't know what either of you are talking about, Andras," Jorge declared angrily. "Lucia, did Gerardo go with Mr. Sanchez?"

"Not Mr. Sanchez no. Gerardo went out half an hour ago."

"But Grandfather's left the top gate open hasn't he, so they can all drive through." Stella insisted. Her grandmother looked at her steadily.

"Some cars came through earlier. It might have been Mr Sanchez. Whether the gate's open, I don't know, you can't see it from here." Her face bore a determined expression, as if she wanted no part in the discussion.

"But Grandfather's going to get muddled up in some trouble, just because he wants to .... to hunt. And you'll be the cause Stella!" Andras almost spat out the words.

"But he wasn't going to be involved. I knew something was fixed for Saturday, Grandfather said he couldn't get involved because of Lucia's party." Stella wailed and sat back heavily on the chair.

"Stella, what's all this about an attack?" Jorge sat down beside her unable to understand. When no-one spoke he thumped his hand on the table.

"Will one of you tell me what is going on. Did Mr. Sanchez actually mention an attack, are you sure this isn't just something you've dreamt up Stella?"

"He….. Mr Sanchez didn't mention an 'attack' but he talked so angrily, about beating them, they were against closing the land to hunting, I thought......,

"Be honest for once Stella, you just wanted to make trouble for the farmers didn't you, just because you want to save your precious carnivores," Andras leered at her.

"They're protected, it's ...... it's not just me."

"So you've organised a little publicity. Did you phone the papers as well? I only heard you phone Emilio, but how many others were there. Quite the little traitor isn't she Dad?"

Traitor! Andras said the word. Now she really did feel like a traitor, unintentionally betraying her own grandfather. Tears brimmed on her eyelids, she was close to crying.

"Be quiet both of you I'm trying to think. Stella who did you phone?"

"Only Emilio, I wouldn't phone anyone else except David and he was away."

"And what did he say?"

"He said he's looking after everything, that I was to keep everyone away from the reserve at the weekend, especially grandfather ....Gerardo.....," She gulped

"He's treating the threat seriously then?"

Jorge looked at Lucia's bowed head, she was completely withdrawn. The mound of empty pods was growing in the bucket at her feet. Peas spun ceaselessly from her hands and rattled into the colander as if she'd divorced herself from them.

"I think so."

"But don't you see Dad, all this is because she's trying to make grandfather scrap their way of life. I'm going to come back here to live!" He glared defiantly at his father "Like grandfather. I'm going to build a reservoir and grow better crops and .....,"

"Don't talk such rubbish Andras."

"But I can, I know I can do it, I can grow things, I'm strong."

"Andras, we've got more important things to think about now," said Jorge. He was only half listening to his son and thinking quickly how to get Gerardo out of the dilemma Stella believed him to be in.

"Andras I want you to go back to your mother and...,"

"But I am strong," Andras persisted shaking his head. "You never take any notice of me, I want to live here with grandfather despite the hardships, but all that will change." Jorge looked at him with an expression of astonishment on his face.

"And why do you think your mother never came back here to live after college. She was only aged 16 when she left, the age you are now Andras."

Andras thought of his mother as smart and scholarly, certainly she always seemed out of place in the cottage.

"And Lucia was the same age as her when she married your grandfather.... Her life's been hard, no running water, no heating through the chill damp of winter, damp clothes, bronchitis. Sure she was sad when Anna left, but she wanted something better for her daughter."

"But she was a girl, I could ...,"

"You could what ...?" demanded Jorge getting increasingly angry, he had no time for this.

"Stella .... get that old coat of your grandfather's from the bedroom, I'll need it on the hill."

Stella was grateful to move, she dashed into the room and took down an old leather windcheater of Gerardo's and another jacket of Lucia's which she had worn when the autumn evenings began to chill. She was about to run from the room when she noticed a large white envelope sticking out from under her grandparent's bed. Sheets of white paper showed through the open flap and the folder looked vaguely familiar. She picked up the packet. As soon as she fingered the mangled pages she knew. Tears sprang from her eyelids. Standing quite still she let the pages slip, one by one, to the floor until her whole biology project lay scattered at her feet. Dispirited and saddened, she was dimly aware of Andras' voice rising to fever pitch. Somehow she stumbled from the room. Listlessly she pulled the bedroom door behind her and turned to watch her brother's face contort with rage.

"You never think I can do anything do you," Andras was yelling at their father. "Well I am going to live here, in this cottage, no matter what Stella or anyone else has done. I want to be like grandfather, work and farm here. I love it here - the cottage, the lands, the woods, it's my inheritance."

"You can't," Jorge said in exasperation. "You talk less sense than your sister. You're living in the past Andras, at least she can see the future."

"Why not -- why not?" Andras screamed "Just because people say I'm a *cripple*, and you think I can't do anything,........You've never believed I can do anything have you?"

There were deep lines drawn across Andras' forehead, his hair hung limply down the sides of his face. Instinctively he caught at his leg and rubbed it fiercely as if willing away the slight deformity.

"You simply can't," his father said.

"Well I'm going to live here no matter what."

But while Andras was savage with anger, Stella was aware of a contradictory sorrow in Jorge's eyes.

"Andras we don't have time for...." Jorge stood up. He noticed Stella holding up the ragged grey coat, waiting anxiously for him to take it, her tear-stained face was almost grey from fear and fatigue. He gave her a weak smile and began struggling into the coat, then he turned back to Andras and sighed deeply.

"You can't live here," he said decidedly, with a quick glance at Lucia.

For one brief moment Lucia raised her head. Stella noticed for the first time that her face was wet with tears, they fell unheeded down her leathery cheeks and onto her apron, visibly dampening it.

"You just can't ...," Jorge repeated " because your grandparents don't own anything here - not one centimetre of soil, not one rock, not one tree. They pay rent they can't afford to an agent of some landlord we've never met. Year after year paying rent for land with no value, for soil that cracks and runs away downhill." Jorge's breath seem to fail him for a minute. He noticed that Stella had begun struggling into her coat, he managed to release his arm from the ragged coat sleeve and held up his hand to her shaking his head.

"Rent for this ruin of a cottage." He glanced at Lucia, at the work-worn hands, the lined face wet with tears. "They don't own one stone, not even one tile of this cottage. If they live for another ten years the cottage will fall down around them. We've tried for ages to get them to move, your grandfather won't, can't bring himself to move. If anything were to happen to him,..... well Lucia knows she's to come to us, so you see you can't live here - you have no *Inheritance!*" Jorge sighed again. "You've got to live in the real world Andras," he said at last, not wanting to see the desperate hatred in his son's eyes. The boy was crushing between his fingers the maps he had laid out so proudly earlier. His eyes, now full of despair, fixed on his father's face. He picked up the loose crumpled sheets and began tearing them apart. Each fragment he threw deliberately into the grate where flames leapt up the paper sending a yellow glow around the room.

"Now I want you to go back to your mother. Tell her.... Just tell her I've gone out to look for Gerardo because there's a storm coming, I don't want her worried to start with and come rushing up here, do you understand."

He turned to look at Lucia.

"All this may come to nothing - I hope it does, but... Tell her that Stella will stay with your grandmother and I'll come back with her. But if

I'm not back by - say 9, when it's dark, then you had better ask her to phone the police."

"I don't think she'll believe me."

"Then you'll have to convince her!" He said sharply, then relented and pulled Andras' drooping form towards him. There didn't seem to be any life left in the boy's slim frame. Jorge spoke quietly, Stella could hardly hear what he said

"Do this for me." He put his hand under the boy's chin and tipped his face up to look at him. It was a pale mask without emotion. Stella felt a brief pang of pity for her brother.

"If not for me, then for your grandfather."

Andras nodded briefly. Jorge ushered the boy towards the door, had already opened it. Andras stood tall in the doorway. He nodded a silent farewell to his father and trudged down the cobbled pathway. Jorge turned to stare at Stella.

"And you can take that coat off young lady. You're staying here with Lucia."

Stella looked at her grandmother. Her head was permanently bowed, the peas fell interminably from her gnarled fingers. It was doubtful she would even notice Stella's presence. Jorge was unprepared for her outburst.

"No, No, I'm coming with you... Even if you don't take me now, I'll follow...,"

"Stella, Lucia needs you here." The old woman shook her head. Jorge couldn't tell whether in denial or at some thoughts of her own. Jorge looked intently at his daughter. Her face was flushed but pale tears streaked her cheeks. He guessed she meant what she said. Perhaps it *was* better to have her beside him rather than let her wander about alone on the hills in the growing twilight.

"O.K., but keep with me," he said sternly. " I don't know what to make of all this but ..... if there's any sign of trouble... any sign at all, then you're to come straight back here, do you understand?"

Stella nodded and buttoned her coat determinedly. Jorge flung open the cottage door and a sharp wind blew round the interior. Stella pulled her coat more tightly around her and stumbled past her father into the gloom of early evening.

Thunderheads piled up hiding the distant hills and the wind was blowing scattered cloud fragments low across their flanks. As they hurried up the track the wind gusted at the branches of the holm oaks making them rage back and forth overhead. Stella and her father had to keep their heads

bent to avoid the streaming dust blowing up from the sandy ground. When
they reached the open hilltop they saw the gate. It was standing open and
shook erratically in the wind. Several car tracks broke the surface of the dry
ground, beside them were the distinct tracks of a heavy lorry. All followed
the gravel road. Jorge decided to do the same. He walked away from the
gatepost and felt a tug on the sleeve of his borrowed windcheater. Stella
stood beside him, the wind was whipping at her hair, blowing it into her
eyes and mouth. She spoke so softly that he couldn't hear her above the
wind. He shook his head when she pointed along the ridge.

"Quicker,.. be...quicker along there." She forced out the words against
the strengthening wind.

He looked back at the road, it descended into the valley after which it
cut back towards the village for another three kilometres before running
along another ridge parallel to the boundary of the reserve. If they followed
the roadway on foot it might take over up to hour until they reached the
reserve and the storm clouds were already darkening over the Tejeda
foothills. Cross-country would be quicker. He nodded to Stella and she set
off in front of him along the ridge. The wind was behind them, it tore at
the dry grass, bending them over and shredding the tangled leaves until
many were whipped up and flew away down the valley slope. When they
reached the ruined shepherd's hut Stella took shelter behind the broken
walls. In the same place, ironically, where she had overheard Gerardo in
conversation with Mr Sanchez.

"What now?" Her father asked.

"There's a track out of the valley," Stella gasped

The path looked uninviting to Jorge, the lower part of the valley was
quite smooth but the top of the ridge outcropped into a crumbling cliff-
face covered with thick gorse scrub. He'd never been that way before so the
landscape was unfamiliar to him. He was already regretting his decision to
follow his daughter's advice. Stella was watching him, noting his indecision.

"You have to skirt round the gorse, there's a goat track." She yelled
into the wind.

Jorge nodded.

"And then?"

"Another valley but the sides are full in oaks and juniper scrub, it's
rocky but the old estate track lies just beyond. The only thing is......I haven't
been across for some time, grandfather took me when I was smaller." The
wind buffeted Jorge's loose coat and tore noisily at the hood. He had to
lean close to his daughter to catch all she said.

"So we don't really know where......?"

"Oh yes, we'll come out just beyond the far corner of the new enclosure. It'll take us about half an hour."

Jorge looked into the distance. He could just make out the tops of the trees in the next valley. They looked a long way off, and he found himself doubting his daughter's estimate.

"Well all right then, we'd better go on - if you're still coming with me that is?"

"I'm coming."

Stella had indeed underestimated the bulk of the gorse scrub and the steepness of the track. The goats usually kept all the small plants in check but when, as here, the young gorse had been protected by the cliff-face the plants grew up large and unruly. Stella had to place each foot carefully in clefts in the rock before pushing round them. Behind her she heard Jorge curse at the huge spines as they jabbed, with malevolent intent to judge by his angry comments, into his clothes and flesh. She reached the top of the ridge where it was cloaked by a dense band of woodland. In the distant past the owners of the estate had made attempts to grow Aleppo pine as a commercial crop. They surrounded the western part of the estate with goat proof fencing. But the pines, suited only to lower altitudes did not thrive in the seasonal extremes. Holm oaks and other trees had seeded into the neglected plantation forming thick stands of saplings and eventually the goat fence too succumbed to the elements.

The wind thrusting up the valley to the south was whistling through the tops of the taller oaks, bending over their huge shaggy tops and scattering hosts of dull green leaves down the slope. Stella sheltered beside a tall tree waiting for her father to emerge from the honeycomb of gorse bushes. As she peered down between the oak trunks she saw that the wooded slope was now just a mass of broken pine branches. The sight horrified her. There didn't seem any way down. All the cast branches were in the same state of decay as if the trees had shed them all in one go; probably in a freak storm Stella mused, feeling an extra tug of the wind. She glanced up at the sky. The wallowing grey clouds had already stripped most of the sunlight from the sky and down in the woodland the oak leaves glowed eerily against the skeletal pines. Stella shivered. From across the other side of the ridge she thought she heard the sound of an engine straining, then a faint metallic clatter but the storm whipped the sound away.

"Dad, where are you?" The wind was growing stronger all the time, it whipped at her face, tearing the words away. She called again.

"Here," Jorge emerged from a grove of sapling oaks just behind her. She noticed that he was rubbing at the fingers of his left hand with a blood-stained cloth.

"Had to take a detour, are you all right?"

Stella nodded, taking his hand.

"You're bleeding."

"Nothing much, a lot of blood for a few scratches." He tried to laugh but his voice sounded hollow and unconvincing.

"There's no path any more." Stella dropped his hand and pointed guiltily down the slope.

"We'll have to go along ......,

He paused as a loud crack echoed from the opposite hillside. Stella jumped out of her skin and clung to his coat.

"What was that?"

"I don't know - a shot?"

There was a further crack, then two more, followed by raised voices shouting against the wind. Her father shook his head.

"I thought I heard engines."

"You stay here, I'll have to make a path."

"No I'm scared."

"Then keep close to me and if I tell you to, just drop to the ground, do you hear?"

Jorge edged between the nearest trees then started down the slope pushing aside the dead branches. He was surprised at first how light they were and after less than ten minutes had reached the valley bottom. Water trickled from the opposite tree-clad slope. Only a faint light was visible now between the trees where water glimmered evilly at his feet. Stella had followed his every step, twisting between the trees and fallen debris. Now she was cowering beside him. While wind still roared in the tree tops it failed to penetrate the lower vegetation and the oak leaves above their heads were quite still. The wind masked all sound from the hilltop. Jorge scanned the trees in front of him, trying to judge the best way to climb the slope.

Without warning an engine burst into life and a harsh grating sound issued from the hillside above them, metal screeching against metal. The engine strained, braked, then suddenly ran free. Tyres throbbed over gravel and a loud tearing sound rent the air. Jorge shook off Stella's arm, gestured to her to stay put and began to clamber awkwardly up the hillside. It took a several minutes scouring through the loose tangle of vegetation for footholes. When he reached the top of the hill, his breath was hot in his throat, his chest sore from unaccustomed exertion. He edged thankfully into the shelter of a fallen branch and tried to catch his breath. He sensed movement near his leg. Stella had disobeyed him. She was cowering beside him, a shocked look on her face.

"The fence!" She pointed to a gap between the trees to the right. The storm was breaking, rain fell in heavy droplets through the trees and padded onto his windcheater. It was so dark now that the pale gravel road loomed at him out of the night. A heavy-duty truck was moving along the far side of the track. Metal clattered behind it. Stella gasped and pointed anxiously. Behind the truck a long line of metal was strung out - now mangled and hardly identifiable portions of chain-link fence. Two dislodged metal posts lay at angles on the ground. Jorge could hear the voices of several men. The truck was barely a hundred metres from them when it stopped and began to reverse. Jorge clutched at Stella's outstretched hand, luminous in the dark vegetation and began urging her down the slope. The rain was beating heavily through the trees and the ground had become slippery so his shoes no longer held their grip. He caught at his daughter's arm as they slithered towards the trunk of an oak and held her fast until he could grip a branch with his hand. They were still near the top of the slope, within easy distance to hear the truck reversing towards the broken length of fencing. The engine revved then idled again. There was a lot of shouting and a sudden thudding of feet on the gravel track. Jorge looked up to see a wall of light sweeping between the trees. The lights of two vehicles sped along the track a quarter of a kilometre away. They were coming at speed, sirens blaring. Men's voices shouted and a shot rang out. One of the lights on an approaching vehicle shattered but it came on as steadily as before, sirens blaring. Then the cars stopped suddenly, less than a hundred metres from the broken end of the fence. Nothing moved on the road until a loudspeaker crackled through the rain.

"Put down your weapons." The device went silent, but a shot rang out and a second of the car's four lights died.

"We want no more violence!" The voice on the loudspeaker implored. "Put your weapons down."

A searchlight at the top of the car was switched on. It instantly became the target of two more shots but the bulbs were bullet proof. They cast a piercing glow across the truck which itself had become enmeshed in the scatter of chain link. Now, the engine was straining, the driver attempting to extricate its wheels. A voice called from the hillside a few metres away.

"Shoot at his wheels."

Jorge pushed Stella's head down behind the tree and huddled protectively over her. The girl was shaking.

"No it's madness, just get away!"

Stella resisted her father's attempts to protect her, she pushed her head up under the nearest low branch. Even through the thudding of the rain she recognised the second voice. She squirmed out of her father's grasp.

"Grandfather, this way."

A kind of staggering movement in the bushes above him alerted them to the approach of the old man. Jorge grabbed hold of Stella's arm again and pushed her roughly behind him. He heard her whimper.

"Grandfather!" Then lightning flashed overhead and in the scattered light he saw a man outlined between the trees at the side of the track. The man held a rifle in one hand and had been just lifting it to fire along the track when he heard Stella cry out. He hesitated and looked down towards them. Jorge watched the man's rifle swing towards him, but at that moment a huge crack of thunder rent the air and dimly beneath it Jorge thought he could hear footsteps running. Someone, a policeman he hoped, shouted.

"Stop or I fire!"

Sounds unlike thunder cracked just above his head, the man with the rifle crumpled and slumped down on the track. Jorge couldn't tell friend from foe. He was desperate to protect his daughter. He clung to her arm and let go of the tree. The girl was too traumatised to resist. She let Jorge take hold of her. The slippery woodland slope and the effects of gravity helped him push off downhill. Above him another flash of lightning lit up the wooded slope. Two shots rang out from the direction of the track then the inevitable boom of thunder burst savagely overhead, momentarily shrouding all other sound. More shots were fired, it seemed only metres away. Their progress down the hillside was halted as Jorge's legs wedged against the trunk of a large oak. He struggled to free himself then, in the pause after the thunder, he heard someone blundering through the undergrowth.

A sudden long moan echoed through the vegetation, as the man fell across one of the chiselled pine branches and collapsed in its shadow. A shot discharged nearby. Jorge heard groaning, then a flash of lightning illuminated the last thing he wanted to see: his father-in-law had fallen against the roots of a huge pine, his limbs spread-eagled on the forest floor.

At his side, half hidden by his arm, lay a shotgun. Jorge let go of his daughter's hand. Pushing her behind him, he attempted to crawl towards Gerardo. Rain pounded on his head and streamed down his face. He was oblivious to everything but Gerardo's face, pale and lifeless, staring at him from the undergrowth. Suddenly a bright light poured down the hillside catching him fully in its beam.

"That'll be far enough!" A voice ordered. Jorge didn't seem to understand, he looked blankly at the light then turned away and continued crawling towards his father-in-law.

"Hold it there or I...,."

"Don't shoot him!" Jorge heard Stella shout behind him. She was screaming as she clambered into the beam of the searchlight. Her shadow wavered over him and a second voice exclaimed.

"Good God...... a child!"

NINETEEN

The sound of wood being chopped came from outside the window, thud, crack! The window faced northwest, its deep embrasure prevented late afternoon sunlight from penetrating far into the room. Unusually, a lamp glowed from a small table at the end of the bed, adding its feeble glow to the otherwise indifferent illumination. Stella found herself musing on the rhythmic blows as Jorge cut more and more logs, now she looked back at the bed. The crumpled bedclothes comprised thick flannelette sheets and a lumpy bedcover stuffed with goose feathers, the colours were drab and faded. The head of an old man lay motionless on the pillow in an attitude of sleep, but the girl knew better. The bedroom door opened. Lucia entered awkwardly carrying a tray. There was just a faint smell of food, soup probably, from the closed pot which stood on the bare wood of her tray beside two wedges of dry bread. Stella edged from the bedside to let Lucia pass.

The old woman hardly looked at her as she placed the tray on a rough-hewn bedside table. The lean-to door slammed and Andras entered, his arms laden with logs. Stella watched him drop them into the fireplace in an unruly muddle. He wouldn't care whether they spilled out onto the floor. She would have to arrange them herself in neat piles. As Andras retreated he looked through the open bedroom door. Noticing the flickering oil lamp he pushed into the room. His oiled, rough woodman's jacket carried the odour of oil and sawdust into the room. He bent down to the lamp. It was too full. He had to be especially careful to trim the flame so it burned with an even brightness. Stella watched her grandmother bend over the bed. She knew the old man would not respond until she had left the room.

"He won't talk to me!" She wailed to the empty darkness rather than to her grandmother.

Lucia simply nodded and shifted the tray a little nearer the bed. Andras was still tending the lamp. As she moved from the corner of the room passing a chest of drawers, she noticed a corner of white paper poking out underneath. Something about its fine white quality drew her attention, she bent down listlessly and pulled at the white paper. The envelope was scattered with grey cobwebs and was quite empty. Clasping it to her chest, she gasped. Lucia half-turned from the bed.

"Where are the pages.......?" Stella began.

"Burnt!" Lucia said sourly. As she lifted the top off the container, soup fumes mingled with the sawdust to cloy the atmosphere in the tiny room. .

"My project........," Stella gasped helplessly.

"Burnt....," Stella almost heard her grandmother add 'and good riddance', but Lucia remained silent, her back turned steadfastly towards the girl.

Somehow Stella's feet took her towards the door. She felt strangely numb, the project had gone but it didn't seem to matter. With all that had happened these last months, very little seemed to matter any more. Her eyes were fixed on the floor but as she took hold of the door meaning to close it behind her she caught sight of Andras' face looking at her. For once his youthful face bore a look of compassion. The grate was full of tumbled logs, she leant down intending to pile them up then realised that she still had the envelope crushed to her chest. She succumbed to the urge to fling it from her, it landed at the back of the grate standing upright as if to mock her. The embers glowed and flames licked at the shiny surface. Stella subsided onto the nearest chair watching the white paper with golden flames licking up before it. The brilliant electric lights of the courtroom were suddenly before her.

Three men stood in the dock. They had just been sentenced to five years apiece for the offences of assault and firearms misuse. A sigh had run around the filled courtroom and one woman on a side bench was weeping softly. The room began to quieten as the implications of the sentences sank in.

"And now I want to say something more."

Some people who had half risen from their seats sat down awkwardly again as the judge spoke. There was muttered argument, but then people began to pay attention to the judge. He had a deep voice and with his polished tones seemed to be talking individually to each person in the room. Mostly though his eyes were fixed on the convicted men.

"There as been one death in this tragic affair, and to my mind - and the court's, that is one death too many."

Stella was seated on one of the side benches. There were just a few empty spaces near her, otherwise the rest of the room was packed with onlookers. Stella's eyes, along with those of almost everyone else in the room were drawn to the woman sitting opposite her. Mr. Sanchez's widow was flanked by two of her three sons. The third son, an executive in manufacturing, had attended the early part of the trial but been called away on business. The woman seemed completely unaware of the room and its occupants. She held her head low, the pale wrinkled face marked by tears. Feet shuffled and people moved irritably as the judge continued.

"This court will not tolerate any more such violence or behaviour threatening the public peace. When disputes are identified, for whatever reason.....," he paused and looked at the mayor of El Rosal, who was also president of the leading hunting society in the district. "Then these disputes should be addressed through the proper authorities, either this Court or higher bodies. Any person, or any group, that thinks they can take the law into their own hands or who endangers the lives of others will be punished with no excuses. I hope I have made the concerns of this Court plain."

He paused and took a sip of water though he hadn't finished speaking. Many journalists at the rear of the court who had been scribbling furiously throughout now began rustling the leaves of their notebooks obviously impatient to leave.

"One thing more. One of the people involved in this case has not attended the court. As I have already said, the age and infirmity of Mr. Gerardo Lopez have precluded him from being present, although he's been legally represented. However, sufficient evidence has been given to indict him in this case. I understand that his son-in-law is willing to stand surety for him, is he in court today?"

Jorge was seated at Stella's side. He stood up briskly and answered the judge's request.

"Yes, your honour. I'm Jorge Martin married to Gerardo Lopez's daughter Anna, she is his only child. He is still in hospital with broken ribs and....,"

The Judge nodded sympathetically. "Well I am sorry for that. But Mr. Martin, have you been notified of the conditions of surety?"

"I believe so Your Honour."

"Then I will bind over Mr. Lopez to keep the peace for six months. Any existing, or even past, firearm licenses......" The judge emphasised the word 'past' knowing full well Gerardo hadn't renewed his licences since before his sixtieth birthday, some twenty years ago, "are to be *revoked*. Mr Lopez will not be permitted to hold or use a gun for the rest of his life." A sigh, more like a shudder, was felt at the rear of the court where the Mayor was seated.

"Any contravention will be punished - despite his age and current infirmity. I hope, Mr Martin, that you will convey this sympathetically to your father-in-law."

Jorge nodded, "I will."

The judge slammed the gavel down on the desk in front of him. The previously hushed court became a noisy melee as people rose and vied with journalists racing out of the room to send in their copy. Mrs Sanchez remained on her bench, unmoved and unmoving.

Gerardo lay in his hospital bed on the day the court's verdict was announced. He had two broken and one fractured rib from the fall against the tree stump, his other ailments were shock, according to the hospital doctors, and unexplained debility. Next day, when Jorge came to tell him of the court's decision, Gerardo lay motionless, his old man's small body scarcely forming a mound in the bedclothes. As Jorge was speaking Gerardo turned his head slowly towards the high windows. He hadn't spoken. Noticing the moisture patches on the pillow beside his head Anna had turned away and wept silently. Only two days later, shaking and still feverish he had insisted on being discharged and was brought back to Holm Cottage in a city ambulance just yesterday afternoon.

The fire glowed dully, the envelope was almost consumed except for a few thin black patches of carbon adhering to the fireback.

"You shouldn't blame Lucia you know, you've torn him apart, you and your conservationists."

Stella remained silent, she had nothing to say to her brother. Andras took off his oiled coat, shook it and placed it on a chairback. He sat down opposite her.

"About your project....," he began. "He wouldn't tell you this himself......."

Stella did not want to listen, she looked from the fire down towards her feet.

"When poor Sanchez came round the Friday before the attack, he had one of their hunting cronies with him. It was before we cancelled the party, because Gerardo let him borrow his second gun, the rifle."

Andras waited for the significance of his words to sink in.

"This man had seen your name on the project and brought it over. Some kind of revenge I suppose, I don't know. Gerardo told me that....that he'd been reading it."

Stella blinked, still she refused to look into her brother's face. The sound of chopping continued unabated beyond the lean-to doorway. Jorge was still venting his energies against the woodpile. Later he would come in exhausted but purged of guilt. She envied him.

"Stella did you hear what I said, look at me."

The girl slowly raised her head. He expected tears but saw that her eyelids were quite dry.

"He read it and still he went out?"

"He was going to stop them. Remember, Lucia said he went off on his own. Sanchez didn't expect him to join them. Gerardo told me that when he got to the reserve they wouldn't take any notice of him. He tried to make them stop but it was too late, he just got muddled up in the whole affair."

Long seconds passed before Stella found her voice.

"But why didn't he say before?"

"He's a tired, sick old man Stella, too proud to admit to the world - to you especially - that he'd changed his mind."

Stella blinked away tears that came hot and brimming into her eyes. *The unchangeable had changed,* she couldn't believe it. A queer kind of laughter bubbled up inside her and burst out painfully in choking spasms. Her small frame shook until Andras became worried she would collapse.

"Calm down Sis, please!"

Stella couldn't remain still, she leapt up from her seat and headed for the cottage doorway.

"I don't know whether to laugh or cry, or both."

"Both," said Andras following her. He held open the door and followed her out of the cottage darkness into the dazzling late afternoon sunshine. He watched Stella walk around the corner of the cottage. Noticing the strange way she looked up the hill and began to climb, he decided to follow her.

"Where are you going?"

He caught up with her by the goat pen. For a moment she stood looking down the pen towards the goat shed, the stone walls bathed in the sunlight. But there were no goats and the usually strong smell was no longer evident. Although the herd had been temporarily removed to a neighbour's home during Gerardo's illness, it was doubtful the goat pen would echo to their strident calls, or the clamour of their raucous bells, ever again. Andras slowly followed Stella to the fence but sensed that she wanted to be alone. She had calmed down now and seemed quite composed. He touched her arm lightly to gain her attention.

"One more thing. David called, this morning, after you left."

The girl stood quite passively without any sign of interest.

"Stella listen to me, he said Dr Mansera has arranged a temporary moratorium on hunting, not just on the reserve but right up to the tops of the Tejeda mountains."

"Temporary...?" Stella interrupted him, her face expressionless, "What use is that?"

"Stella, Stella - it might last several months then David expects the nature reserve status to be confirmed - on a permanent basis with compensation payments for all the farmers? Aren't you glad?"

Stella turned slowly. She looked back to Holm Cottage and thought of her grandparents and all the memories that sad little building evoked. Andras sensed her mood. It would take time for her to digest the news. He gently removed his hand from her arm.

"Little Sis, always in the wrong place for all the right reasons."

As he turned to go Stella watched a deep brotherly smile cross his features.

"What will you do?"

Andras knew what she meant.

"There's no future here for me - I was stupid to believe it. It was a nice dream for a time."

"College?"

"Oh, I'm not giving that up. I'll need to make a go of it now more than ever. I'll just have to start on another project - why you've no idea how many plans Theo has, he's just a minefield of information."

"A mine, not a *minefield*," Stella corrected mischievously. Brother and sister looked at each other laughing aloud. She watched him walk back towards the cottage. He went through the gateway and she waited until he turned to wave. He seemed to be growing taller every day. He swung proudly down the lane in the direction of the village. You would hardly guess he had once been labelled a cripple.

Stella passed the end of the goat pen and reached the top of the field where she sank down in the new lush grass. Her eyes played over the distant hills now green after the rain of recent weeks. Earlier, thick clouds had been tumbling over the mountain tops. Now long thin white streamers were spreading away to the east as the white limestone hilltops soared clear against a fierce blue sky. The late October sun began to sink behind the westerly hills. 'Moratorium'? The word was unfamiliar but she knew it meant protection for wildlife. All the land up to the Tejeda mountain peaks would be free of hunting for ever. Somewhere up there, Pardito would be beginning his evening hunt for food, his footfalls soft on the drying earth, the rustle of resin-drenched trees above. Somewhere up there, he was free and safe - for now at least.

=o=o=o=o=o=o=o=

Kris Slokum, Nov16